OVER MY GOD'S DEAD BODY

BY JOEL SPRIGGS

Copyright © 2018 by Joel Spriggs

All rights reserved. No part of this book may be reproduced or used in any manner without written permission of the copyright owner except for the use of quotations in a book review. Use of this book does not guarantee future employment opportunities.

Joel Spriggs
Lebanon, IN 46052
www.joelspriggs.com

Acknowledgments

I took a lot of late nights and odd times to research, write, edit and revise this novel. It has been a very educational, eye-opening and rewarding process. The whole concept and execution of this novel did not take place in a vacuum. I have many people and experiences to thank and rely on for inspiration of characters, situations, scenarios, creatures, etc.

I'd like to thank my wife Sarah and our children. They put up with my laptop keys clacking on for my restless nights and didn't complain. Kids, you'd better not read this book until you are much older. College age or older may be best. But you three should know that you helped make any children portrayed in here more believable, especially with the rhymes about Mama Mia's Pizzeria. Don't fret random reader, you'll get the inside joke later in the book.

I'd like to also thank my brother, Seth. I know I made a pseudo-villain of an Egyptian God named Seth, trust me, the name is where the comparison ends. The real Seth, my brother, was a great sounding board for a lot of my ideas and the source of a few running gags and good one-liners. Except for any Star Wars jokes, I don't think I can emphasize enough how much he hates Star Wars.

CONTENTS

Chapter 1	1
Chapter 2	5
Chapter 3	14
Chapter 4	22
Chapter 5	35
Chapter 6	46
Chapter 7	52
Chapter 8	64
Chapter 9	80
Chapter 10	88
Chapter 11	105
Chapter 12	111
Chapter 13	125
Chapter 14	133
Chapter 15	144
Chapter 16	151
Chapter 17	164
Chapter 18	174
Chapter 19	187
Chapter 20	192
Chapter 21	202

Chapter 22	206
Chapter 23	213
Chapter 24	224
Chapter 25	232
Chapter 26	236
Chapter 27	239
Chapter 28	242
Chapter 29	252
Chapter 30	258
Chapter 31	264
Afterword	275

CHAPTER 1

JACK AND THE SQUATCH

Two figures walked through the dim street lights late on a Thursday night. One silhouette loomed over the other and ambled with a long gait. He was extraordinarily furry and wore an old ammunition belt slung like a sash across one shoulder. The street lamps glinted off a small trophy the shorter carried. He wore a white long sleeve shirt with an old black leather vest and some dark jeans tucked into riding boots.

"See, wasn't that a lot of fun?"

The tall hairy creature looked down at him and let out a low, gurgling roar. Mentally, it was heard by his friend as, "It was a lot more fun than our usual round of grabbing some Happy Meals and hanging out in your dusty old apartment. I had never been to a party with that many humans. They were fun." He lifted the ammo belt with a thumb. "Why did we have to get dressed up though?"

Jack thought for a second to parse the question. "Well Ned, normally the GDI house is just a good frat to hit for Thirsty Thursday. Next week's Halloween though and fall break for Baldur College. The frats are going to get their costume parties all out this weekend. The GDI's kick it off, and there's one every night 'til Sunday."

"Raaadraradraa," replied Ned, which Jack understood as, "that sounds like a good roll, we should do this again. Who are we supposed to be again?"

Jack chuckled. "I don't know how you've gone around for nearly sixty years and not seen Star Wars. We're supposed to be Han Solo"--he pointed to himself and then to Ned— "and Chewbacca. They're a pair of smugglers that become heroes in those movies."

"Rarrrr, draaadraaaraaa," he replied, which Jack heard to mean, "bah, all movies are shit compared to real life. Why did we go drink and party with them, anyway? I thought you were supposed to be a respectable professor here or something."

They walked away from campus down a side road that led towards the college football and practice fields.

"I don't know Ned, I guess I always liked getting down and crazy like that. I did it a lot in my college days, and it's fun. I'm not too worried about partying too much with those guys because, well, it's not like I'm seeing them in a lecture hall to teach them philosophy or brain surgery. I teach phys ed, so I guess I like that they can see that not all of their professors are these snobby bookworms."

"Grarararrrrraaaaa." Jack heard, "good point." With that, Ned slapped him in the crotch and took off in a loping sprint across the fields. Jack felt the breath go out of him. He dropped the little trophy for best couples costume and started sprinting across the fields. Jack began to get his wind back and tried to catch up to him.

Around the fifty-yard line of the main football field, he leaped hard and latched onto the back of the tall sasquatch.

The sudden weight toppled him forward, and they fell together into a heap. "I got ya. Ha, I got ya again," Jack yelled triumphantly.

He rolled off Ned, and they lay on the dark field looking

at each other, "draaaarararaaaraa." Jack understood that as, "that was a good run, but you got me, now what you gonna do with me?"

Jack knew this trick too well, this was how their relationship began when they found each other in the wild. That felt like years ago now, even though it was just last summer. "I think I know what you're looking for Ned." Jack gave him a kiss on his neck and raked his hands through the beast's fur. He started kissing down his chest, moving slowly further down.

"Orroaltrrra," which has no translation, it was just Ned moaning and caused Jack to crack a smile hearing the exact same sound in his own mind.

Suddenly the lights all around the football field clicked on, humming audibly. Ned sat up suddenly. The thrust made Jack choke before he could get the sasquatch from his mouth. They both looked around blinking, temporarily blinded by the brightness of the lights.

Then they heard it, the sounds of chuckling from the sidelines, and saw the five people. Just a group of kids. Jack recognized one of them as a Freshman from one of his classes. "Dude, that bum downtown was right, this is where the big show is tonight," they heard one of them say through the laughing.

Ned grunted, trying to get a better look at them.

Another kid stopped laughing. "I think we just found out who shot first, and it definitely wasn't Han."

Their laughter doubled at the joke, Ned roared furiously. "Grarararar!"

In all of their minds, including Jack, they all heard the same message clearly. Jack was shocked, but all of the students were just surprised to hear the squatch scream in their mind, "motherfuckers."

They took off running and were over the fences before Ned could reach them. He leaped the fence to follow. They split and all went into different directions. Ned followed one of them.

Jack tried to keep up, but the squatch outpaced him easily

between his rage and long stride. When he did finally find him, Ned had chased down the one student he'd recognized in the group, freshman Billy Turner. Ned had broken one of the boy's legs and was straddling the kid. As he approached, he saw Ned was squatting over Billy's head.

Jack heard Ned uttering a low guttural growl, which he also heard in his brain as, "that's right boy, I'll teach you not to cut in."

He cried because Jack couldn't think of anything else to do. He saw the scene and could see his teaching career going straight down the drain. He leaned onto a nearby tree. Jack looked back at Ned, on the student again, and threw up. He swayed, dizzy and light headed, and Jack slumped down into his own vomit. Rocking back and forth in the dark, he kept saying between sobs, "oh Billy, poor Billy."

CHAPTER 2

⚡

LOKI

Loki stumbled through the door of his motel room. He was so tired that he missed the single queen-sized bed as he tried to fall forward onto it. He slipped past the foot of the bed and landed on the floor with a thud. He lay prone on the floor for a moment, a lean, tall, long dark-haired man flat in the short pile of the dirty red carpet. He could hear the bug-zapper hum of the neon Vacancy sign outside on the motel roof above his room. Loki opened his eyes. If he could hear the sign, that meant he left the door open.

He pulled himself up and closed the door. He felt tired in the cold dark room of the Hamilton House Inn. Instead of turning up the heater and crashing in bed, he stared daggers at the mirror. He knew his night wasn't over yet. It was time to pay the piper; he had to check in with the boss. He hated the boss, Seth. Here he was, Loki, immortal frost giant and honorary Asgardian, highly regarded in myth, reduced to petty jobs.

He flicked on the bedside lamp and stumbled over into the bathroom, then turned on the cheap neon light. The cheap grey linoleum felt slick with dirt and perspiration. He picked up a cup from the teal green ceramic sink. Loki pulled the watercolor brushes from the container, knocking the dampness from them on the sink while he up-ended the brownish-red water from the cup into the matching teal toilet.

He picked one of the brushes out and wiped it against his grungy sweatshirt to dry out the bristles. He stopped for a moment and stared at himself in the mirror. He gazed into his own gaunt pallor staring back at him.

"I must be tired," Loki said to himself in the mirror. Even under the wiry bristles of a long, dark beard, he could make out faint scars that he could typically suppress with just a minor effort of will. The scars were the clear reminder of why he had to continue tonight, to pay off the debt.

Loki held the brush firmly and walked back out to the main room. Dodging the bed, he opened the small dorm-sized fridge sitting on top of a cabinet. He pulled a small baby food jar out. It had no label, its original contents had been cleaned out, and it now contained a viscous red liquid.

He placed the jar and brush on a nearby short dresser with a large mirror back. He dug through a few pockets of the grubby black overcoat he wore. Eventually, he produced a pair of tea light candles and a small book of matches with the name "Double V" printed on the back.

He reached into one last inside pocket and pulled out a small leather-bound volume. As he set the book on the dresser, it expanded to the size of a vast encyclopedia. He browsed the pages and found an oft-used entry. The page title read, "The Rite of Ombus Setekh." He knew most of the rite by heart, having performed it hundreds of times. It called for a half gallon of pure virgin oxblood, a large mirror, eight candles and pillars to set them upon.

He knew all of this was pure bullshit, as over the last millennia, Loki had discovered the only thing you really needed was a mirror of any size, two candles and about 2 ounces of badger blood. Seth had dictated the rite to numerous authors, wanting them to have to make a more magnificent spectacle than necessary to contact him. The rest of the ritual, as recorded, called for the invoker to use the blood to draw a series of symbols on the mirror and call forth a chant to gain an audience through the mirror with Seth.

Loki would have to sketch the symbols and those he hadn't entirely committed to memory. He'd tried going from memory once. A pair of symbols being reversed resulted in his interrupting a wendigo in the middle of an awkward meal, so he always consulted the manual now.

Loki lit the two candles. He opened the jar of badger blood and painted a scrawl of symbols on the mirror of the dresser. He sat back into a cheap dinette chair that he'd pulled over from the other side of the motel room. The simple part of the rite was over, now he just had to wait for Seth to answer. That was what never got written down in these elaborate rites to talk to other beings, that it wasn't a phone call, and the other end picked up immediately. It was more like a shitty pager that only blinked mildly at the being you were paging. Seth may respond quickly, or Loki may be sitting in front of this damn mirror for eternity. Still, he had to admit a boring eternity in a shady motel room was better than an eternity of being scarred by acid dripping from the fangs of a serpent as penance for a crime.

He shut the tome again and tossed it back on the farther side of the dresser. Something slid out and fell on the floor. He picked it up; it was the map he'd bought of the town from a nearby gas station when he'd first drifted in a week prior. He unfolded it to study again while he waited for Seth's response. There were numerous little circles and notes in the margins around the map. Baldur College and its various buildings had most of the notations, while there were still other small marks all around the town. He found where he was at present, a circled little house icon labeled "Hamilton House Inn." It sounded quaint on the map but didn't accurately portray it as an old motor lodge motel that will rent rooms by the hour.

Loki checked the mirror. The symbols pulsed dully in the gloomy light. A strange idea struck him, something he hadn't done in years, centuries really. He picked up the spell book again and flipped through the various conjurations, definitions, and directions. He found the one he was searching for, "Revelation of Blood Ties." A simple little spell, the instructions called for a reasonably accurate map of the area to explore, four drops of blood and a trivial incantation. He'd used this spell on others before to help them find a missing family member or reveal paternity if a child's parentage was in question. Every time he'd tried it on himself, nothing had ever shown. He wasn't surprised, his lineage as a Jotun meant that not many of his family came to this realm and his own children had been either killed or sealed away.

He had time, and he was bored though, so Loki pulled a small multi-tool from his coat and slid the blade out from the side. He pricked his thumb with the point and squeezed a drop of blood at the cardinal points of the map, north to south, then east and west. He shut his eyes and whispered the short incantation three times over. Loki knew what he'd see when he opened his eyes, the same map, all the points he'd circled and little notes. The only thing new would be the four drops of blood.

He opened his eyes, they went wide with surprise. A few blocks from Baldur College's campus, in a small residential area. They shouldn't be there, all logic dictated that the map should be the same, but there they were. Two little dots of color pulsated in the same small area, distinct in color, one red, and one blue. It meant that in that home resided a male and female that both shared his blood. He faintly became aware of some noise nearby him.

"Loki," the mirror thundered, pulling him from his fixation on the map spread in front of him. Seth stared back at him from the mirror, the hooded person was brightly lit, and Loki could make out his image. A head that looked like a massive black, slick-furred fox stared back.

Loki shook off the sudden surprise and dropped the map to the floor. "Seth, I do have some news to report."
Seth's ears shot up, flaring out from under the hood. "You found what is left of Horus?" he asked eagerly.

Loki sighed. "No, not specifically. This town is strange, there's a lot more going on here than I'd expected."

Seth's ears fell flat around his head. "What do you mean strange? You are not coming through very clearly; did you use the whole half gallon of ox blood?"

Loki rolled his eyes. "I've told you before, there's no need to use that much, and oxblood isn't the best medium either."

Seth threw his hand forward pointing at Loki. "Do not start on your shit about badger blood again. You still have yet to convince me."

"Look, regardless of what blood I use, you wanted me to be inconspicuous. How much attention do you think I'll start making for myself if I go around a small town bleeding random oxen and carting around gallon jugs of blood?"

Seth waved his hand airily and backed away in the mirror.

Loki leaned forward and spoke up. "This town is odd, spiritual entities are showing up regularly. I found evidence in the cemeteries of voodoo practitioners. The college this town surrounds is centered on a confluence of lay lines, making it a major hub for magical energy. I even caught some gym teacher at the college engaged in a very sexual relationship with a Sasquatch."

"You caught a human boning a Sasquatch," Seth shot back suddenly interested.

"Umm, other way around I'm afraid and same sex."

Seth raised a furry eyebrow. "So, wait," Seth said intrigued. "Did you, uh, catch the Bigfoot actually in the middle of it all?

Loki leaned into his hand covering his eyes. "I'd really not go into it. It's not a pleasant thing to watch."

"No, no, I get it, man," responded Seth. "But I have to ask about Sasquatch penis. Did he have like a normal human looking penis or was it like one of those red rocket kinds you see on dogs?"

Loki looked horrified at the mirror, turning up his lip in disgust. "Come on, Seth, there are just some things you don't ask, alright?"

When Seth started to try asking again, Loki shot back sarcastically, "You know, you have a part of the body of a fox, do you have a normal penis, or is it a red rocket dick?"

They sat silently across from each other on either side of the mirror for a moment. Finally, Seth spoke up. "So the intel was right? Someone may have the remains, or they could be at that college."

Loki nodded. "It's not outside the realm of possibility, but it's not confirmed and guaranteed either."

Seth interrupted, "Remember, the absence of evidence IS NOT evidence of absence!"

Loki hesitated then continued carefully, "Yes, well, your friend was right, a lot is going on here. I have never sensed this amount of magical and supernatural beings roaming around the same general area together without it being a battlefield before the treaties. Beyond the interspecies erotica, I could smell elven blacksmithing on one side of town and in some random areas I could even hear the night cries of at least two chupacabras. This isn't just abnormal, it's downright dangerous."

"You are right," agreed Seth. "I am coming to you; I will make the preparations and travel there directly this weekend."

"What? No, I don't think that's a good idea. This is a bit of a powder keg situation; we don't want another situation like Detroit on our hands."

"I will make sure Apep gets left out of this, but I need to come for myself. If anything is left of Horus, I have to be sure to destroy it before Isis can create another heir. I must retain the throne; they still make a point to announce me as the "acting king" here."

Loki sighed and looked at the ceiling. "And you still want to see if you can confirm this Sasquatch dick issue, right?"

Seth jabbed a taloned finger at the mirror. "Fuck you, it was a valid question."

"Alright, alright," Loki said pleadingly. "We also have to talk debt on this set of tasks."

"What about debt? I own yours, and as long as I do, you will do whatever I ask."

"Right, that's what I'm getting at. I'm very thankful you got me out of my unfortunate imprisonment, but that was two thousand years ago now. Surely by now, my debt's been paid off, right?"

Seth crossed his arms in the mirror. "Maybe we could arrange a decade break if you come through for this one."

"Look, I liked the decade breaks you'd give me now and then, but I want my actual freedom. This place is complete batshit. I'll be lucky to live through this if someone gets tipped off on what I'm doing."

"We will see, but it depends on how secure my throne is when all is said and done."

With that, Seth disappeared in a puff of smoke in the mirror. Loki waited a moment to make sure Seth didn't pop back up suddenly in the mirror. When he didn't, Loki grabbed a wet towel from the bathroom and cleared the badger blood sigils from the mirror to make sure Seth didn't pop back in randomly. He threw the towel back in the tub and grabbed a clean watercolor brush and the cup from the counter before heading back to the mirror and the map.

He opened the knife and cut a small slit on his forearm. Loki clenched his fist, letting a stream of blood flow down into the cup. He whispered a short incantation, and the cut sealed itself. He picked up the map from the floor and stared at it again. The two points still shone brightly in red and blue, both still at the same location on the map.

Loki dipped the brush in the cup of his own blood and began to paint a new set of symbols along the sides of the mirror. He whispered briefly and blew a gentle breath across the mirror's surface. It shifted hazily, Loki's reflection disappeared, and he began to see two separate scenes. Both images came into focus showing bedrooms.

On the right side of the mirror, a dark bedroom came into view. A prone man lay stiffly on his back dozing in a barely disturbed queen-sized bed. The room around him was immaculate. A desk nearby showed a satchel and a book, but no papers or pens on the desktop. A digital alarm clock glowed 2:56 a.m. dimly in orange light on the nightstand next to a lamp, but nothing else. Well that's just boring, thought Loki as he looked at the scene unfolding on the mirror.

On the left, another bedroom sharpened into focus but appeared much different. The room was still lit by a floor lamp near the bed. Dirty laundry seemed to litter the floor, sports bras hung from the corners of the metal framed bed, and a nightstand was barely recognizable under a small landfill of food wrappers and empty Starbucks paper cups. The covers of the bed were disheveled and strewn about. A woman in her twenties sat cross-legged in a pair of panties and a green tank top. Her kinky brown hair was pulled back loosely into a ponytail, and she was transfixed on a screen of a laptop computer glowing brightly in front of her.

"This one is much more interesting," Loki said aloud to himself. "But who are you and why do you look familiar?"

He whispered another short incantation and dabbed a new sigil in his blood underneath the woman in the mirror. The sound suddenly began coming through the mirror along with the visions. From the right, he heard only soft snoring. On the left, he heard soft music playing while a song started to fade out. Loki saw the woman's eyes dart down at the phone playing the music.

She began singing right to the beat of the new song. "Yo, tell you what I want what I really really want," she started belting out. Loki listened intently as he watched her sing along with the Spice Girls enthusiastically and dancing her shoulders back and forth while focusing on the laptop screen and randomly typing.

The voice conjured a memory, someone he'd known and actually loved nearly a century before. "Beatrice," Loki whispered softly and leaned to look closer at the woman in the mirror.

The song ended, and a new one began, an upbeat electronic number started. The right side of the mirror erupted with sound as the man in the bed abruptly sat straight up and screamed, "COME ON BARBIE, LET'S GO PARTY!"

Loki fell off his chair from the unexpected interruption. He quickly wiped all the symbols from the mirror, the sound muffled and fell away while the images of the two bedrooms faded away, revealing Loki's own reflection again in the faint light of the old motel room.

He clambered over the floor and into bed, kicking his boots off along the way. Loki clicked the lamp on the bedside table off. Shutting his eyes, he whispered, "Sleep now, learn more about them tomorrow."

CHAPTER 3

ESMY

Esmeralda Hansen slumped over on the toilet; she felt her eyelids weigh heavily before they closed shut again. Her twin brother Jake started banging on the paint-chipped bathroom door. She woke groggily, staring at the floor.

Jake pounded on the door again; a few chips of the white paint fell onto the old pink tile. "Come on Esmy, we BOTH need to get ready for work."

Esmy woke groggily to that and said, "Sometimes I think that if I had a dick, I could just pee standing up and this sort of thing wouldn't happen." Esmy realized she said this out loud, though she only meant to think it. "Jake, I think I'm still asleep."

"Anyone can fall back asleep standing just as easily as sitting, Esmy, especially you. Now quit the toilet philosophy and let me get moving!"

Esmy gave the door a snide glare, ruffled the frizzy dark brown hair out of her face and got moving again.

Esmy stumbled past Jake in the hall, he wore a white terry cloth robe and carried a small shower caddy. "Your majesty." She presented the bathroom to him with a flourish and headed back to her room to dive through the closet. More often than not, she turned to the bucket of clean laundry she hadn't put away yet to find something to wear for the day. Today confronted Esmy with a strange situation.

It was Friday, which meant casual Friday at work. She wished it would allow for student casual, but she didn't have a set of pajamas or sweats anymore without either a hole or stain.

Esmy dug through the closet, then the bucket of clean laundry by the bed that had been sitting there since Monday. She found a Rolling Stones t-shirt that looked vintage, but she'd bought online last year. No jeans in the closet or bucket, but the pair from the other night on the dresser had only been worn for two hours, which was close enough to clean. The same decision was made for a sports bra over any of the underwire pieces sitting clean in a drawer. Unable to find a suitable and clean pair of panties in the bucket of fresh clothes or dresser, a choice presented itself: slutty thong or dirty panties. Esmy went for the thong. The boss she reported to preferred her to keep her shirt tucked in, even on a casual Friday, so at least she wouldn't have to worry about some sophomore trying to ask her to a frat party again.

Esmy heard Jake leaving the bathroom and checked her watch. He'd been in the shower for fifteen minutes, which meant the old house's water heater would give her ten minutes of decent hot water, fifteen if she let it go colder. She swore Jake was worse than most women about getting ready for a day. She grabbed her shower cap and stuffed her wavy shoulder-length amount of brown hair into the cap. No time to shampoo, condition and shave with only ten minutes. That came down to just enough time to wash her body and face, do a quick shave of the pits and ankles to calves. No point to do the whole legs and waste the hot water time.

By the time she was ready to head out the door, Jake had already left. "Must be a nice day out," Esmy said to herself. She found a note deposited on the counter next to her keys.

Esmy grabbed her keys and the note while heading to her car, a faded red Nissan Stanza that followed her through college to now. She was convinced that the car was only still running because of the easy availability of junked Stanzas that the mechanic could pull random parts from when it broke down. Still, he likely sacrificed a few chickens to a lesser demon each time. However, the demon's prices must have gone up to three chickens and at least one goat given how much more Darrel's last bill was for a water pump and heater core.

    She read Jake's note while starting up the car.

    Esmy,

        Need to borrow the car tonight, got a date. Meeting her at a place a few miles away, too far to walk and going to have to hazard her seeing the Stanza. Leave the keys on the counter please, catch you at the house later

    Love,

    Not the Fatman

    Esmy knew he used the joke signature so she couldn't get mad for him taking the car on a Friday night. She hit autopilot driving to work and thought it's not that big of a deal, no plans for the night, anyway. Maybe it would give her time to get her laundry done and actually folded. Esmeralda made up her mind that there was at least the same probability of that happening as cosmic beings coming down from the heavens or winning the lottery.

    The weather was beautiful though, so she'd likely toss on some running clothes, stash her debit card and house key in her phone case and go for a five or six-mile run.

    Closer to dark, she'd probably grab a coffee and come home. Once home, Esmy planned to catch up on some games she'd been neglecting, but in reality, she knew she'd find herself attempting to solve some issue from work. She would then spend hours trying to work through why something wasn't running correctly and lose track of time trying to fix it.

If she were lucky, Jake would get home late at night from his date and shake her out of the coding mode enough to realize the time and get some sleep. If she were unlucky, Jake would get lucky, and she'd pass out around dawn when Jake might be heading home. The short drive blurred by, and she was soon turning onto the campus of Baldur College.

Esmy was staring out the windshield, talking out loud to herself while looking for a parking spot. "The good thing about this scenario is the odds are in my favor that Jake doesn't get lucky because he'll try to be too much of a gentleman and won't get the hint. If she even drinks one glass of wine, he'll worry so much about it being date rape that he'll be home before midnight."

She parked the car in a nice shaded area, which was great as the interior started to smell like sour yogurt if it sat in the sun too long. Three points for Jake and his date tonight, thought Esmy. She hopped out of the car and attempted to stash the keys in her pocket before grabbing her bag. Her hand rebounded past the fabric of the fake pocket, and she tried two more times to shove the keys into pockets that wouldn't open. It wasn't meant to be, and before she realized she was saying it out loud, Esmy shook the keys at the sky and shouted, "Fuck women's pants and their lack of REAL. FUCKING. POCKETS!"

"Perhaps you need to invest in some cargo pants if you care to permanently eschew purses, Ms. Hansen," said a voice behind her.

Esmy inhaled and closed her eyes; she recognized the voice and the strength behind it. She turned slowly and looked up into the elderly face of the college president. "Good morning, Dr. Longfellow. Please excuse my morning cursing of the heavens, I haven't had any coffee yet," she said sheepishly, finally hazarding to open her eyes.

He was lumbering in his height and broad as an ox in his shoulders. Esmy wasn't sure how old he was, no one really knew. He'd just always been there as the college president. Dr. Longfellow had a habit of looked her square in the eyes; it was a feat for which he had a particular knack. Most people feared that look; it could make you feel five years old in a heartbeat, as though you'd been caught with your hand in the candy jar, even if you were more penitent than Mother Teresa. He also just didn't act old either. He looked somewhere between sixty and eighty but was known to outpace some of the college athletes when he wanted to get in some exercise.

Dr. Longfellow spoke warmly to Esmy, "Nonsense, my dear. If the gods were to actually take offense to it, then you could apologize. But I can't recall any recent memory of someone being struck down with a bolt of lightning for cursing the heavens." He looked down at his watch briefly. "Please give Mr. Mordido my regards, and remind him of his obligations to attend the board meeting later today."

"I'll be sure to let Jesus know, Dr. Longfellow," Esmy started to part ways with him.

"Thank you, and be sure to curse some more gods for me today, some of those bastards deserve it!"

Dr. Longfellow headed up the steps to the building known to campus residents as the Old Bastard.

Esmy paused for a moment to listen to an upperclassman giving an early morning tour to someone. She thought maybe it was a prospective student and quickly decided the story made it more likely a younger brother.

"It's called the Old Bastard because, aside from the library and the Wellhouse, it was the only building on campus that never burned down entirely and has been around for more than 20 years," said the upperclassman.

"Really? That's kind of impressive."

They stood near the building. "A whole side of the building made a good attempt at burning down back in 1922. It was rumored that a biology professor was prepping some lectures at night in a third-floor office. This particular biology professor still preferred to work by lamplight because it kept his office warm. Part of his lecture included a squirrel he caught on campus that day. Supposedly, the squirrel got loose, it bit the professor and leaped for the window. On its way to freedom, the squirrel ran into the lantern, coating the fluffy tail in oil and becoming a very powerful and swift living torch, during a time when heavy curtains weren't only fashionable, but useful for a heating and cooling strategy."

Esmy decided they must be brothers and the older one had been practicing telling this tale.

"The end result was a series of interesting rumors ranging from the most likely that the bio professor had to receive some very early and painful rabies vaccines to the highly imaginative were-squirrel theory. The other end result was that natural sciences were moved across campus to a different building."

"Weresquirrels?"

"Big ones," the older brother kept spinning the tale as they began to walk on.

Esmy finally hurried on, laptop slung over her shoulder, down the building's hidden back stairwell to the basement. She stopped just at the door. A flurry of a dozen students flashed past her, rushing down another set of steps. She looked over at them, but when she looked directly to where she had seen them descend another staircase, all she saw was a brick wall. Esmy turned her head slightly and looked askance from the corner of her eye. Looking this way, she could see a sign labeled "Subbasement (PN Sciences)" and a set of stairs. When Esmy tried to look directly at it again though, it was just a brick wall. She checked this oddity in her vision a few more times.

She passed through the door on the stairwell, strode past the offices for a few Math and Computing professors and through a door labeled "Information Technology Department." Jesus was already in his office, the door was cracked, but that was about the only visible indicator, she had to peer into the dark room to see the soft glow of a pair of monitors and a small desk lamp.

Esmy nudged open the door. "Y'know boss, I was just complaining about the lighting in the basement last week to Fred in maintenance."

Jesus didn't look up right away from one of his monitors. "You mean how there's too damned much of it? I keep telling Fred the same friggin 'thing."

Esmy scoffed at him. "Well, if you weren't a damned vampire, we wouldn't have this problem in the first place."

At that Jesus looked away from the monitors and square at Esmy, pointing a finger at her. "Damn it, Esmeralda, you know vampirism is an irreversible syndrome, quit being so damned insensitive to the handicapped!"

Esmy laughed. "Hope you are ready for the weekend, you've got a fantastic start to it today! Dr. Longfellow wanted me to stop in to remind you about the Board of Regents meeting this afternoon."

"Oh, fuck me sideways," Jesus said cupping his face in his hands. "I thought that was next week. Shit, shit, shit, I hate how long those meetings can go and that awkward Dr. Neidermeier."

"Hey, while you're in a fantastic mood." Esmy decided to take a stab and just ask about it. "What's in the subbasement below us? I swear I see it sometimes and sometimes I don't. Like just now, I saw some students rushing down a set of stairs that weren't there when I looked. I can see a staircase and a sign if I don't look directly at it."

"Huh, most folks don't notice them at all. That's interesting."

"What's interesting?"

He sat back up and shrugged off the question, "Nada, it's one of the departments for the school. Natural Sciences got moved back in the 20's to Miller Hall, but they left the School of Preternatural Sciences here in the subbasement."

Esmy looked perplexed. "What does one study in a School of Preternatural Sciences?"

"Do they ever complain about WiFi or tech support?"

She thought it over. "No, no one's ever come up for that."

"Then it doesn't concern us much. If you want to find out more about that department, you can check with the registrar." Jesus tossed his hands up, leaning back in his office chair. "Hell, enroll in a few of their classes if you get interested. Just remember, unless you can make it pertinent to your job, you only get the twenty percent college employee discount. If you can convince me it'd be useful in your role, then I can have the department cover it in our continuing-ed budget."

Esmy thanked him and headed back to her desk to set up and get the day figured out. She wrote out a quick reminder on a post-it note and left it on her monitor to check with the Registrar's office about the School of Preternatural Sciences.

CHAPTER 4

DOLORES

"**M**ommy, when will daddy be home?"
It was the fifth time the eight-year-old sitting on the kitchen island asked the question. It was the first time the issue really registered to her mother though. Dolores heard her daughter ask, and recognized it was the same question again, but only now realized what question Sofia asked.

"Oh, sweetie, he's on a long business trip this time." She shut off the water, realizing the dishes were done and turned to talk to her daughter. "He just left on Wednesday Sofia, and his company was sending him all the way to China this time. That's a long flight, and why are you sitting on the island? Get down from there." Dolores furrowed her brow and gave a puff of breath. She knew she wasn't mad at Sofia, but her frustration with her husband's constant business trips put Dolores on edge, especially after finding a condom randomly in his luggage.

Sofia knew this was Mommy's angry, worried face. She knew most of her mother's mannerisms after spending eight years with her as the only child. Sofia was used to most of them, including this one, but she wasn't used to Mommy being as distant or having to ask past the fourth time. This was the only time she could remember asking for the fifth time to get an answer. Something was up.

"Geez, Mom, I've been sitting here on the counter all morning eating breakfast, and you just now noticed?" Sofia even added an eye roll to let her mom know that she was advancing to a level of sarcasm and snark well beyond her age.

Dolores felt her lips purse and twist to the side. "We sit on the stools if we are eating at the island, thank you, or we don't sell cookies this weekend. And you know that if we don't sell cookies this weekend, your troop won't get top in the state again."

Sofia could tell when her mom really meant something; she hopped back down to her stool immediately. She wasn't going to risk the cookie goal; it was a fun activity they both seemed to enjoy while dad was on one of his frequent business trips. Sofia was so eager to get onto moving boxes of cookies that she was wearing her girl scouts uniform to school. Her whole troop would be to drumming up word of mouth that cookie sales were kicking off this weekend.

"Where are we going to set up this weekend, Mommy?"

Dolores mulled the question over for a moment. "I'm not sure yet, hon. I'm going to run the numbers from last year and look over some spots while you're at school today. Don't you worry though, by the time we rally the troops this weekend, I'll know a spot in town that will pump our numbers. That troop over in Scottsville will look like rookies."

Sofia and Dolores exchanged a wicked grin at that; they both shared a deep loathing for Scottsville. Dolores encouraged the rivalry, in the belief that it would be good for her daughter's ego. Sofia didn't know why they should hate Scottsville so much, but she really liked to share the feeling with her mom.

Sofia even kept a diary hidden under a drawer in her dresser, where she wrote a prayer a day, wishing new horrors onto the people of Scottsville. Her ill will gained strength recently. It started when she was able to write with a simple prayer of agitation that read, "I hope your poop gets poop." Last night's entry involved wishing that each family would be forced to feast on a bland chili made of the stewed meat of their maternal grandmothers. The diary alone could easily be a basis for no less than three doctoral theses in child psychology.

Dolores straightened the sash across Sofia's uniform and told her to go grab her backpack. "Your bus will be here any minute, and you don't want to be late!"

They finished getting Sofia ready for school, taming some knots out of her slick black hair and into a tight little bun that the hat of her uniform sat neatly against. When she saw her daughter hop onto the bus, and the bus start to pull away, Dolores closed all the curtains in the house.

She went upstairs to her bedroom where she started her preparations for the calling.

Dolores started with the foods; she took them up in a laundry basket and spread them out across her bedroom on the various dressers and nightstands. She made sure that there was fresh water, imported from an island spring, running through a small fountain on the dresser opposite the king-size bed.

Knowing it would be more sacred, she emptied space between the bed and the dresser with the mirror. Once the area was thoroughly clean, she took out a large bag of flour, opening a corner into a spout. She shook the bag and walked around, drawing on the floor. Once done with that, she bathed and put on a silky flowing gown of greens and yellows.

She was putting her hair put up in a coral red wrap when there was a rapid DING DONG DING DONG DING DONG DING DONG DING. Immediately, Dolores said out loud, "ahh, shit." She wondered if she remembered to lock the door after Sofia caught the bus.

The front door creaked open, "Knock, knock, Dolly, I know you're home, girl," a cheery high-pitched Texan voice called up from down the steps near the living room.

Dolores went to her bedroom doorway and called down the steps, "I'm a little busy, Samantha, what's up?"

"Don't you remember hon? We are supposed to have lunch today, don't tell me you forgot."

"Crap, Sam, I'm sorry," Dolores called back down again, trying to find some way to get out of it or just get her out of the house altogether. "I got busy with a few things, and I'm right in the middle of something."

Sam shut the front door, and Dolores could start to hear her mounting the steps. "Don't you fret, Dolly! My Nana always said a job's easier to knock out with a friend. We'll get done and still be able to hit Jackie's for lunch."

Dolores slammed the door in a panic. "I'm, umm, not sure this is a job you can really help, uh, out with much. It's a little hard to explain."

"Now Dolly, just let me in. We've done all sorts of things together before, and I'm sure this ain't any different from that. Hell, you remember that time I threw my back out, and you helped wax my legs and bikini zone?"

Dolores remembered, it was a bleary morning that would haunt her on strange sleepless nights for years, which can speak volumes when she had seen many notably horrible things living, dead and undead in her initiation years. She put her back to the door to brace it shut. "I really don't think you'd quite understand this one, Sam, maybe we can just do it next week."

"Bullshit, Dolly. Now let me in, or I'll have to shoot the door down, my backs not up to ramming you off the other side today."

Dolores paused for a moment to consider that. Samantha was a very tall woman, broad-shouldered and athletically built. She wasn't overweight, but she definitely had more mass to her than Dolores's willowy frame. Dolores also needed to consider that the Dallas native may actually be packing heat. "OK, no laughing, no judging and you have to listen to everything I say, got it?"

Sam called back on the other side of the door, "On my mother's grave, you got it."

"Sam, your mom's still alive, she called you on Tuesday,

and she's supposed to visit next month."

"Well shit, Dolly. We gonna argue semantics or we gonna get this done? I've been looking forward to a buffalo wrap all week."

"Fine." Dolores opened the door. Sam poked her head in first and gave a puzzled look around the room, then stepped in. She was wearing jeans and a green flannel shirt with a tank top underneath. Her massive chest tested the strength of the top set of buttons of the flannel shirt.

"Now what in the world do you have going on here?" Samantha was staring around at everything in the room trying to make sense of it all.

Dolores quickly stepped in front of her, putting her hands up. "First off, try not to touch anything. It took a long time to set up, and if anything is out of place it can really screw up the ritual."

Sam looked at her with a cocked eyebrow. "Ritual?"

"Look, you know how Jack and I got married right after college?" Sam nodded. "Well, my education was a bit non-traditional. I majored in some strange things, I was always interested in African and Haitian cultures, Creole too, a lot of my mother's side."

Sam backed slightly towards a corner. "And that's what this is, some sort of weird Satan ritual?"

Dolores put her hands up pleadingly. "No, nothing to do with Satan, we're not Satanists, that's a whole different thing. This is Voodoo; the most common term for me would be a practitioner. Technically, I am a bokor, which marks me as a sorcerer able to work in, well, many different fields. Though, some like to sell themselves as priest or priestess, even king or queen of voodoo. I excelled in being able to contact a number of the Loa, hell, I interned with a prominent queen in Haiti."

Sam remembered something Dolores mentioned and barked out a quick question. "You weren't on a mission trip for your semester away like you told us about, then?"

Dolores turned the phrasing over in her mind. "Well, it

was a sort of mission, more of a personal mission to find a job and the credits to graduate."

Sam sighed and gave Dolores her "don't give me your bullshit" look. It worked, frighteningly well. Dolores saw her use it on a used car salesman to instantly drop a price by about 10 percent.

"Look, I have a pretty good talent for this. I had plans to travel, learn more about the rites, but..." She looked around and held her hands out.

"You got knocked up and decided to settle down instead," Dolores summarized shortly.

"In a nutshell. Josh and I, things went really fast, and next thing I knew, I was pregnant. I never once thought about not having her. I just thought about how I could leave and still do what I wanted, but that wasn't a life for raising a child. I decided to just alter how I defined priestess to me, to include motherhood."

Samantha was focusing on Dolores but still looking back and forth around the room. "Does Josh know about ... this?" She waved her hands around the room.

"In nine years of marriage, he never found out about it." Dolores felt herself smile in light of the deception. "I wasn't sure how he would feel about it, so I kept my practice secret. I'd wait for him to be away if I wanted to do a ritual I could do at home, or I made up the need for a spa day if it was a night time ritual that required a different venue."

Sam gave her a hawkish stare. "By different venue you mean..."

"Graveyards, yes. There are powerful Loa and spiritual connections that happen in graveyards. Some rituals have to be done at certain times, and that can be very late into the early morning hours."

Sam scoffed and looked around incredulous. "Ok, Sam, you're skeptical, I get that." Dolores paced. "Oh, speaking of that time your back went out you just mentioned? Do you remember how the day right after you had me help you wax, it suddenly all felt better?" Sam nodded suspiciously. "And your chiropractor was amazed at the recovery, that you were able to still go run the Mini Marathon down in Indy the next weekend?"

"Horseshit."

"Hear me out. Do you remember after we got done, I walked around your house burning what I told you was incense, and you said it smelled like we were hip deep in a Grateful Dead concert? I was actually performing a ritual to Loco, a healing Loa, asking him to fix your back."

Sam rubbed her back thinking back to the pain and the sudden relief.

Dolores motioned towards her ritual setup. "This is a pretty standard ritual I've done a lot, with a Loa I call on often, Erzulie."

Sam gave her a confused look and sat down on the bed next to her. "Well, you got my interest, but we should hurry it along. I'd like to hit lunch still, and Jackie closes up by two. Give me the short version, like what the heck a Loa is and what we have to do with this Erzily fella."

Dolores nodded her head and stood up to face Sam. "OK, Loa is just the term for the spirits or gods in the Voodoo pantheons. There are five. Think of it not really as though they are all equals, but a big corporation and they make up departments with various roles. Not everyone has the same amount of power or ability, but they make up the whole of the organization. The one I'm looking to deal with today, Erzulie, she's from the older set, the Rada pantheon. They are easier to deal with but can be confusing at times."

She motioned to the drawing on the floor in flour. "This is a veve. It's a set of symbols associated to the Loa and can help to call them to this specific place. For Erzulie, it's an ornamental heart pierced by a sword, and she likes to be called from a bedroom."

Sam cocked an eyebrow at that detail and gave a slight smirk.

"OK, yes, she has associated with some family planning related activities, but in this case, I'm calling on her for prosperity in other ways. She can show me the means for success in some things. In this case, where to…" She covered her face with her hands, realizing what she was about to say out loud.

"Where to what? Don't leave me hanging now."

Dolores dropped her hands and looked up at the ceiling. "Where to sell cookies." There she said it, and she looked back at Sam who was giggling now.

"You go through all this just to help your rugrat sell more cookies?"

She pointed a shaking finger at Sam and slung her other hand to her hip. "It's a lot tougher than they tell you when you sign up, just trying to foist those damn boxes on strangers. So, yes, I call on some extra help to know where will bring me some better sales. We've been the state's top troop for selling now for three years thanks to Erzulie, thank you very much."

Sam stopped giggling and asked, "Alright, what do you need me to do?"

"Usually, I call Erzulie into me. She eats the food I've put out, and I ask her favor by either a note or something obvious in the room." She hadn't set that out yet, but she lowered her eyelids and looked over at Sam. "That's where you being here may make this a little weird. Did you ever experiment a bit when you were in school?"

Sam gave Dolores a confused look. "What, like drugs? I tried pot a few times, but it just gave me a nasty headache the next day."

"No, not drugs." Dolores sat down next to her and gently touched Sam's knee to let her get the drift.

"Oh… This goddess is a lesbo?" Sam managed to cock one eyebrow high enough that it jumped behind a lock of hair.

"She favors both sexes but is known to be very flirtatious with women and can be pretty forward."

"OK, thanks for the warning. What else do you have to do? I hope you're not planning to slaughter a rooster in here or anything, because, let me tell you, blood doesn't come out of white sheets. Ever."

Dolores laughed. "No, no, regardless of what you've heard, a number of the rituals can be done without sacrificing an animal or blood. For Erzulie, it's a matter mainly having the right symbols, the right foods, clothes, and some good jewelry laid out. She likes to ... feel pampered. Look, you just stay where you are, I'll call her into me. She's a bit needy at times, so just give her the foods, maybe put some jewelry on me for her, and tell her she looks lovely and what not. Then ask her to show me where I'll be most prosperous for my weekend. She'll determine from there what I want to see."

"And if she starts getting all horned up, what do I do?"

"Whatever you want to do. If you're not comfortable, then just tell her it's not your preference. But, if she gets your interest, feel free to have a bit of fun." Dolores gave Sam a wink.

"Oh that's not even funny. Girl, you're like a sister to me." Sam closed her eyes for a second, and the image kept there. "Ew ew ew ew."

Dolores giggled some more at the reaction. "I'm sure you'll be fine. She may ask something from you, but just barter her down and ask her my question."

Sam thought for a second. "What about zombies? I thought voodoo was a lot to do with raising the dead and shit like that."

Dolores shook her head. "No, that is something a bokor can do, but it's only one thing a bokor can do. Kind of like... your plumber can install a toilet, but he doesn't just install toilets, he can fix a pipe, replace a tub, unclog your sink, etcetera."

"So, zombies are like toilet work?"

Dolores chuckled again. "They aren't the easiest things to work with; they're hard to control without assistance. Good luck running more than one human zombie at a time, as bad as a kid on crack."

"Actually, now that you're here"--Dolores looked around and trailed off on thought--"you've given me an idea." She picked up a large gold locket in the shape of a heart with a diamond shaped emerald in the center. She handed it to Sam.

"Instead of asking her, tell her I'd like a ride along instead. Tell her I would like her to possess this as an Ouanga for me. That should cut her cost down."

Sam nodded. "OK, ask her to hop in as an Oh-Anga thingy. Got it."

Dolores stepped over to the veve and looked at herself in the mirror. Sam sat, watching on the bed. Dolores started swaying from side to side on the balls of her hips rotating her hips.

She called out, "Erzulie! Ori ye ye o!"

Sam stifled a short giggle, but it didn't distract Dolores. She continued swaying and started to wave her arms in motion with her hips. She called louder, "Erzulie! Ori ye ye o!"

She began swaying faster, keeping a mental rhythm of drums speeding faster in her head. She stopped suddenly and shouted at the top of her lungs, "Erzulie! Ori ye ye o!"

Her body collapsed and curled up on the floor. Sam leaned over across the bed to get a better look. Just as she could see her, Dolores slowly rose. When she turned, her eyes rolled back, far enough that only white was visible.

"Dolly, you in there?"

When she spoke, the voice sounded an octave or two lower than Dolores usually sounded. "Ooh, chil', what yo 'frien' got you inta wit Erzulie naw?"

Sam took a moment to process that statement. Thick accents were more comfortable for Texans usually, but this one could be used to fill potholes.

"Well, ma'am, Dolly wanted me to ask if you could help her out, hopping into that locket there." She pointed to the necklace. "To be something like an Oh-Wanga."

The spirit inside Dolores closed her eyes and gave a soft chuckle. "You must be new," she said as she rubbed her hands up and down her body. "Oh, and the Bokor wasn't expecting you." She opened her eyes and curled a serpentine smile. "She's not wearing any underwear."

Sam's eyes widened as Erzulie sauntered toward her.

When she was close, Erzulie whispered, "Or was she hoping to catch you in a web to pull you in like the cunning little spider she is?" She licked Sam's neck, and Sam jumped back.

"Now, look, I'm a married woman," Sam said shakily.

Erzulie purred, "As am I. The bokor should have set out three rings, one for each husband: Damballah, Agwe, and Ogun. The bokor is married as well." She rolled her eyes. "Though unhappily so."

Sam cocked her head and gave her a confused look. "You folks get into that more than Mormons anymore, do ya?"

Erzulie just trilled a laugh.

"Look, I'd love to help my friend, but one partner in my life is enough for me. Now, there are cakes and all kinds of stuff that Dolly said you'd like here. Would that work, maybe I could do your makeup or somethin'? Maybe rub your shoulders?"

Erzulie slumped and pouted. She sighed. "I must be getting old, I can't even seduce a prime Amazonian like you. I thought the bokor was happy enough with our last interaction that she might finally bring me some company, but you don't even want to play along."

Erzulie sat on the bed and started crying. Sam was thoroughly confused and felt further out of her element. She was unsure how to act around a spirit possessing her friend, but she was starting to think that this girl was more emotional than an after-school special.

Sam put her arm around her possessed friend. "Look, it's not you, it's me. I just got hit with all this voodoo stuff being a real thing a few minutes ago. Plus, I've always been into guys, not gals. I tried that drink when I was younger and did not care for it, if you get my drift."

Erzulie calmed her sobbing. "Re-really?"

"Yeah, but don't get me wrong. If I were into the ladies, I'd totally take you up on it. You made Dolly seem downright sexy."

Erzulie stifled her wails a bit more and wiped her eyes with her palms. "Do you really mean that?"

Sam gave her another squeeze. "Of course I do, sweetie.

I'd be spreading for you like butter. Now, could you help out my friend?"

Erzulie smiled. "Well, I'll make you a deal. Put the locket on me and give me a kiss. It only has to be one kiss, but you need to really make it worthwhile. Surely, you couldn't grant me a kiss?"

Sam grimaced. "One kiss and we're good? No hanky-panky?"

"That depends," Erzulie trilled, winking Delores 'eye at her. "Ever get your butthole licked out by someone being possessed by a multi-dimensional sex fiend?"

Sam gave her a stern look. "I'm not looking to have my butthole licked out by anyone," she said flatly.

Erzulie made a pouting face and drew a cross over Dolores's heart with her finger.

Sam walked over to the dresser and took the locket. She knelt down next to the bed. Erzulie looked down. Sam clasped the necklace around Dolores's neck, and then gently pulled Dolores's face back up with her index finger. She looked into the eyes of Erzulie, then closed her own.

Sam leaned in, tilting her head slightly and leaned in to gently embrace her lips with her friend's. They were soft and tinged with a muted salty flavor of dried tears. They both welcomed the warmth of the gesture and pulled in closer. As Sam was about to release, she felt sudden hotness on her tongue and saw a soft glowing luminescence through her eyelids.

Dolores rocked back and looked confused at Sam. "OK, please tell me we weren't about to go full tilt there. Did she agree to it?"

Sam sat back on her knees and pointed at the locket, the gemstone gave a soft green glow.

Dolores jumped up. "You are awesome Sam! Let me change, and we'll grab lunch. I owe you lunch for, like, the next three weeks."

Dolores ran to the bathroom to change. Sam just turned to sit back against the bed, now suddenly wondering what it would be like to make love to a spirit like Erzulie. Maybe it wasn't such a stretch.

CHAPTER 5

ESMY

It was about half-past one when Esmy walked into the library. She wove around the counter and ducked under the opening towards the back. Esmy could smell the odor of melting plastic as she made her way behind the work-study student. She saw he had a textbook out that he was making the utmost impression of studying. However, he also was browsing with five tabs open on the computer next to the book. By the icons, she could tell three of them were Reddit, one was Facebook, and the last she couldn't discern as she walked through the door with a laminated sign reading "Staff Only."

She crossed the room, past the new books that were set to receive barcodes, past the older books that were pulled for their wear to have their spines mended, and found Jake in khakis and a green polo. He appeared to have finished laminating a small stack of new signs and was diligently trimming the excess material from the edges.

Esmy plopped down into a wheeled office chair and rolled the last 10 feet to Jake. He didn't seem the least bit distracted or surprised by her arrival. Without looking up from his trimming, Jake asked, "Hey sis, what's up?"

"I've come on my search for incidental and trivial knowledge. I have brought my customary payment, the currency that I believe is accepted by all librarians universally!"

She set a banana that she'd been carrying next to Jake and gave him a wide grin. Jake sighed and leaned over to check that he switched off the laminating machine. He turned towards his sister and looked down at the banana. "It's still green."

Esmy gave a tsk and folded her arms. "Just once, only once, I'd like to come in, do that and the only thing you say is 'ook'. Is that so damned hard for you?"

Jake gave a small laugh. "Well, for one thing, this isn't Unseen University; this is the Baldur College library. For another, I am not an ape." He looked her up and down for a moment. "Stones today? Was Bowie dirty?"

Esmy pursed her lips quizzically. "It wasn't in the clean bucket, but I haven't seen it in a while. If it wasn't for him dying last year, I think only the staff would recognize him."

Jake looked back down at the laminated signs and went back to paring the edges down carefully.

Esmy made her move at maneuvering the conversation. "Hey, speaking of staff and the college, have you ever heard of the Preternatural Sciences department?"

Jake didn't even look up from his cutting this time. "You mean the folks that caused the were-squirrel incident of 1922? Not much, just they got booted out to Miller after that."

"No, that was the Natural Sciences department, there's apparently a Preternatural Sciences department."

Jake looked up at her again, one eyebrow crooked up dangerously close to his short hairline. "What would a Preternatural Sciences department even study?"

Esmy hopped up from the chair. "Thank you, I was wondering the same damn thing. It kept me off task most of the morning."

"What was the task?"

Esmy sighed heavily and dropped her arms like they were lead weights. "Old Dr. Jeffords again."

Jake leaned onto the counter. "Again? He's not that old, he can learn to use an email program, can't he?"

"There are three things I can't really stand about Jeffords. First, he's always wearing sweaters, even in the summer. That's not right. Second, is that the sweaters are all lower cut than anything I own. Between the chest hair and that gaudy gold medallion he wears, it's a big bucket of nope all around."

"Yeah, he doesn't look that old, but I suppose his fashion sense is dated about thirty-five odd years." Jake agreed, somberly. "Is the third thing the computer issue?"

"Yep, I don't get it. Why Jesus lets him get away with it is beyond me, and even more beyond me, is why his secretary puts up with it. The poor woman prints out every email from the previous day in the morning. He reads them all, writes out the replies on the same damn pages in cursive, and then makes his secretary transcribe all that crap back to send out replies."

"How does that end up causing you issues, then?" Jake asked.

Esmy buried her face in her hands for a moment. "That's the stupidest part. He won't touch a computer to deal with email, but he thinks he can fix printers. They have a separate printer, so they don't ruin the toner budget for the rest of the building. When the toner runs out though, he doesn't understand that you need to either get a new cartridge or refill it with actual toner. Somehow, he keeps trying to refill the cartridges with ink for fountain pens. They try to lie about it and play innocent, but I caught him one time. He had an awl and this old ball peen hammer. It looked like he was preparing to cobble shoes, but he was trying to bust a small hole into the print cartridge."

"Maybe he was about to perform trepanning on his secretary." Jake muttered. "What did you do?"

Esmy shrugged. "What could I do? He has tenure. I can't exactly get them to penalize or fire him for just being a Luddite. I know it's horrible to say, but annoying pains-in-the-ass people like him just mean I have more job security. Hell, I don't even know what he teaches."

Jake thought about it. "I think he teaches one history class I know of, but I'm not sure that he's an actual part of the History department."

"Hmm. That still doesn't help us to know anything about this department of Preternatural Sciences."

"Where did you even hear about this department?" asked Jake.

"I was asking Jesus about the subbasement in the Old Bastard," Esmy replied.

"Wait, there's another basement below you? I never noticed."

"You never come to visit me, I always have to come to you Mr. Center-of-the-known-Universe. Come down the stairs sometimes, and you'll see another set of stairs going further down. But here is the strange thing, you can't see it if you look directly at it." She turned her head sideways. "You have to look at it from the corner of your eye. I kept seeing a set of students going down there all the time and asked Jesus about it."

Jake was getting curious now, too. "What did he tell you?"

"The same thing I'm telling you. He told me they were majors in Preternatural Sciences. He wouldn't say anything about the department, just told me to take it up with the registrar."

"That's awfully cryptic, ironic coming from that specter."

"Vampire," she corrected him. "But, yeah it is. So I decided I'd take him up on that, but came by here to see if you knew anything about it first."

Jake thought about it for a moment more. "No, never knew about the subbasement and hadn't heard about that department. Makes me curious though if they have different books than what's in our collection here. Want some company going to talk to Mrs. Pilleteri in the Registrar's office?"

"Sure, let's head over to the Old Bastard and see what she can tell us."

Esmy headed for the door, as Jake grabbed his jacket from

his nearby chair and threw it on. They walked out of the back room to behind the counters again. The student that had been acting to study was packing up and letting another student take over. She glanced at the screen again and caught two strange images. The first was what looked like a wasp nest. The second appeared to be a picture of an old dark blue or purple van, airbrushed with a picture of a wizard and a unicorn. She did a double take, but by the time she whipped her head back, the tabs were closed, and he was logging off the user session.

Jake followed Esmy's gaze and saw the pair of students swapping seats out. "Done for the day, Kyle?"

The student packing, looked up suddenly. "Oh hey Mr. Hansen, Dr. Gene texted me. Somebody found a giant wasp nest in a field, and he wants me to try to retrieve it for study before the farmer kills it." Kyle spoke in an accent vaguely northern, and Esmy wondered if he was from Minnesota or somewhere in Canada. "Judy's going to take over for me, and I'm going to take some of her Saturday hours."

Jake nodded and motioned for Esmy to keep walking. "Alright, be careful out there. It'll be hard for you to shelve books covered in wasp stings."

Jake and Esmy walked out the door and headed across a set of neatly manicured lawns towards the broad, dark bricked building that earned the nickname of the Old Bastard. It was large and foreboding with a slate roof that stood up to centuries of storms. The building felt oddly shaped like a stepped pyramid. At its widest points, the building was three floors high, adding stories as you came to the center of the structure. At the center were six stories total of class and office space. Jutting out above that sixth floor, visible to the whole campus, was a bell tower that rose well above the rest of the building. There was no clock on any face, but the bells atop the high spire still rang loudly, precisely on the hour.

Esmy and Jake walked in a back entrance of the Old Bastard and headed towards the center of the building. They passed through the center stairwell. The grand mahogany staircases ascended and wrapped around an opening that ran through the center of the whole building. Esmy stood at the bottom and saw straight up to the sixth floor. The first flight of stairs started in the center and rose to the back wall where it split off to two flights for students to head left or right. At the center of that was a large bronze bust of a Norse god, Esmy knew was the college's namesake, Baldur. A student shuffled up the staircase and rubbed Baldur's discolored nose as he strode past. "Must have a test," Jake muttered.

 They headed past the staircase and went down the next hallway where the registrar kept an office. Inside, they found Mrs. Pilleteri, a raven-haired, overweight Greek woman in a blue floral dress, seated at her desk. She peered at them from behind heavy curved glasses. "Ah, ze twins! What can you do for me today?" Her voice was low and husky, with a slight accent that was vaguely European.

Esmy and Jake both forced grins and pushed back the agitation of the greeting. Esmy started, "Hi Mrs. Pilleteri."

She cut her off quickly. "Please, Ezmeralda, call me Betty when we aren't around students."

 Esmy winced at her whole name. Betty's smoky voice made it sound too formal, and she rolled the name smoothly with the 's 'making a slight 'z 'sound. "Then please, just Esmy. Jake and I randomly heard about a major in Preternatural Sciences."

 Betty's eyes twinkled, and she hopped in. "And you wondered what constitutes a Preternatural Science?"

 " In a nutshell, yes."

 Betty steepled her fingers and stared across her desk at them. "You should have some clearance about that department, how did you find out about it, Ezmy?" She motioned for them to sit in the pair of seats behind them.

 They pulled the chairs and sat. "I was asking Jesus about the subbasement this morning, and he mentioned the students heading down there were Preternatural Sciences majors. Jesus told me I should talk to you about it."

Betty scoffed and rolled her eyes. "That damned vampire will be the death of me yet." She sat back in her chair and stared at them, her green eyes seemingly piercing them.

Esmy chuckled a bit.

Betty took off her glasses and rubbed the bridge of her nose. "What is so funny, Ezmy?"

Esmy sat up straight from her slouch, as though she was just scolded. "Oh, I always joke about Jesus being a vampire, too. He keeps that office darker and colder than any IT person I've ever known."

Betty smiled at that. "Usually, students aren't allowed to take courses from that catalog. It's kept separate for an excellent reason. Most students never even know it exists. I'll say Mr. Mordido just gave you the clearance by telling you about it in the first place."

The twins sat forward with anticipation.

"There are some subjects of study that are not generally accepted in your normal scientific research, nor generally well..." She searched for a word. "...received by the general public of students learning."

Esmy and Jake looked at each other. They both looked puzzled and turned back to Betty.

She searched for a better way to explain it and leaned forward. "OK, let's say you go to the Natural Sciences building. You'd go to take classes in say Biology, Physics, Astrophysics, and Chemistry, right?"

The twins nodded in agreement.

Betty continued, "Well, in the Preternatural Sciences department, you'd instead take classes in..." She looked over a course catalog for a moment. "...Cryptozoology, Metaphysical Manifestations, Cross-dimensional Astrophysical Travel and General Thaumaturgy." She clasped her hands and leaned back in her chair.

Esmy and Jake alternated looking at each other and looking back and forth at Betty for a moment grasping at what she just said.

Jake leaned forward so far he almost fell out of his chair. "Wait, everything you just listed is basically magical or supernatural in nature. We don't actually teach that here."

Betty pointed a sharp red painted nail at him. "That is exactly why we don't publicize this and announce the major to the world, that closed-mindedness you just pushed back my way. Of course, we offer this, I just told you we did, but you tried to shove it back in my face and say it isn't offered."

Esmy found her voice now. "Umm, so Cryptozoology, that's studying Yetis and gnomes and such, right?"

Betty winced a bit. "Yetis, yes, gnomes, no. Gnomes would fall under Cross-Realm Humanoid Biology and Medicine."

Esmy pushed a bit further. "Cross-dimensional Astrophysical Travel would be…"

"Wormholes, essentially. I never took the class, but that's how I've heard Jeffords explain it in the abridged version. He could probably go on for hours about it."

Esmy felt her jaw drop off her face. "Dr. Jeffords? The same Dr. Jeffords that can't be bothered to actually respond to emails and makes that poor secretary print it all out, that Dr. Jeffords? Jeffords can create a wormhole to travel through space?"

"Time, too. How else do you think he gets those absurd sweaters. He won't shop at the vintage stores. Those things are fresh from the seventies, great prices he says, but finding old currency, so you don't cause a time paradox is a pain." Betty shifted her expression to be a bit compassionate. "And you really shouldn't give him such a hard time about the computer problems. It's a side-effect of a failed attempt by an ill-prepared student a few years ago. If he actually touched a computer, at the very least it would destroy the device's usefulness. The circuits are the issue, too close to unshielded electricity and strange things happen. We think he may have touched a TV once after the accident and it vanished. It's still unaccounted for."

"He can accidentally drop electronics through space?"

Betty nodded. "Like I said, we don't know where it's at, but we also don't know where the TV is at either. It could pop back on the same table tomorrow, or it could be sitting in the middle of an Apache or Miami encampment in the fifteenth century, though no accounts found have mentioned an ill-gifted Toshiba thirty-two inch TV."

Esmy was getting the hang of this now. "Metaphysical Manifestations, would that be ghosts or out-of-body experiences?"

Betty grinned wolfishly at Esmy. "You see, you are catching on. Ghosts and spiritual communion is in MM one, OBE's are held for a special study in MM two. Now, the problem is that this is just general ghosts and spirits of this realm, divine contact, pacts, and summoning are taught in specialization to the different religions and outer realm studies. Some, we teach every year, some we only teach for certain years when certain lecturers are available."

Jake looked dumbfounded. Esmy just nodded some more. "And General Thaumaturgy, what does that entail?"

Betty spread her hands. "Well, you have General Thaumaturgy or GT, then Thaumaturgy One or T1, then T2, and Advanced Thaumaturgy, AT. These are your classes around sorcery and spell casting, using material elements and symbology. For example, Runecraft is taught in T1, in GT, you can expect how to mix some entry-level potions. They generally have prerequisites such as Preternatural Botany or Arcane Linguistics."

Esmy nodded some more. She found this really interesting. Jake tossed in, "I've never really seen any of these topics in the library or the campus bookstore. Are there textbooks for Yeti biology? A special collection I don't know about?"

Betty chewed over the question for a moment. "A lot of students are able to get their required texts from professors, in our special collections housed under the college, or they just order them on Amazon like everyone else. Cryptozoology is a pretty easy one to pick up on Amazon, though you have to get the right ISBN numbers. I've had so many complaints of kids getting the fourth edition on accident."

Esmy and Jake sat stunned for a moment, mulling all of this over. Betty sighed. "Look, you both are nice young folk, and we like you here. If you really want to look into it more, think over what we talked about today, and we can talk about maybe enrolling you in some of the base courses. You get your college employee discount, you know. Right now though, I have reports to print out for the board meeting this afternoon."

They both still stared at her, not sure what she meant. Betty pointed to the door. "If you would please, I will have more time next week. It's been great talking. Ezmy, let's maybe have coffee and discuss it more, but next week, eh?"

Jake and Esmy finally got the hint, stood up, and shuffled out of the room. Betty got up from her seat and shut the door behind them. The pair walked stiffly down the hall to the central staircase. They turned to stare at the bust of Baldur a flight up from them. The ancient Norse god was staring down at them, past a tarnished nose.

Jake turned back to Esmy. "Esmeralda, did we just really have that conversation with Betty? That we are sitting on something like a miniature advanced Hogwarts blended into a regular college?"

Esmy blinked a few times. "Yes, we did. It sounds too good to be true, doesn't it?"

"It sounds insane, Esmy. I don't believe it. It's impossible."

Esmy chuckled. "The impossible does often have a kind of integrity to it which the merely improbable lacks."

Jake sighed. "You stole that from Douglas Adams."

"It's not stealing it, I'm quoting him."

"You didn't attribute it though, Esmeralda Hansen!"

"For fuck's sake, Jake, it was one of Dad's favorites. I thought you got the reference. Look, I've got to wrap up some stuff downstairs. I'm going for a run later."

She tossed the keys to the elderly Stanza to Jake. "Have fun on your date tonight; see you when you get home. Be careful driving OK? Don't forget the raincoats, eh?" She winked conspiratorially at him.

Jake caught the keys nimbly and nodded. "You, too. Wear something reflective this time. I don't want to get called away from my date to identify your body. I'd have to take that Metaphysical Communications or whatever class just to call you back and yell at you!"

She yelled back to correct him, "Metaphysical Manifestations!"

CHAPTER 6

KYLE

Kyle was barreling through the countryside. Led Zeppelin's Physical Graffiti album blared through the front of the van, vibrating the plastic paneling violently. Behind him, he heard a different sort of violent vibrating. Thousands of wasps were darting around a large plexiglass crate labeled "Baldur College Bio – Dr. Gene." Kyle barely noticed some errant buzzing and specs flying around the cabin of the van through the netting attached to his pith helmet. The slender steering wheel was hard to grip in the thick leather gloves. Kyle jabbed wildly at the cd player buttons in the thick leather gloves. He gave up, deciding he'd have to wait to hear Kashmir again.

The intense decibels of classic rock was all Kyle could hear, not the sirens approaching from behind. He squinted through the mesh veil to see the road ahead of him. The side mirrors were harder to see with the helmet on, he would see a random flash of red or blue but not wonder about it.

Only when the deputy passed him, did Kyle see the speeding car, with lights flashing and turned off the music. He was even more shocked when the car slowed in front of him and finally brought him to a stop, two miles from the city limits.

Deputy Frank Harwald, a stocky middle-aged man with a crown of white hair encircling his pink bald head, exited his vehicle with his sunglasses on. He reached back into his car and drew on his campaign hat before strolling back to Kyle's van, resting his right hand on his pistol and his left on a can of mace as he strode.

Kyle, for his part, didn't notice this gesture as he was busy knocking his head on the steering wheel of the old Dodge Street Van repeating the same phrase, "Oh shit, oh shit, oh shit."

He was mid-oh-shitting when the deputy knocked on the window. "Son, can you turn off the engine and hop out of the van?"

Kyle obeyed the officer without question and hopped straight out of the van. He still wore the entire apiary suit when he tried to address the deputy. "Sir, is there a problem? I thought I was driving about the speed limit."

The deputy stared back at the young man as Kyle shut the door. Kyle was a tall, lean wisp of a young man, at six foot even, he stood a head above Deputy Harwald. "Son, what's your name?"

"Kyle, sir," he answered quickly. "Kyle Voortman."

"I'm Deputy Harwald, Kyle. Now, I have a couple of questions for you. First of which..." He drew his sunglasses down his wide nose; they were dangerously close to slipping off his lightly stubbled face. "Why in the hell are you wearing that thing?"

Kyle realized now how ridiculous he must look. "Oh, this? It's an apiary suit, eh. It's for beekeeping and such."

Deputy Harwald sighed. "I know what a beekeeper's suit is for, but why on Earth are you wearing it driving? You know I've been following you for the last three miles? I was tempted to shoot your tire out. Hell, I thought you might be some kind of weirdo meth runner hopped up on angel dust out here when you didn't stop."

Kyle ripped his pith helmet and veil off in a bit of a panic, realizing he may be in serious trouble now. "I'm so sorry, deputy, I didn't mean to ignore you, but there are a few stragglers still in the van. I figured it was better to wear this than get stung while driving."

Deputy Harwald looked back and forth between Kyle and the van a few times. "Stragglers? Son, you mean to tell me, you've got a full, living hive in the back end of that ... the thing just rolling around?" He was leaning back now.

"Oh, no, no. It's secured in a crate; I can show you if you like. It's half-inch plexiglass, so you can watch the hive. It's truly fascinating to watch the colony feed if you give it a fresh chicken."

"Bees eat chicken?"

"Naw." Kyle chuckled. "A wasp nest! Big one, too. Sucker almost didn't fit."

The deputy held his hands out to pause Kyle. "No, that's fine, I don't need to see any of that. Now, you don't sound too... local."

"Oh yeah, I'm Canadian, born and raised in a suburb of Toronto. My Dad immigrated up there to marry Ma back in eighty-four. Dad graduated from the college here so I could get some good scholarship opportunities as a legacy, and my Uncle Ray still lives local up in Mississinewa. I'm all legal, so no worries, eh."

Deputy Harwald nodded skeptically. "Uh huh. Now, son, do you know why I stopped you out here today?"

"Well, you thought I was some sort of meth runner, but I have no idea what would ever give you that idea." Kyle was talking fast and pointing at the van and up and down the road. "I was going the speed limit. Do I have a tail light out or something, eh?"

Deputy Harwald stepped around him and used two fingers on his right hand to wave him over to the side of the van. "I pulled you over to ask you, what the hell is that?" he pointed at the side of the vehicle.

Kyle scoffed. "You like it? I just got it done last month, and it cost a fortune for that beauty! Came out wonderful though!"

They stood next to the van, a 1978 Dodge Street Van.

The entirety of which was painted midnight blue with a night sky as a background across the whole of it, the back of which had a single octagonal window blocked by a thick purple velvet curtain. The side of the van was airbrushed further with a mural of a wizard and a unicorn. The wizard was behind the unicorn, and both were wearing expressions of deranged pleasure.

"You actually wanted someone to paint a wizard buttfucking a unicorn on your van?" Deputy Harwald cocked an eyebrow high, almost to his hat. "Son, I thought you were a victim of some sick vandal."

"Naw, that's a piece of priceless art."

Deputy Harwald stared intently over his sunglasses at the scene for a bit more. He turned to Kyle and looked him square in the eyes. "THAT is art?"

Kyle smiled brightly down at the deputy. "It's a beautiful scene of high fantasy, depicting man's ability to overcome the unknown and really gain conquest over the whole realm of the natural world."

The deputy shifted his hips to stand fully facing Kyle, pointing at the van he was starting to raise his voice a bit. "Boy, that's a wizard fucking a unicorn! He's hiking up his robes and giving it to him. I can see his stubbly legs and socks behind the thing, and that's the goofiest goddamned o-face I've seen on anything, let alone a unicorn! You can't defend that as high fantasy art. It's a public nuisance."

Kyle knew deep down that the deputy is right, he thought the same thing when he picked up the van. He spent a significant amount of money on the mural to be painted by the sort of people that don't like to hear complaints. However, Kyle also knew that while it suggested one thing, there was no actual nudity shown. So, he decided to adopt the artist's arguments in his initial reactions, which were similar to Deputy Harwald.

"Well, sir, the wizard is celebrating that he's cast a spell to create a homunculus. See the sparks coming off the staff and the starburst from the unicorn's horn?" He pointed to the parts of the mural. "That shows the viewer that the spell was a success!"

Deputy Harwald cocked an eyebrow at him. "So, he creates a hummonuclus."

"Homunculus eh," corrected Kyle on instinct.

"Whatever. Your wizard creates that thing by cornholing a unicorn? Naw, son, that's just perverted. I should run you in for causing a public nuisance and indecent exposure."

"Well, you could, but there's nothing illegal about the painting. Regardless of how suggestive the mural may be to some people, there's nothing actually shown. As much as you may think this is a piece of trashy porn, it is art to me. So ticket me if you want to, but we'll both be wasting our day in a traffic court where a judge decides if this piece of art is protected by the first amendment or not."

Deputy Harwald sank back and crossed his arms. Kyle knew he got him with that argument. Even though the deputy now looked like he'd be happy to shoot him for being an ass. He would bet that the deputy didn't like spending time waiting around in traffic court. It was a gamble, but Kyle thought it was a good wager that Deputy Harwald was the kind of man that hated doing unnecessary paperwork.

"Kid, anyone ever tell you you're an asshole?"

Kyle smiled back at him, realizing he likely wouldn't be getting a ticket today.

Deputy Harwald sighed deeply. Realizing he'd been beaten on his main issue, he resorted to the one thing he could do, become a bureaucratic headache.

"I'll need to see your license, registration, and proof of insurance please, and we'll get you and this ... art on your way."

Kyle complied and went to sit in his van while the deputy ran his plates and license for any outstanding warrants or suspensions. He assumed the deputy was so thorough now just to be annoying. It was taking a very long time, and Kyle thought he could see the deputy was napping in his car.

Eventually, Deputy Harwald ambled back to the van and handed Kyle back his documents. "Looks like you're all in order here. Two things before I let you take off though. First, keep your ass out of trouble. You do not want me to pull you over in this ... thing again."

Kyle shook his head. "Yes, definitely officer, no speeding, no worries. What's the other?"

"I think your van is a gaudy piece of dumpster graffiti that really ought to be in a compactor."

Kyle shook his head again. "Yeah, art generally has its critics and its fans."

The deputy continued, "But would you mind taking a quick picture of me with it?" He was holding up a cell phone.

Kyle stopped shaking his head, and his jaw dropped. "But you just said it belongs in a trash compactor, eh?" Kyle got out of the van and waved the deputy over to stand by the driver's door.

"Yeah, but nobody, I mean no one at my office, not even my wife, will ever believe that I pulled over a shitty old van painted with a wizard fucking a unicorn."

"OK, well, say cheese." He took a couple of quick snaps on the cell phone camera and handed the phone back. "So, nobody would just believe you, have faith that you saw my majestic vehicle?"

"Sometimes, seeing is believing, and I don't think I could give this ... thing justice in words. This," he held the phone up, "is worth way more than any thousand words I could use to describe."

They got back in their vehicles, the deputy drove away first. Kyle settled into the seat, purple Naugahyde squeaking and groaning under him. When the deputy pulled far enough away, Kyle queued up some more Zeppelin and started heading back to the college.

CHAPTER 7

THE BOARD

Betty Pilleteri pushed a small cart covered with a thick white tablecloth out of her office, down the main hallway of the Old Bastard. She passed the central stairwell and took the elevator. It was late enough on the Friday afternoon that students had mostly vacated class buildings campus-wide.

On the elevator, she licked her finger and pressed the button labeled B2. The button glowed pink, and she felt warmth against her fingertip. There was a ding and the door shut much faster than it usually would. Almost immediately, there was another ding, and the doors sprang back open.

Betty exited the elevator into a dark hallway. Sconces along the wall lit as she stepped off. Her heels echoed off stone walls in the cavernous halls as she walked down wide planked hardwood floors.

She walked halfway down the hall and turned to a door. She knocked her heel twice, and the thick wooden arched door swung open. A large chandelier above a long stone table lit the room. Betty started to push the cart, but the front wheels stuck on the threshold. She gave it a shove and jumped the casters back into motion.

She started prepping the room for the upcoming meeting. She moved the old heavy chairs with thick padding, pulling every other one on the sides away to the walls on either side of the large table. To the left, she flanked the chairs around a smaller buffet table. To the right, she flanked them around a hearth situated in the middle of the room. She left four chairs on each side and one at the head of the table opposite the door. In front of each chair, Betty placed a short, typewritten agenda upside down. The ordinary ballpoint pens she left with each agenda looked strange among the rest of the room. An odd modern element in a medieval setting.

Placing the agenda at the head chair last, she glanced behind herself at the giant head mounted on the wall. The room was tall and wide, but the head of a massive serpent filled the space. The cured leathery green skin with brown diamonds had hung there for untold years, possibly centuries, and showed a single deep crack across the center of the massive head. Glass eyes gleamed and sparkled from light bouncing deep inside them. The fangs in the open mouth were cracked but still bore light brown stains from ancient kills. It always gave Betty an uneasy feeling, she always felt like the eyes of the damned creature was following her.

She shivered but kept on her task. She thought of lighting the fire but felt that it wasn't cold enough in the fall to need more heat. She laid the white tablecloth on the buffet table and started unloading the rest of her cart. She placed a carafe of coffee, followed by a set of cups and saucers. There was the bowl of various sweeteners and a small pitcher of cream. Next was a plate of raisin cookies. Then she set out a plate of smoked meats and smoked salmon. Finally, she took a silver bowl filled with ice and contained two units of type O blood from under the cart and placed it at the end of the buffet table.

As she was pushing the cart out of the way and wrapping up, the members of the board started to shuffle into the room. Betty grabbed a cup of coffee and headed to her seat at the table.

Dr. Longfellow was the first to arrive, followed by Professor Mull and Dr. Walker. The pair contrasted each other sharply; Dr. Walker is a tall, young black man with a bald head, and Professor Mull looking like a dwarf copy of Colonel Sanders, aged 60 years more and considerably more substantial.

Dr. Jeffords strode in, followed by a slender young stick of a woman, whom he turned to address, "Professor Cross, Claudette, how are the plants?" He tried to lean in for a hug and to give her a kiss on the cheek, but she deftly swayed back out of his reach.

"My specimens are just fine, Fred. Please keep your hands to yourself." She darted away from him and sat on the other side of the table, avoiding the concessions and settling herself in. Fred scowled briefly and then turned to grab some coffee.

Jesus Mordido strolled in, followed closely by a tall skinny man with a bushy brown mustache, brown curly hair and thick plastic glasses. He was dressed in jeans and a yellow plaid flannel shirt. They both approached the buffet. Jesus picked up the pints of blood, sloshed them both in his hands for a second, then put one back.

The man with the glasses next to him finished pouring a cup of coffee and addressed Jesus. "Only a pint low today, oh Prince of Darkness?" he asked airily.

Jesus chuckled and patted his stomach. "Watching the waistline a bit, Dr. Gene. Human blood can just get so fatty sometimes when it's consumed directly like this. They test for diseases when people donate, but I don't get a listing of the person's cholesterol or triglycerides. It's not like they put nutrition facts on units of blood."

"Huh, does that make a big difference? In the flavor and the digestion?"

Jesus sighed. "Yeah, everyone thinks, 'oh you're a vampire, and you just stay one way forever. 'Hell, we may not be able to die from heart disease, but we can still get fat, overeat, and end up needing to lose some weight. It is a more straightforward process for sure, but the flavor too. Ugh, last week, I swear I drank a unit from someone with a diet of soda, Cap'n Crunch, and Fruity Pebbles. It was like drinking sugar water."

The pair kept a quiet discussion going of the distinctions of blood across various species and diets but found their seats at the table.

Last to walk in, was a tall woman with an oversized bone structure. Her forehead and brow hung over her wire-rim spectacles like a cliff threatening to crush a small village. She carried a thick messenger bag that looked to be strained by the weight of its contents and hurried to find a seat without making eye contact with anyone.

Dr. Longfellow noticed her nonetheless. "Dr. Niedermeier, how wonderful for you to join us," he said across the noise of small talk. "Now that everyone's here, perhaps we can get this moving along? Betty, can you kick us off?"

Betty and a few others at the table flipped the typewritten agenda over to read through it. "Alright everyone," Betty began in her smoky European accent. "We have a short agenda today, some new items and some old ones. Let's start off with an oldie but a goodie. Item one is a petition brought by the students to change the school mascot."

Dr. Longfellow didn't bother looking up from the page as he responded, "Nope. There is nothing wrong with this school's mascot. We go through this every year."

Dr. Walker spoke from the end of the table. "Jim, maybe we should think this through. Students keep petitioning on this year after year. Maybe the college could use a bit of a makeover."

There was a general nod of agreement from other chairs at the table. Jesus spoke up next. "Jim, I know you're really tied into being the War Goats. I get it, plus you've still got the goats, but the kids these days, they just don't get it."

Dr. Longfellow covered his eyes with his hand and sighed. "What is there to get? They are goats that fight in wars, pull chariots and haul carts."

Professor Cross cleared her voice. "Jim, a lot of the

student body wasn't alive when wars were fought with goats, and they've never even seen it in their history books. They just don't associate the two. What if we just change it slightly? Fightin 'Goats might be a college mascot they can get on board to support. We could hire a marketing firm to make up some new logos and drum up support for the name."

Dr. Longfellow stroked his chin. "You may be onto something there, Claudette. I don't like marketing firms though. I think these are things we can take care of in-house. Is the student body support something we can do as a class project in thaumaturgy?"

Claudette thought it over for a moment. "Yeah, I think we can integrate it into the lessons before finals, sometime after Samhain. Might be closer to the Yule break."

"That'll work." Jim turned to Betty next. "For a new logo, there's some kid in the bio department." He nodded over to Dr. Gene. "Reginald, one of your normal students I think, I don't know his name, but he drives a van with a fascinating mural on the side."

Dr. Jeffords spoke up, eyes brightening. "Oh, the 70's van with the wizard screwing the unicorn!" Faces around the table darkened with realization, and someone muttered, "Oh that one."

"Kyle," replied Dr. Gene. "I've told him he really needs to cover that up a bit, it seems disrespectful."

There was a slight murmuring around the table and some nods of agreement. "Nonsense," replied Dr. Longfellow. "I loved the concept when I saw it, very spunky, reminds me of something my uncle would have painted." Dr. Longfellow paused on that though, appearing suddenly dimmed at mentioning his own family.

Betty broke the silent moment. "So we should ask this Kyle who did his van, with this mural of a wizard fornicating with a unicorn, to make a new logo for the college?"

Dr. Longfellow brightened again. "Yes, but let's leave out the bestiality when we talk to him. It sounds horrible the way you said it."

Betty made a few notes. "Moving on to the next item on our agenda, Professor Briggard has caused some complaints from students, and unfortunately, they have been raised by both groups in and out of the Preternatural Sciences majors."

Dr. Longfellow chuckled briefly. "What's old Jack gotten himself into now?"

Betty took off her glasses to stare across at Dr. Longfellow. "Jim, he was caught in some inappropriate behavior with a sasquatch."

There was a general inhalation of disgust around the table. Dr. Walker leaned forward. "What was the exact nature of the act and how were the uninitiated handled?"

Betty stared pointedly down the table to Dr. Walker. "Anton, he was fellating a younger sasquatch. We don't know how long it's been going on, but Jack's apparently been bringing him back to campus on weekends and keeping him in his quarters at the rec center. We assured the students outside of PS that it was just a very hairy younger gentleman."

Dr. Longfellow leaned back in his chair and gave a look of disbelief. "Jack was blowing a bigfoot?"

"To put it bluntly, yes," responded Betty.

"OK, I guess we have a few issues there. Does it violate any of our treaties with their people, for one? Do we know how old the Sasquatch is? It may be that he was not actually doing anything wrong, outside of just unfortunate viewing."

Betty consulted some notes. "None of the treaties with their people explicitly ban relations with humans, but I believe it is taboo for them. We don't know the age, only that it appeared young, male, and very well endowed. One student's complaint said, and I quote, 'Coach Briggard has a better gag reflex than I've seen on internet porn. I won't be able to ever look him in the eye the same again'."

Professor Mull spoke up from next to Anton, waving his finger to be noticed. "When I was a little girl, being caught in such a display would mean a shotgun wedding, be it man or beast!"

Dr. Niedermeier's nasal voice broke through, "Well, this country only recently legalized same-sex marriage, I believe interspecies marriages, even with sentient beings may be a while off." Nobody laughed, and everyone stared at her briefly in silence.

"What I don't get," Dr. Longfellow continued, with Betty ignoring the other comments, "is why didn't he just make sure his curtains were closed?"

"It didn't happen in his quarters," Betty continued. "They were discovered together on the fifty-yard line of the football field late after a fraternity Halloween party off campus."

Dr. Longfellow cocked an eyebrow. "Apparently, they went together as Han Solo and Chewbacca," said Betty. "The group that found them made some bad remarks."

There was a collective inhalation. "Did the squatch kill anyone?"

Betty shook her head. "The squatch, Ned, only caught up to one of them. A student named Billy Turner. Billy suffered a broken leg, and then Ned held him down to 'teabag 'him. We wiped that part of his memory. Billy just thinks he fell severely on some roots of an old tree when he ran away. The mental scarring of Sasquatch sexual assault should be gone."

There was some more bickering across the table around the unique intricacies involved in how to start a relationship with a Sasquatch. Finally, Dr. Longfellow cut them off, "Enough, Betty, tell Jack to bring this Ned back for us to check into this further. In the meantime, he's on paid leave. Get the other phys-ed staff to take on his classes. Was he teaching anything this semester for PS?"

"There is one, Basic Hand to Hand Combat with Deities, Demigods, and the Supernatural."

Dr. Longfellow pounded his fist on the table. "Excellent, I'll take that one over!"

The rest of the table looked surprised. Professor Mull croaked out from the opposite end, "Aren't you a little old and busy to take that on, Jim?"

"Jerry, I only feel young when I'm bashing on something, you've known that forever. And this job," he waved a hand over the paperwork and the room, "well, it's a lot of paperwork, but I've been doing it long enough that I can take some time away to help teach one class. It'll do me good to get back into it."

Dr. Neidermeier burst into laughter, snorting intermittently. Everyone at the table stopped and stared at her. "For heaven's sake," she choked out between laughs, "shouldn't it be a fair fight?" She looked around the table and realized she was the only one laughing. She stopped suddenly, and looked across at Professor Mull. "Was it something I said?"

Jesus coughed. "Jim, not that I think it's a bad idea, you do have the most experience to teach it. But that might be the problem, that you may be overqualified. These are kids that have barely been in fights, ever. I don't know that they could really fare well against you."

Dr. Neidermeier scoffed at that idea. "You all really think it's a good idea to allow a slew of early 20-somethings to beat down a ... an octogenarian?" She stumbled at the end, realizing she'd tread too deep into murky waters.

Dr. Longfellow looked across and back to Betty. "Betty, how long has Julia there been with us?"

"She's been in the Math and Computing Department for four years, three of which as an adjunct, and teaching for one year in the Preternatural Sciences. Classes include Arcane and Non-Euclidean Geometry," responded Betty. "This is her second meeting of the board."

"Not fully tenured into the PS program then?"

Betty shot a glance over to Dr. Neidermeier. "No, Jim, not fully tenured."

Dr. Longfellow leaned forward and looked around the table at the other board members. "I'll remind each of you that there are facts and truths we only reveal tenured members. Until Dr. Neidermeier receives full tenure in this department, you will refrain from voicing the concerns of this matter in front of her, we can continue those discussions one-on-one." He looked down at Dr. Neidermeier. "Julia, if you feel the students are a threat to this 'old man, 'then you are more than welcome to join them on the training field and judge if I need to be sent off to the old-folks home." He stared down the table directly into her eyes, leaving her with chills.

The room was quiet for a moment. The awkward silence was broken by a sound of a straw sucking an empty cup. Jesus put down the unit of blood and mouthed, "sorry."

Betty picked up her agenda again. "Moving on again, our third item on the agenda is a vote to allow Professor Emeritus Crowley back for another semester to teach a course in general arcane philosophy and ethics."

Dr. Jeffords leaned forward and smiled. "Aleister! I thought this was an incorporeal year for him!"

Dr. Neidermeier gave a quizzical look around and leaned back over her chair to whisper to Dr. Cross sitting next to her. "Surely, they don't mean Aleister Crowley? I thought he died in the 30's."

Claudette leaned over to Julia while the table was discussing the matter at large. "1947 actually, and death hasn't really stopped a lot of other staff from picking up a course here and there. I wish it would sometimes, the years they have Nixon in for Advanced Interdimensional Politics are horrendous."

Julia looked aghast and was about to ask another question, but Dr. Cross put a finger across her lips for silence.

Dr. Walker spoke last. "Before we vote on it, can we stipulate that his continuing ability to teach be dependent on him not being allowed to take part in any student clubs or organizations? I don't think we want a repeat of what happened when he was somehow allowed to be a sponsor of the Catholic Student Organization, Bacchus, and the Jazz Band, do we?"

There were murmurs of agreement and another confused look from Dr. Neidermeier. Then Betty asked, "OK, noted, so let's vote. All in favor of approving Aleister with the restriction from student organizations?"

Everyone except Dr. Neidermeier raised their hands; she stared around the table and rested on Betty's steely gaze directed at her. She timidly raised her hand half-way.

"Motion is passed with all yeas." She scribbled a few more notes. "Onto item four," Betty read from the agenda and pointed down to Julia. "Dr. Neidermeier is seeking approval for a guest speaker. Could you give us more details?"

Julia coughed. "Yes, I would like us to host a set of guest sessions for both normal and PS students. Dr. Derrick Boule has a few days open in his schedule that he could be on campus next week to do two separate sessions."

She looked up at the table and saw a lot of confused faces still. "He specializes in mathematics and archaeology, with an emphasis on ancient Egyptian mathematics. So he would be discussing that, with some interesting insights for our PS students on topics with Egyptian cosmology. It's a bit ironic since we were just discussing ol 'Aleister." She attempted a giggle. At least the confused faces now fell to more flat expressions.

Dr. Longfellow picked up a pen and wrote a short note on his agenda. "Dr. Boule, what dates will he be here?"

"Monday and Tuesday next week."

He looked up from his notes and down at Julia. "Dr. Neidermeier, you should have put this in at the last meeting. We don't like surprises on the week before fall break and the annual Samhain outings."

"Of course, it was very last minute. I've known Derrick since my undergrad days, and he just mentioned his schedule was clear and would be in the area."

"This will be the only time I want this to happen on such short notice and please be sure that he is off campus before Wednesday."

"Yes, he will be. Thank you." Julia folded her hands back and looked down, feeling ashamed but exhilarated.

Betty jotted a few more notes down. "Finally, our last item on the agenda is the annual Samhain outing for the PS students. We're set for a record turnout; about 97% will be in attendance. Not a surprise though, we usually get a big turnout when we make the New Orleans trip. Our bus down leaves Tuesday night, we have a full schedule with local vodouns and the NOLA alumni panel, and bus back on Sunday afternoon."

Dr. Longfellow sat back in his seat and bridged his fingers. "We have a minor change of plans with the trip. Dr. Neidermeier," he nodded down to her, "was already set to be staying here as well; I'd like you to make certain your guest is on his way before you take off for break. Dr. Cross and Dr. Jeffords were already down for chaperons, as are Betty and Dr. Gene. Professor Mull and Dr. Walker, would you be so kind as to take on that role as well? Unfortunately, Jesus and I must remain behind for the duration of the break."

Dr. Walker and Professor Mull gave a conspiratorial grin to each other and nodded agreement. "I expect you two to be role models for the students, and that means you may need to watch your elder there a bit more closely, Anton. He can get a bit wild when he's down south."

Professor Mull blushed, skin reddening considerably under white whiskers.

Betty scratched a few more notes onto her now full agenda sheet. "Is there anything you need me to put on the record about this, Jim?"

"Nothing official. We received a late request for a private viewing of a piece from our collection, a potentially dramatic donor that would like to remain confidential. We decided the weekend of Samhain would be best, not many students and staff here. Jesus and I can manage the security of it all on our own. We'll let you know if anything comes of it when you all get back."

Betty finished jotting down her notes. "OK, well, that concludes our general agenda. Is there anything anyone would like to add?"

Everyone glanced around the table, and most everyone was shaking their heads. Dr. Longfellow started to stand up, "Then I think we can adjourn."

Betty cut him off, "I do have one last item I need to bring up."

Jim sat back down. "Go on, Betty."

"I was visited by the Hansen twins earlier today at the Registrar's office. They were asking about the PS classes, mostly Ezmeralda, but the brother, Jake, was interested as well."

Jesus sucked in a breath.

Dr. Longfellow stared thoughtfully at her for a moment, glancing over to Jesus. "Do we have a problem? I thought they were just vanilla folk, a librarian, and a computer geek."

"They were before they walked into my office today. Apparently, Ezmeralda asked Jesus about the subbasement, and he sicced her on me, she just brought her brother along for edification."

Jesus spread his hands pleadingly. "Jim, she seemed to have known about me being a vampire for a while now, and it never freaked her out. I figured maybe she's in the know and just went with my gut on it."

"She mentioned that while she was in my office, that she always joked about you being a vampire, too."

Jesus folded his hands over his face and whispered, "Dios Mio."

Dr. Longfellow looked back between the two, then erupted into a full-bellied laugh. "That. That is hysterical. OK, it's alright, the Hansen twins are good people. The librarian can be a bit high strung, but they're both good people. If they want to take classes, we'll put them through orientation and see how they do. Anything else?"

No one spoke up this time, and Jim stood again. "Great, meeting adjourned." Everyone began to mingle and start to shuffle out. Only Dr. Longfellow noticed that Dr. Neidermeier didn't stay for small talk or another cup of coffee, she seemed to be the first out the door.

CHAPTER 8

ESMY

Esmy wrapped up her afternoon at work and headed home. She made the short walk from campus across the small downtown area of Baldur at a brisk pace. She came in through the perpetually unlocked back door.

After another quick rummage through clean clothes, then dirty clothes, checking the bucket of clean clothes next to her closet, Esmy finally decided to settle on a set of running gear. While only part of them were clean, she decided that the pants that hadn't been washed recently were at least dirty long enough to not smell, and maybe they aired out just enough. She popped her phone, driver's license, and a debit card into her armband and grabbed her Bluetooth headphones.

Esmy checked that the front door was still locked before heading out the back door. She started stretching in the backyard, wondering if she should hire some neighbor's teenager to mow the grass she kept putting off mowing. Suddenly, she heard a noise over the privacy fence of a man grunting.

She walked over to the fence. "That you Billy?"

The grunting changed to just some heavy breathing.

"Yeah, Esmy, just me so far."

"Geez Bill, you sound like you're about to blow an o-ring over there. I thought you guys at least had indoor plumbing." She leaned her back against the fence and continued some more stretching. It made no sense to try to peer over the fence.

Bill walked over to the fence, too and peered over at her. His head appeared floating over the six-foot-tall privacy fence. Bill didn't hang on fences either, not just due to height, but they didn't tend to hold his weight.

He caught his breath and stopped wheezing. "Naw, we got rid of the outhouse ages ago."

Esmy quietly hoped he was joking. "Big plans tonight then, over there?"

"Maybe, just the normal weekend kegger. My place is up on rotation for a party house, so I was just moving the third keg around. You're more than welcome to come. Hell, your brother can too, we promise not to bite ... again."

Esmy laughed at that. Jake was nervous the first time they met the neighbors behind them, which turned out to be a biker and his mom, whom also turned out to be a biker.

"I dunno. I might swing by later after a run and some food. Jake will probably be a no. He has some date tonight."

Bill grunted an approval from behind the fence. "Same girl still?"

"I think so, but he hasn't let me meet this one yet. I think this is their fifth date now, too."

Another grunt from the fence. "Gettin 'serious then, before long he's gonna be askin 'for her to move in. Then you'll have to start actually doing your laundry."

Esmy choked and looked at the fence. "How would you know my habits that well?"

The voice from the fence barked a bit of laughter. "Caught ya!" He laughed a bit more. "Hell, Ma's been single for thirty of my thirty-seven years. You think I don't know there's not much difference between a bachelor and a bachelorette? I'd guess at least something you're wearing now hasn't seen a washer in a while."

"Shit Bill, here I thought you were just psychic." Esmy wrapped up her stretches and took a few steps. "I'll be back later if your crew sees any bitches trying to break into my place, you be sure to cunt-punt them for me."

Bill laughed, as he always did at that line. "Shoot, Esmy, you know I can't hit a woman. Now Frogger's old lady though, she can lay Shamu flat out in one hit. So we got you covered."

Esmy chuckled back. "Thanks, Sir Billiam. Take it easy." Billy went back to working on his kegs, and Esmy took off on her run.

She turned on her running playlist, a mixture of electronica, dubstep, rap, rock and most any genre that wasn't country. Esmy ran her normal path around some of the neighborhoods of the small city. She went around the park, listening for the intermittent pings from the app on her phone telling her the current stats for her run at every quarter kilometer interval, enjoying the consistent flow of data.

Esmy added a few extra blocks in the middle of the route, so when she started to approach the downtown area, she could slow for a cool down and walk home the last few blocks. She heard the little voice click on in her headset that she hit eight kilometers and stopped to turn off the app and shut off her headphones.

Esmy was happy to see she guessed right on her stopping point, within two doors of a bakery and coffee shop just off the downtown area. She stood outside of Baldur the Beautiful's Bakery and stretched, looking through the glass to make a decision about coffee and the oversized cinnamon rolls mocking her just 20 feet away.

In the late October evening, darkness began to fall over the city. Esmy turned to continue some more stretching and avoid the icing glare of the rolls. Across the street nearby was Morrigan's Family Funeral Home. It sat stalwart and tall on the corner of the block. It was a tall old Victorian home with intricate woodworking and a very reserved coat of white paint with a dark green accent. In the small yard in front of the funeral home was a simple little fixture, a slight flare of a fire, not much more than a gas light built into a pedestal. She saw it many times on her runs and walks through the town, and Esmy knew from the plaque that it was an eternal flame installed by Doc Morrigan. Doc was the oldest of the Morrigan family still alive and was the primary mortician for over sixty years. He put the flame in the yard sometime in the mid 60's as a memorial for everyone that passed through their doors to eternity.

Sitting on that well-kept lawn, was a man, tall and pale with a long, dark beard. He wore jeans, a faded red sweatshirt and a flannel hunter's cap over long black hair.   More remarkably, he speared two hot dogs on a long, sharpened stick, trying to cook them over the eternal flame. Esmy could hear him singing something lowly in a gruff voice, and she thought it sounded familiar.

He started to sing a bit louder, in a hoarse voice. As Esmy kept listening and got closer, she did recognize the song. The homeless stranger with the crazy look in his eyes was belting out the entire first verse of Wannabe by The Spice Girls, and nailing every single syllable. The man stood up tall and waved his hands and hot dogs about, continuing onto the chorus. He was completely oblivious to anyone watching or gathering for his bizarre flash performance. At that moment, a sheriff's car drove by, turned around, and parked in front of the funeral home. The man apparently sensed he was in trouble, and settled back over the fire, humming the next verse of Wannabe.

The stout Deputy Harwald got out of his cruiser and rounded it without grabbing his hat. He approached the man who had now quieted down and hunched over his hot dogs on the fire.

"Mister, do you realize you are trespassing and desecrating a local memorial?"

The mysterious stranger didn't look up from his hot dogs at the office. "No, I am just making dinner."

"Well, the county lockup offers dinner as well, and maybe

you need a night to see my point of view."

He was reaching for his cuffs, when Esmy, against her better judgment, ran across the street shouting, "Professor Paulson! Professor Paulson!"

She stopped in front of the lawn standing between the stranger and the deputy. "Professor Paulson, we've been looking everywhere for you. I'm so glad I finally found you." The stranger picked up on the con very quickly and didn't flash any confusion.

"Esmy, you know this person?" asked Deputy Harwald, pointing up at him.

Esmy turned to face the deputy. "Yes, Frank. This is Professor Robert Paulson. He's visiting for a while this semester from a sister college over in Norway."

Deputy Harwald crossed his arms. He didn't like being called by his first name while in uniform. "Uh huh, and what's our professor here teach?"

Esmy chuckled. "Survivalism. His main teaching areas are in nature conservancy, but he's here to help out with a set of survivalist boot camps the college is offering. You're lucky those are hot dogs. With the size of squirrels around here, this scene could've been a lot more gruesome. Right, Professor?" Esmy turned back to the man at the fire as he studied his hot dogs.

"Well, the traps were all empty tonight," he croaked out, shrugging his shoulders and raising his eyebrows.

Esmy turned back to the deputy. "Uh huh. Look, Esmeralda, just get him out of here and keep him from roasting anything else over the eternal flame. Next time, I will run him in, visitor or not. Hell, I've had enough of foreigners tonight between this and that boy with the van."

Deputy Harwald turned to walk away, and Esmy swore she heard him mutter something about wizards fucking unicorns. She turned back to the man at the fire who looked at her meaningfully and croaked out, "Thank you, young lady."

"Frank can be set in his ways. Sorry he harassed you, but we better get out of here before he comes back around."

She looked at his meager dinner and felt sorry for the man. "How about we go grab a burger over at Brick's cafe, and you tell me who you really are so I can lie better next time around."

He stood up, towering over her from across the eternal flame. He nodded his head and looked out past her, down the opposite corner of the block. "There?"

She followed his pointing and saw he was pointing at Brick's Cafe and nodded back. "Yeah, I don't have any other plans, you could probably use a good, hot meal, and I like to hear a good story."

She started walking, and the stranger followed her. Passing storefronts as they walked, he found a trash bin and deposited his stick and hot dogs. He stepped close behind her, like a looming specter of darkness.

They walked into the café. Esmy could smell bacon and fry grease in layers. The paneled walls matched the wood grain of the chairs and stools. Esmy headed toward an empty booth on the left. She looked over to the right and could see Brick, an older man with a large potbelly wearing an apron over a t-shirt and jeans, with a cigarette tucked behind his ear, stood at the open grill. He nodded at Esmy, and she held up two fingers. Brick threw some patties on the griddle.

Esmy saw the man staring over at the cook. "That's Arnie Brick. He's ran this diner for ages. Don't worry, they tell me he stopped smoking at the grill a few years ago when the county health department finally came down on it."

Her companion looked around the rest of the cafe a bit. There was a sign above the door to the rear of the cafe behind the bar. It was a simple wood sign engraved to say, "Arnie doesn't need the money, he just loves to cook!"

There were some pictures of men standing around in front of an M1 Abrams tank, he noticed one of them was a younger version of the man at the grill. He pointed to the picture. "Is that Arnie there?"

"Yeah, Arnie was a tank guy back in the late 80's and got pulled into another tour of duty for the gulf war. He got discharged after the war and opened this place."

The stranger nodded and looked thoughtfully over at Arnie again.

Esmy shook her head and decided to dive straight in. "OK, I need a few things answered. Who are you? Where are you from? What are you doing here?"

He turned back to look at her, itching his neck under his beard. "Of those three questions, which one do you think is the most important, Esmeralda Hansen?"

She cocked one eyebrow at him. "How the hell do you know my name?"

"Four questions now. One is more important than the rest and can answer the rest. Which one?"

Esmy thought on that for a moment. A bell dinged and made her jump a bit. A few seconds later, the waitress brought a tray with plates of burgers, fries, and drinks over to them.

When the waitress walked away, Esmy picked up a fry and pointed over at the man, "Name. I think if I got the name, I might get some of the others figured out."

"Some names have been applied to me. I think the most likely for you to recognize is Loki." He started eating large bites of the double cheeseburger.

Esmy thought about that for a moment. "Loki? Do you have a last name Loki? Is that the last name and you have a first name? Because you can't possibly be that Loki, that's just..."

Loki stopped chewing, swallowing roughly, and said, "Not possible?"

Esmy nodded her head and picked up another fry.

"Think it through Esmeralda."

She did, and he continued eating the rest of the burger, then started picking the fries.

Finally, she started talking again. "Loki? The Loki? Brother of Thor, Son of Odin, trickster, and villain in the comics and mythology?"

Loki leaned one elbow on the table to look straight across at Esmy, pointing a fry back at her. "History has done more injustices to me than I've done to anyone else." He was waving the fry around to emphasize these points as though it were a wand. "The mythology is flawed from generations of personal retelling, with each generation adding their own 'flair. 'Don't get me rolling on the comic books and movies. They needed a proper villain, and my story fit the bill. They got some minor things right. Thor and I treated each other as brothers, but the All-Father and I were more like... you would call us ... really close drinking buddies."

Esmy looked a bit shocked at that and finally picked up her burger. Loki looked disappointed at that. "You guys have some weird ways to relate to each other."

Loki nodded. "It's complicated. Think of it this way. We live indefinitely. So, it is not hard for us to build bonds of brotherhood over centuries together. I became like a brother to Odin and many decades later became like a brother to Thor as well, and some other Aesir. I don't think many humans can equate that sort of continual existence."

Esmy chewed her burger and started talking with a half mouthful. "I can see that, it's more like you are integrating some new releases with legacy code and having them all work together eventually."

Now it was Loki's turn to look puzzled. "What?"

Esmy swallowed. "Sorry, I'm a computer nerd. Basically, you and Odin were featured in an old legacy system. Thor was a new feature that got developed. After working through some bugs, it all got merged together, and now you all can mesh and about the same level together. Not really a hierarchy, as much as an equal set of features."

Loki rolled his eyes around, mulling over the analogy. "In a way, yeah, I can see that, but Odin definitely can pull some rank on things. He does have more on the rest of us due to his age and magical abilities."

Esmy picked up on that bit and started pointing a fry again. "Magic, that's something that has been coming up lately. Is that how you know my name? Magic? Are you using that to stalk me or something?"

He bounced his head back and forth and smiled a bit at that. "Yes and no. It's a sort of magic. I wasn't stalking you, just needed to find you or your brother, Jake. I am able to use some small bits of blood magic to know the names and locations of relatives."

Esmy dropped half a fry back on her plate. "I'm related to a god?"

He bounced his head again. "That's an overused term, god. We can get into that another time. Might be good to talk about that more with your brother around. I hate repeating myself."

"How are we related?" she asked, now visibly more excited.

"I'm kind of your great-grandfather."

"Shut up! No, you are not!"

"Does your family ever talk much of her? Beatrice? She was quite the beauty. Did they say what happened?"

"Grandma said her mom died in childbirth and she was raised by her sister's family. No one ever knew about the father, Beatrice never talked about him. She went away on her own and came home very pregnant. She fell ill before the baby was born and lived just long enough to say she had her father's eyes." Esmy looked across the table and recognized the same glacial blue eyes of her grandmother staring back at her. Her eyes turned from intrigue to wonder and anger.

Loki knew the next topic by the new look across her face. "I met Beatrice a long time ago. We both happened to be in Boston at the same time. She was there for school; I was, well, just there. We became an item. My kind aren't normally able to reproduce easily with humans. It takes more than one time, and we, as a rule, don't let ourselves get involved like that. Beatrice though, we had some good times." He stared off wistfully for a moment.

Esmy threw a fry at him. "Focus up here, what happened? Why weren't you there for her?"

Loki looked gravely at her. "I got called back. There were problems, and I couldn't stay here. I tried to leave her a message to wait for me. When I came back, she was gone. No one knew why I never got any forwarding addresses. I figured she just forgot me and moved on. We had fun, but I'm used to people just moving on from me."

Esmy sighed deeply. "So your defense of abandoning a daughter was that you never knew? Even though you could find me so easily?"

Loki sank back in his chair. "It isn't so simple. I only randomly found you. And it took a decent amount of my own blood to do that and get your name. To know I was a father to a newborn daughter, when I hadn't even thought we could conceive was impossible."

Esmy appeared to be settling down but was still visibly angry. Loki reached across and held her clenched fist in a giant hand. "Look, your grandmother seemed to grow up well without me. She seems to have gone on to have a good life and a good family. I would have probably made that more complicated and worse. I'm not looking for a family reunion or to become your father or anything like that. I came back to Midgard to take care of some things and coincidentally found out I had some family I didn't know about. It's as simple as that."

"So, how long are you here for?" She started picking back through the fries.

"I'm not sure just yet. It could be a few days; it could be a few years. It all depends." Loki cleared his plate and pushed it off to the side.

"Do you have a place to crash or are you going all creepy hobo style everywhere?"

Loki stared back at her for a second. "Are you offering me a place to stay for a while? Should you talk to Jake first?"

Esmy shrugged her shoulders. "We bought a house that has more bedrooms than we really need. We always kept an extra bedroom made-up in case our parents were in town or for the occasional drunk friend. It's by no means the Hyatt, but it's better than a park bench in late October."

Loki nodded in agreement. "Still, I don't want to be a bother. I may be in and out at odd times; I have a couple of things at the college I have to sort out. Are you sure we shouldn't chat with Jake first?"

"I'll handle Jake, don't worry about him. What kind of business do you have at the college. Jake and I both work there."

Loki waved it off a bit. "Not a big deal. I'll tell you about it when Jake's around too. There's some big hullabaloo about an old thing they have. It's best not to have to repeat it a lot. I'll tell you both about it later."

He sipped at his water, trying to avoid it a bit longer. Esmy finally broke the silence again. "OK, well, like I said, no big deal to crash with us a while. The bathroom might be a bit tight. We only have the one shower working. Hope you don't mind pink tile."

Loki snorted a bit of laughter. "Clean running water is more than I could ask. You mentioned you both work at the college. What do you do there?"

Esmy rolled her eyes. "Well, Jake's a librarian. Fascinating work there, wink-wink. I'm in IT."

Loki was confused. "You are in what?"

Esmy laughed at him a bit. "When were you on this planet last?"

Loki puffed his cheeks and thought. "Sometime in the eighties."

"1800's or 1900's?"

He scowled at her. "1980's Esmeralda."

"If you haven't been back since the 80's, how did you know that Spice Girls song so well?" she asked, pulling a fry in half.

"BMG music club. They could actually still ship tapes interdimensionally until the late 90's," he replied, matter-of-factly.

"OK, well, I mean Information Technology. I work with, y'know, computers and such. I have to deal with networking issues, but I mainly work on custom programming for various departments around the college."

Loki leaned forward. "So you go in and out of the information of all the departments and your brother is a librarian? That's a lot more than you think Esmeralda. That can be extremely useful."

She nodded considering the thought. "Perhaps, but there's still a crap ton of secrets there I never knew about."

"Like what?"

"Hell, we just found out today that there's an entire department we never knew about. Preternatural Sciences. It deals with all kinds of stuff from magic to ghosts to bigfoots. Or would it be bigfeet?"

"Sasquatches," he corrected her quickly. "That's fascinating though, they actually teach those things there to students?"

"Oh yeah, apparently. Jake and I got the whole thing unloaded on us today when we asked the registrar about it. I'm thinking about taking a course or two, but I have no idea where to begin. It's not like I can hop on Amazon and find the 'Idiot's guide to spell-craft 'or 'A Field Guide to Crypto Critters.' I mean, imagine the cover art." She chuckled.

Loki stared at her briefly. "Why would you go to a river for a book?"

She snorted another laugh. "I've got a few things for you to read to acquaint yourself with modern society."

A waitress came by to collect the plates and drop off the check. They paid at a register on the bar and headed to the door. Esmy turned to him as they walked outside. "So, will you be heading back to the house with me? You can take the spare, and I'll tell Jake when he gets in."

"Sure. Which way do we go?" She pointed the direction, and they began walking, cutting through the town square to head to her sleepy neighborhood.

When they reached the house, it was dark, and the neighborhood was quiet. She looked over to Loki. "That's odd,

Billy was supposedly having a party tonight. He's the neighbor behind us, over the fence. Good people. Other neighbors don't seem to like them much, but Billy and his mom seem a lot nicer than most around here, tattoos and bikes or not."

Loki nodded. They approached the house; the front looked a bit like an old storefront with big picture windows and an overhanging porch with columns. There was a covered balcony on the second floor that was set up with a few pieces of wicker furniture as a secondary porch. The house seemed like it would be more appropriate to New Orleans than it would in Indiana.

"Nice house. I like the balcony."

"It's no Valhalla," she turned the lock and opened the front door, "but its home."

"Asgard," Loki corrected her. "The 'gods, 'the Aesir live in Asgard. Valhalla is a meeting hall for the great warriors of Midgard to go when they die.

"Ah." She flicked on some entryway lights and grabbed a small tablet from a side table. "Here, I'll show you up to your room, you can get the rest of the tour tomorrow."

She pointed him upstairs where her room and Jake's were, where the bathroom would be for him, and which door was the spare room. She turned on the light in the room, which was sparsely decorated with a bed and a desk.

"It's not much, but here, you can use this too. It's called a tablet, this one's an Android model. The last time you were here a computer with the same power as this probably weighed a couple hundred pounds at least."

"I wouldn't even know where to begin with this thing. What can it tell me?"

She opened a web browser and set a few pages for him. "That should give you a start. It's connected to the internet, which can give you endless information, tell you endless lies as well, or show you endless and totally unexpected pornography. Search engines can help you answer questions, just type it in and find pages to answer what you need. The news is always available, and there are resource sites that people maintain for history and info as well. Just remember, not everything you read is true, anyone can put crap online."

"That's nothing new, people used to believe just because a book said something it was true. I know many, including myself, who have wrongly been painted a villain in that manner." He turned the tablet around in his hands and sat on the bed. "If people have these things, what do they do with them? Is everyone becoming smarter? Able to access information and knowledge with such speed and ease?"

Esmy laughed again and snorted. "You crack me up. No, most people use it to post pictures of their ass or laugh at memes of cats. I'll teach you about memes tomorrow if you don't Google it tonight."

Loki nodded, unsure of what she just said. "Cat pictures?"

"Yep, just because the tools are better, doesn't mean folks use their brain better."

Loki set the tablet on the desk. "That is true, now I have a gift for you. Were you really serious about taking those classes? Learning magic?"

"Yeah, it sounds like a cool thing to pick up."

Loki took a small bag from his pocket; it looked like a coin purse with a rope tying it shut. "You are in luck then, the talents do run in your bloodline. And you can have this." He unwound the string and opened the bag. The bag looked as though it should only open a few inches, but he kept stretching the mouth of it. He pushed it in different directions for a moment, and it stretched large enough that he could reach in with both arms and his full torso. He came out with a large leather-bound book.

"This will get you a start; it has instructions for basic magic, runes, and syntax for runes, along with some primers for magical creatures and other world realms."

Esmy looked the book over for a minute. "It looks old. Will I destroy it reading it?"

"It's a magical tome. It can't be easily destroyed. In fact, here." He touched a pattern on the cover of the book, it flashed briefly. A duplicate copy of the same book sat next to it. "There, this is a copy of the book. You can utterly destroy this version of it, and you won't affect my copy. It's as good as it was first printed." He handed her the copy and dropped the original back into his bag, closing the strings back shut.

She looked at it skeptically. "Cool, cool. Well, I'm going to go give this a bit of a read, and I'll see you in the morning."

Esmy picked up the book and headed for the door. Loki sat down and started poking at the tablet. "Good night, Esmeralda, talk to you and Jake in the morning."

She was shutting the door. "Yeah, morning, maybe afternoon. I might be up for a bit reading."

She shut the door to the spare bedroom and went downstairs. It was only about ten at night. A headlight glowed through the front windows briefly. She held the book in one arm and waited by the front door.

Jake walked in, locking the door behind him. "Hey sis, exciting night?"

She bobbed her head and frowned. "Meh, not too much. I ran into a friend, and he's crashing in the guest bedroom. Date go bad?"

Jake yawned, as he kicked off his shoes and hung up his jacket. "She got sick, needed to head off early. I'm beat though, so I'll meet your friend tomorrow." He started heading upstairs to his room.

Esmy caught up with him. "Hey, Jake, do you still have that scanner you brought home from the college?"

He stopped and thought. "That one for the loose manuscripts and periodicals?"

She lit up. "That's it, you can just feed it a stack of paper double sided to scan automatically right?"

He yawned again. "Yeah, I'll grab it for you." He ducked into his room briefly. Jake emerged with what looked like a large printer. "Here, just put the stack of papers in the top, and it'll spit them out the bottom."

"Thanks, Bro, night."

Jake shut his door, and Esmy bounded back to her room. Before she realized it, it was three in the morning, but by then Esmy scanned the entire book into a format that she could search and index on her tablet. Esmy was also over a hundred pages into reading and only stopped to grab something to eat and a notebook to jot down a few ideas. By four, she finally slumped over and slept, drooling on her brown curls that sprawled over the desk in her bedroom.

CHAPTER 9

JULIA

In the dwindling daylight of Friday evening, a small dog sat on the back of a sofa in a little cottage home. The creature was a fat chihuahua that ambled about the space, when needed, with the grace of a walrus. His name was Brutus. Brutus's black fur, where there still was fur, on parts of his back and side was thin and ratty. Long tufts of white and grey hair popped from his ears. He lay, staring out at the road on a knitted afghan on the back of a floral sofa. His bulbous eyes would follow cars as they passed, headlights gleaming. Every third car, a long tongue would shoot out over his pronounced underbite to wet his nose.

A dark spot on the back cushion marked a brother-in-arms, missing for some time now. His fallen comrade was another little dog, a mutt mix of a chihuahua and a small bulldog. The result looked like a miniature accordion that spent too much time with a drunken sailor. Brutus slid his head to look at the dark spot where Caesar once held this lonely vigil with him and sighed gently.

Finally, he saw a set of headlights pull into the driveway. The lights were on a lime green Ford Festiva. Dr. Julia

Neidermeier wrenched herself out of the car and reached back to pull out a purse and a satchel from the vehicle. She got the bag caught on the handle for the car's emergency brake and almost broke the strap trying to wrench it free. Brutus sat up and started yapping loudly.

She scrambled up the walkway and fumbled her bag while grabbing the mail from the small metal box next to the door. Julia kept dropping pieces of mail while she kept hunting, scratching across the deadbolt face, trying to slide the key into the lock. She finally made it into the house and dropped everything onto a small polished wooden table next to the front door. Brutus hobbled down from his perch and was waddling excitedly around her ankles.

"Not now, baby," Julia told the small, obese canine. She picked him up and carried him belly-up like an infant. "Mommy's just had an exciting day, and she needs to get in contact with our special friend."

Julia cradled the dog in one arm as she went to the kitchen and rummaged through the refrigerator for something. She emerged hefting a large mason jar filled with oxblood and kicked the fridge door shut behind her, heading out the back of the kitchen.

In the back bedroom of the house sat eight large blood-red candles, each on its own cement pillar. She followed the circle of candles, lighting each one carefully. Brutus skipped over to an overstuffed armchair in another floral print, turned a few times and lay down once more. She sat the bottle of oxblood next to Brutus. The dog sniffed at the jar and licked the outside a bit, his bug-eyes staring back at Julia for any reprisal.

Julia walked over to the closet of the small bedroom. She disrobed, hanging up all of her clothes neatly. When completely naked, Julia took a simple grey, hooded robe from the closet to wear. She walked around the room, lighting each candle with a new match from a book in a pocket of the robe.

With all of the candles lit, she gave Brutus a quick pat on his head and picked up the jar. Julia opened the lid and started to finger paint a series of glyphs and symbols down each side of a full-length mirror in the middle of the ring of candles. When finished, she closed the jar and let the dog lick the last bits of ox blood from her fingertip. She sat down in the armchair with Brutus and put her hood up.

Julia picked up a large leather-bound book tucked under the chair. She flipped to a marked page and read over a section titled "The Rite of Ombus Setekh." Comparing the figures on the page to the ones she had just finger painted, everything looked correct.

"Brutus, I know that this way of contacting him can take a while for him to respond, but that lag always makes me wonder. Did I use big enough candles? These are half-melted all over the floor, maybe I needed new ones. Maybe not enough oxblood." She scratched Brutus behind the ear, his bulbous eyes shut, and a thin tongue lulled out to the side.

Minutes ticked by, but before Julia could get bored of sitting, she heard a strange noise like a Theremin. She looked up from Brutus to see the mirror shimmer, and the image of herself and Brutus went out of focus. When she saw the picture sharpen it was replaced with a dimly lit room, with a shadow of a person facing her. A dark torso was naked, and the head of the black fox stared back through the mirror. The mouth curled to an eerie smile, spittle glistened from the fangs.

"Good evening Julia," he spoke with a deep rumbling tone. "I hope you have good news for me tonight."

She stood up from the chair and approached the mirror. Brutus rose his head briefly, then, recognizing the speaker, turned over to lay on his back.

"I'm afraid the news is both great and grim," she began. "The good news is I have secured your cover story. You have a background that they aren't suspect of and will have three days to roam the campus with me, but you will have to give at least two guest lectures on ancient Egyptian mathematics."

Seth rolled his eyes. "I think I can manage that well enough, I only lived through the whole of their history. If that is the bad news, then we should be in good shape."

Julia took a step back from the mirror. "Actually, that's not the bad news." She braced herself and reminded herself not to fidget with her hands. "The bad news is we were discussing the upcoming schedule at the Preternatural Sciences Board meeting this afternoon."

Seth's smile visibly dropped off the fox face and his ears drooped. "Continue."

"Well, Dr. Longfellow announced we'd be hosting a private donor that wanted to see some specific pieces from our artifacts collection. He didn't specifically say that the private donor would be Isis, or the artifact would be the remains of Horus, but it seems to match with your concerns."

She stepped back further. Julia could see Seth's eyes shift from black to red and his tall pointed foxlike ears slick back flat to his neck. Suddenly, the mirror shimmered more than usual and appeared to become liquid. As though he were pulling himself out of a pool, Seth reached through the sides of the mirror and pulled himself through. The mirror went translucent behind him and faded back to a regular mirror. He stood nearly seven-foot-tall in front of Julia, naked except for what appeared to be a belted skirt like she saw in hieroglyphics and paintings.

"We must move swiftly then. I knew Isis was planning to travel for quite some time; she does not leave our realm without a large retinue anymore. This may be where she's going."

Julia staggered back and sat in the armchair. Brutus hopped down at seeing Seth in the room, ran over to him, and began humping his leg.

Julia reached out to grab him. "Brutus, bad boy, no rumpies! Remember what happened to Caesar when he did that?" She certainly did. While she now realized that Seth didn't like his leg humped, she wasn't eager to scrub more blood out of carpets. It was surprising how much one little chihuahua bled.

He picked up the small dog by the scruff of the neck, staring at the animal as it trembled in his fingers. "Are you still committed to my cause, Julia?"

"Wh-What would make you think otherwise? I came to you, I killed Dr. Smith, I combed through that massive inventory of rare and magical artifacts to find a single line reading 'Sarcophagus and remains of H. 'Does that sound like someone with questionable dedication? Hell, I didn't just kill that man, I got him blown up!"

Seth scratched at Brutus's belly with a long dark claw. "Do not forget who most of those actions benefited. You are far better off now than when you first contacted me. Then, you were only an adjunct professor. Now you are tenured and about to secure your own chair of a whole department. As for Dr. Smith, you got lucky. Though Foxglove poisoning can be harder to detect, it is not impossible. The fact the man dabbled in chemistry and alchemy worked to your advantage that the poison would kick in when he was mixing such combustible elements."

She reached out to take Brutus from his grasp gently. "Yes, it has come to my advantage, but some of the stuff I have to do to work with you can be a little hard. Do you know how far I have to drive to get the volume of ox blood you require just for a chat? It's not like they ship it from Amazon."

"I could care less of your problems. I have watched kingdoms rise and fall, I have raised pyramids, killed entire civilizations and watched war wage on in my family's names for centuries. The plight of your drive for an hour does not matter to me. If you wish to keep my help and not let on how you had a hand in a murder to secure your career, you will do everything I tell you. We have to get me on campus to start looking around by tomorrow."

She weighed his demands and leaned forward in the chair. "We have two things to consider here. One is that come Wednesday night, most of the department flies off for a Samhain trip to New Orleans. The only members of the faculty left behind will be I, Dr. Longfellow, and our IT director Jesus."

Seth shifted his weight and put a hand on his hip, staring

down at her, his red eyes changed to a fluid green. "Oh, well that does not seem so bad. What is the other thing?"

Julia pointed at his face. "You've got a damned fox head! You'll stand out a bit going on campus like that. Can you change something about it?"

Seth clicked his tongue and rolled his eyes. He closed them and turned around in place. By the time he'd rotated back to face her, he became a muscular olive complected man, about a foot shorter. His head was smooth and completely bald, but his eyes still gave off a sly liquid green glow.

"Is that better?" he asked holding his arms out.

"Much," she replied.

"OK, now tell me about these two." Seth sat on his knees in front of Julia. "Why is an IT director even on the board for Preternatural Sciences? Does he actually teach anything?"

"Well, he's a tricky one. Apparently, Jesus is a vampire. He doesn't teach anything himself, but he gives guest lectures on his kind to different classes. I think they like him because he makes it easy for someone to be on call day and night."

Seth perked up. "A vampire? Really? I didn't know any had survived the westward expansions. They can be tricky but not impossible to deal with. What about the other one, this Dr. Longfellow."

Julia leaned in closer. "That's the one I'm not sure about. See, he's older, I would say between sixty and seventy, but seems spry for his age. Not really decrepit or anything. He is the college President and chairs the department of Preternatural Sciences."

Seth cocked an eyebrow. "That doesn't seem so bad, just a vampire and some old guy."

"That's the thing though, I think there's more to Longfellow." Julia got up and started pacing behind the chair. "We were forced to put a P.E. coach on administrative leave this week and--"

Seth interrupted her, "Why?"

"Oh, apparently he was caught blowing a bigfoot." She made the statement as though it was as common as getting gas.

Seth yawned. "Heard about it already. Unless you have some of the juicy details to tell me about it, I already had that information."

"How did you already know?"

"I have another person in the town already."

"Why do you need me then?"

"My other guy, he is not in your inside position. He is good in a pinch, but I would not say I trust his loyalty completely. I just own his freedom and can compel him to do tasks for me."

"You have slaves?"

"You say slave, I say contractually obligated to serve my purposes. Why was the old man worth mentioning with the gym teacher though?"

"It's not important. What is important is that he was teaching a course this semester in hand to hand combat with … I believe they put it as deities, demigods, and the supernatural. Anyway, Longfellow just said he'd take over the course and looked like a kid at Christmas." She began pacing.

"Is this Longfellow person someone that was in the military? Does he have experience with those kinds of fights?"

Julia stopped pacing and chewed on a nail. "Weird thing: I asked if it was wise for him to be working on hand to hand combat with kids half a century younger than him." She looked directly into Seth's eyes. "Everyone else in the room basically laughed me off, they were more concerned for the student's wellbeing."

Seth didn't say anything; he just blinked confusedly at Julia.

"I know. I don't get it either. So I looked for something about him, and I couldn't find any history on Longfellow. He's just listed as Dr. James Longfellow, and it's listed in the blurbs about the college that he's been president for over thirty years now. Apparently, it's a family thing too, because it lists a different Longfellow as president for intervals of 45-75 years since the founding of the college over two hundred years ago."

Seth stood up and grabbed her by the shoulders to stop

her pacing and fidgeting. He fixed her with his eyes. "Look, it is just one man and a vampire. He may even be a powerful man. He may be a wizard that fakes his death every few decades or even a demigod himself. But we have something they will not. Julia, we will have the element of surprise."

"That does make me feel a bit better. How about we get you some clothes and you can tell me more about your friend and discuss our plans over some dinner?"

"I would rather just get some sleep. The hop through realms can really wear a god down. Your bedroom is through here, right?" Seth walked through a hallway to the living room. From across the house, he shouted, "I will take the bed, you can bunk down out here with that chinchilla thing on the couch."

Julia heard him slam the door. She looked down at Brutus. "Guess we're hitting the couch then, boy. I'll get the blankets in after I clean up."

Brutus waddled his fat little Chihuahua body over to Julia.

"You coming to cheer up mummy?" She held out her arms to have him jump in them. He instead ran to her leg and humped it with incredible vigor.

CHAPTER 10

ESMY

Esmy was jarred out of sleep by heavy bangs. She wasn't sure how long he was pounding on the door. Jake would stop intermittently to say through the door frame, "Esmy, wake up and let me in, we really need to talk."

Finally, tired of the continual beating, she sat up and headed for the door. She wiped the drool from her chin and realized it was in part of her hair too. Esmy opened the door to see Jake in the hallway with a worried and drawn expression on his face.

"Would you stop with the banging? It's a door, not a high school prom date. Shit."

He pushed the door a bit and slipped into the room. He started pacing between the bed and the desk, being careful to step around the two buckets of laundry. He was wearing khakis and a blue sweater.

She shut the door. Staggering back to her bed, she sat on the end of it and stared at Jake and his pacing.

"If you need something constructive to do, you can fold the laundry." She wasn't sure if Jake understood this though, partly because she was still half asleep and knew she mumbled it; partly because Jake stopped pacing and stared at her.

He finally grabbed the desk chair and rolled it closer to the bed to sit across from her. "You said last night you ran into an old friend that you were letting crash here. Wait." He turned to the desk again. Jake pointed over to the scanner he'd loaned Esmy the night before. "What did you do there?"

She stretched to wake herself up again, mid-yawn Esmy started to answer him, "I got a book, no digital edition, and so I made my own. Now I can do the full-text searching and read it in bed or wherever. A lot of good that did me."

Jake stared at her in wonder. "The binding looks like it's hundreds of years old! You hacked the damn thing apart with a razor blade to scan it, are you nuts?"

Esmy stared at him blankly for a moment and then blinked. "Yep, and nope."

This time it was Jake's turn to stare and blink. "Do you realize it could be valuable? Even priceless?"

"It was already a copy of another one, so I didn't think it was that big of a deal."

Jake stared blankly at her again. "There were two copies...wait, let's go back to the first problem. You said an old friend of yours was crashing."

Esmy walked over to the buckets and started to root around a bit for some change of clothes. "Yeah, what time is it? I feel like I slept only a few hours."

"It's nine thirty. Didn't you go to bed around ten last night?"

She grabbed a pair of jeans and a different grey t-shirt. "You were heading to bed at ten, I didn't crash 'til, shit, it was four or five. Man, why did you have to wake me up this early? It's Saturday Jake, frackin 'Saturday. I don't pull this shit on you."

"Well, no, you don't, but I don't let complete strangers crash in our home either."

Esmy stopped looking for a towel and looked back at him. "Oh, you met Loki."

"His name is Loki? What the hell? Where did you dig up a

guy that calls himself Loki?"

Esmy finally found a towel. "That one deputy was harassing him. Dude was trying to cook up some dinner, and Harwald was going to bust his head."

Jake looked very confused. "What?"

She sat back down on the bed. "Yeah, he was just trying to cook up a couple of hot dogs on the eternal flame at that funeral home, and you'd have thought he was pissing in Harwald's Cheerios."

Jake cocked an eyebrow. "Esmeralda, last night you said an old friend was crashing. I got up this morning, went for a paper and some donuts. When I came back, I found some guy that looked like the result of a fistfight between mid-nineties grunge and goth making coffee."

Esmy narrowed her gaze. "So you're pissed because he made coffee. That's fucked up bro, Loki's being nice."

Jake waved a hand. "You're missing the point. You let a hobo stay in our house. We are lucky to have not been robbed and murdered."

She stood up and headed towards the bedroom door. "We'll sort this out after I get a shower. If you feel safer, hang back in my room while I get cleaned up. I smell like ass from not getting a shower last night. And hey, I lied OK, he's not really an old friend, but he is family."

Esmy began to open the door. "Family? What do you mean?"

"He's our great grampa." She let that bomb fall on him, shutting the bedroom and bathroom doors across the hall in rapid succession.

When she came back to the bedroom twenty minutes later, Esmeralda was dressed in her t-shirt and jeans but was still towel drying her hair. Jake was mesmerized at her desk.

"Esmy, where the hell did you get this book?" he asked.

"Oh, Loki gave it to me last night. Why?"

She walked over and saw what he was doing. Jake took the time she was gone to try to organize the pages and assess the damage to the book.

"OK, few things. First, the book has no name, but the chapter headings are really weird. And there's this." He motioned her next to him.

Esmy clearly remembered cutting all of the pages from the book with a razor blade the night before, but the sheets of thick paper were firmly bound in the volume she saw on the desktop. Jake picked up a page. As he brought it closer to the open cover, the page shook and pulled from his hand. It fused with a popping sound back into the spine.

"Damn, he said it was pretty hard to destroy, but Loki didn't say it would fix itself. That's sweet."

She picked up the stack of pages and brought them all closer to the near-empty spine. The pile started vibrating as she brought them within inches of each other and shot out of Esmy's hand. There was a series of popping sounds, followed by an odd slurp and the book was entirely together once more.

Esmy picked it up and tossed it at Jake. "Read it if you want. I made myself a digital edition." Esmeralda picked up her tablet and unplugged the charging cable.

Jake fumbled with the book for a second. "Esmeralda, I need you to back up a few paces. The man downstairs making coffee."

"Loki." Esmy stared daggers for saying her full name.

"Right, Loki something or rather."

"No, just Loki, as in Loki of the Norse mythology." Esmy tapped the power button on the tablet and pulled the notification tray to check for new email while Jake processed this information.

He gaped at her for a few seconds, and Esmy could pinpoint the moment his brain rebooted. "So, what you are trying to tell me is that Loki, the trickster god of the Norse pantheon, is crashing at our house, making coffee, and is actually our great grandfather."

"Yep." She put the tablet back on the desk and folded her arms.

"How do you know that?" Jake started pacing again and stopped. "Did he tell you this, and you took his word for it?"

"Do you remember the last thing great grandma said before she died?"

Jake chewed his lip. "She said grandma had her father's eyes. What's that got to do with anything?"

Esmy pointed to the floor towards the kitchen. "You didn't notice anything about the pale blue eyes on Loki when you ran into him?"

This time Jake crossed his arms. "I'm sorry Esmy, I don't tend to stare longingly into the eyes of strange men making coffee in my kitchen."

Esmy scoffed. "It wasn't only the eyes. He knew about us, and he knew great grandma's name was Beatrice. That she was in Boston for school. Remember, from what the family has said about her, she went to a college in the Boston area on a scholarship. She did come home pregnant and not willing to talk about the father at all."

Jake was nodding now, rubbing his chin. "I'm not entirely sold, but I'm also not sure how much of that knowledge could be connected to us through info on the internet, old newspapers, and local records."

"If you want some more proof of all of this, maybe we should go talk to him together. He said he needed to talk to both of us together, anyway. He said something about explaining things and not wanting to do it more than once."

Esmy picked up her tablet again and headed to the door; she held it open for Jake and motioned for him to exit ahead of her. They walked downstairs together and led into the kitchen. The kitchen was one of the few parts of the house that wasn't in need of any redecorating. New stainless-steel appliances, white cabinets, and smooth white marble countertops shone brightly. In contrast, there were a few crusty bowls in the sink, but they smelled a fresh pot of coffee. Jake followed Esmy cautiously past the refrigerator, into a breakfast nook big enough for a black table and four black chairs that overlooked the backyard. Loki sat at a chair in the nook, sipping a cup of coffee and reading something on the tablet Esmy handed him the night before.

He looked up when he heard them enter. "Esmeralda, good morning. I must really thank you for loaning me this thing. It is amazing how far things have come along. I used to have to buy newspapers, now I can go to the Google and find a bunch of interesting articles."

"That's wonderful." Esmy reached towards the cabinet to grab a coffee mug. She found no mugs and checked the dishwasher where she grabbed two large ones with little owls painted on the sides. She spoke loudly so Loki would hear her. "There's a lot out there, so I hope it's not too overwhelming." She handed Jake a mug and poured them both some coffee.

"Yes, I've seen that. I spent almost half an hour trying to figure out why I should care about these Real Housewives of somewhere before figuring out that I shouldn't. I have cream and sugar on the table."

Esmy and Jake came into the breakfast nook and took the other seats at the table. Jake brought with him some packets of artificial sweetener and poured some cream into his coffee. Esmy brought a spoon, adding what seemed like a quarter of the sugar bowl to her coffee, she stirred it together and chanced a sip. Esmy headed to the fridge and came back with two ice cubes. She dropped them into her coffee.

"So," Esmy began, "I didn't formally introduce you two. Jake, this is Loki. Loki, Jake," she said, nodding back and forth.

"Yes, we almost met this morning, but I may have startled Jake a bit. I'm sure you have questions. Would it help if I changed a bit?"

While they sat, Loki's hair began retracting. His beard disappeared, and he now appeared clean-shaven, with a long, thin face. His dark hair stopped to a much shorter cut.

Esmy sipped her coffee and regarded him with a grin. Jake looked dumbfounded. "See Jake, things keep getting more interesting, don't they?" She nudged him a bit with her elbow.

Jake shook off his confusion. He set his cup aside for

a moment. "Loki, I need to start with some facts here." He pointed to his sister. "Esmy tells me you are actually our great grandfather and that you are a Norse god."

Loki held up a hand. "I never said god, did you say god Esmy?"

Esmy looked at Jake. "I never said god, I said 'figure in Norse mythology 'to be exact."

Loki rolled his eyes and bobbed his head a bit. "Yeah, I can't argue that. Not a god though. Hell, none of the gods you were told to be gods are really gods truth be told. That was a bit confusing though, wasn't it?"

Jake tore open two packets of sweetener and poured them into his coffee. "OK let's table that for the moment. What about this claim that you are our great grandfather? How can we believe that?"

"Well, I'd offer some sort of biological proof, blood test or something," Loki started, adding, "but it would probably show inconclusive."

Jake asked back, "Why is that?"

"Your human DNA has forty-six chromosomes. The DNA of Asgardians, Jötnar, Alfheimr, and Svartalfheimr all have forty-eight. Some other realms have that same issue as well. Basically, you humans are the exception to the rule; you got that special break of showing us all what you can do with those 46 chromosomes. It's interesting though, it makes you compatible enough to be impregnated by beings from other realms, where we wouldn't be as compatible directly."

The twins processed this for a moment. Jake spoke first, "so, blood tests would be inconclusive because you couldn't really compare our DNA to yours."

Esmy snapped her fingers. "Shucks, guess Maury Povich is out."

"What?" asked Loki.

"Nevermind. Is there anything at all you can give us to prove you are who you say you are? Esmy told me about the eyes, and you do have eyes very similar to our grandmother, but we also saw you change your own appearance."

Loki mulled it over for a moment. He stood up and walked away. He came back a moment later with his own copy of the same book Jake got from Esmy. Loki opened the front cover and pulled a small square envelope out. "This may offer some reasonable proof."

It was a picture, an old faded and yellowed black and white print. "Here this may help," Loki said as he touched his index finger to a corner of the photograph. The faded tones gradually became darker, and color flooded the image. Soon, the picture was clear, a couple sitting at a cafe table sharing a cannoli. The man was clearly Loki, with the same glacial blue eyes, but his hair was long, black, and tied in a ponytail. The girl was a ravishing brunette with wild curls and reminded Esmy of her own hair.

Esmy poked her brother. "Jake, that's our great-grandmother. We've never seen this one, but that's her from the other pictures grandma used to show us. Here, hold that still for a second." Esmy took out her phone and snapped a picture of the colorized photo.

"How did you do that?" Jake asked, pointing at the picture.

Loki took his finger off, and the image yellowed and faded once more. "Magic. There are many other ways to describe it, but in this world, it's easiest to batch a lot of things together and call it magic. I share a memory with this photograph. I was there. I can remember everything down to the smell of the perfume Beatrice was wearing even over the coffee in that cafe. I impress that memory as an overlay of that image."

Jake, for a moment, caught a scent of jasmine, potent enough that it flooded his senses. Loki turned the image over. In a neat cursive script was written, 'Loki, never forget the cannoli. Love, Beatrice'.

The twins read the note and stared at each other briefly. "OK," said Jake, "Let's come back to that, suppose you are our great-grandfather. Fill in the rest for us. How are you still so young looking? Are you immortal? How do you know so much about us? What else don't we know?"

Loki sipped his coffee. "That's a lot of questions and an awful lot of answers. The first few are pretty easy. Yes, I am kind of immortal. There are many other realms. In other realms, you have other beings. Humans generally have some of the shortest lifespans. Other realms can range. The elves of Svartalfheim and Alfheim live much longer, but still grow old and die of old age after a few centuries. Dwarves can last almost as long. To be honest, I'm Jötnar, which means I shouldn't be immortal but die after a few millennia, but I have an agreement with the Asgardians."

Jake and Esmy were both nodding and trying to keep up.

"Basically, I became excellent drinking buddies with Odin a very long time ago. In a way, I became a brother, cousin, or uncle to most of the rest of Asgard over time. Well, the good people of Asgard aren't technically immortal, they can age. They don't grow old because of one special person, Idunn. Idunn, and only Idunn, can harvest these sweet golden apples. They restore life and preserve youth. As long as they eat them, they are immortal. So, they shared them with me."

Jake nodded again. "Yes, I do remember reading that in the mythology, about Idunn. I thought it was a symbol for something else like clean living."

"No, it was very literal. They are very juicy apples and hard to mistake for anything else. Anyway, I know about you because I used some blood magic. I took some of my blood, applied my will to it against the environment and area I was heading. The spell gave me an image in my mind of the two of you and a pair of names. I looked the records up to backtrack your parents, grandparents and so on. When I hit your great-grandmother, I understood immediately. The date of birth for your grandmother, Beatrice's date of death, and the timeframe after our last time together. All the pieces fell into place."

Loki sipped more on his coffee and stare into the mug. "As far as what you don't know, well, we could spend centuries on that topic."

Esmy leaned forward and folded her hands together. "So, let's start off with the obvious. Gods. How did that work?"

Loki grimaced. "It's complicated. Let's start with saying that your world, I call it Midgard, you call it Earth, is a nexus. A central node. We can travel directly to it from Asgard. We can travel directly to many other realms directly from here as well."

Jake leaned on an elbow. "So we're like an interdimensional hub for of these other worlds?"

"Yes, yes, like a hub, your world is in the center, and you can jump through various means to these other worlds. When we started coming to Midgard, our way of travel got called a Bifrost by those you know as the Vikings or the Norse. We tried to explain it to them, but it took this tree analogy."

"I can see where that would help," replied Jake. "Is that how they picked up some oddities of their myth? Like Ratatoskr, a great squirrel that can climb the world tree to deliver messages?"

"No, that one is also quite literal too." Loki chewed on his words for a moment. "In the other realms, flora and fauna grow similar and very different. For example, Thor raised these two goats Grinder and Snarler. You could kill them and cook them nightly. As long as the bones were unbroken, Thor would make them rise again with his hammer Mjolnir. Ratatoskr is literally a massive magical squirrel. They took that one literal, as he is *literally* a big fucking squirrel."

"So how did you guys end up as 'gods 'to the Norse?" asked Esmy.

"Last time I was here, on Midgard, there was this movie I saw. I don't know if it got too popular, it was called 'Ghostbusters.'"

Esmy slapped the table. "It became a cult classic. It's one of our all-time favorites, Jake and I have seen it about 20 times."

"Well, in the words of Winston Zeddemore, 'When someone asks if you're a god, you say yes.'"

The twins nodded together.

"So it was kind of what happened. We showed up out of nowhere, the locals saw us just show up, hell, they saw us resurrect the goats, and they even saw Ratatoskr. If we said, 'Nah, we're some guys that happen to live a really long time given the right circumstance, 'we'd probably been imprisoned, killed, or worse."

Jake furrowed his brow. "How often has that kind of thing happened? I mean, you popped out in the Scandinavian areas. What about, say the Roman or Greek gods? Egyptian? Aztec? Jesus?"

"That gets a little more complex." Loki started to tick through them on his fingers. "Egypt happened about the same, Aztecs too, but they got hosed when they asked Cortes and his men the same thing, and he slaughtered them. Roman and Greek are basically the same, they rolled over from one civilization to the next, but they basically did the same thing, they had an open entryway at Mount Olympus. The Judeo-Christian area gets a little tricky."

"Tricky how?"

"Tricky as in we made them up, mostly."

Esmy quirked an eyebrow. "Mostly?"

"It's complicated. Some of it, that whole mess about angels and demons and what not, that's real, but they are out on their own and often bicker back and forth. They have their own realms, and those beings go on and on. So, we borrowed some of their stories and characters, massaged some others in and boom we had a story. It was all meant to take the spotlight off all of us, Asgard, Duat, Olympus, Alfheim, all of them. We figured, if we shove most of the world we interacted with, over to some form of the same thing, we could go back to a more incognito role."

Esmy waved the subject off. "OK, gods aren't gods, great. I can get on board with that. What about some of the other stuff. Fairies, elves, werewolves, ghosts? How much of them are real? I know vampires are real. Apparently, my boss is one."

"Basically, all of it." Loki looked at both their faces drawing surprise. "Most of your myths have some basis in reality. In fact, all of them do. So there are some inaccuracies and some straight-out nutty conspiracy theories. Vampires do exist, werewolves yes, and other were-creatures. Elves come from Alfheim and Svartalfheim and are different natured. We'll hit a lot of it in time."

"OK, the history and everything is fascinating." Esmy looked at her hands and the tablet she brought with her. "What about that book you gave me last night? It's interesting, but I'd like to see some practical application."

Loki stretched his arms above his head. "We have been talking for quite a while. I need some exercise. I see your backyard is fenced in." He stared across the yard from the breakfast nook windows. "How about we go do some lessons in the yard?"

The twins nodded.

"Before we head out, I gave Esmy the book last night. Would you like a copy, Jake?"
Esmy replied before Jake, "It's cool, he's got my copy, and I made my own." She held up her tablet.

Loki narrowed his eyes. "May I see that for a moment?"

She unlocked the tablet, pulled up the copy of the book and handed Loki the tablet. He started swiping around and making gestures with his fingers on the screen.

"This is truly impressive Esmeralda. I knew the book was intelligent, but it managed to learn from your devices as well and imprint itself accurately. See here." He pointed at a page with a spell for flight. "See how it says to combine attunement spells for levitation and motion? It also links them so you can click on them to take you back to those reference spells. The physical book has the same aspect, you can tap the word, and it would reshuffle the pages to that spell."

Jake picked up the copy Esmy gave him from the kitchen counter. He turned to a random page with a listing of potion ingredients. He touched the word aloe, and the page shifted to show a definition for aloe, where it can be found and an image of the plant.

He shut the book and carried it with them as Esmy led him and Loki out the back of the house into the yard. Loki looked around at the yard for a moment.

"OK, so the book will teach you a lot if you read it cover to cover. There are many types of magic and many ways to cast it. You can use enchanted items, you can use runes and symbolism to map spells together. If you get really talented, you can cast spells simply by mental focus and pushing your will into it. There are also beings with certain innate abilities. Vampires, for example, can move extremely fast and have less of a toll for most spell casting. One thing you have to remember is that you cannot get something for nothing."

Esmy quirked an eyebrow. "So, like I have to sacrifice a chicken or get some cow blood?"

Loki chuckled. "Well, you would if you were trying to trade and barter with certain demons of the pits or dealing with the vodouns. But no, in most cases, if you need blood it would be a simple drop of your own."

He let that sink in for a moment. "Now, what you use will become dependent on what kind of magic you end up becoming comfortable using and what you intend to do. For example, let's say you want to mow your yard as it is a bit high right now, what will we do?"

Jake and Esmy looked around. They had been at a stalemate for two weeks now on whose turn it was to do the final mowing of the season. Esmy hazarded, "Necromancy. Raise a zombie to get the mower out and take care of the yard."

Jake shook his head. "Nah, we can't do that. We'd need a corpse first of all. We'd have to raise it and bind it to ourselves. If we can do that, we have to worry about the zombie actually mowing and not running off to eat the neighbors. Also, would he have the muscle and agility to push a mower? If he ran over his foot, would he keep going?"

"Jake is right, here Esmy. Necromancy isn't always the answer, and in this case, we have some other things we can try. Any other ideas?"

Jake tried an idea, "Well, we can enchant the lawnmower to run itself and mow the yard without us around. Like a Roomba for the yard."

"That's a start, but you are still relying on a lawn mower in the garage. Is there anything you can think of that doesn't end up relying on a machine that requires fuel and can break down?"

The twins thought for a moment. Esmy hazarded an idea. "Well if it's dry enough, we can burn it with fire magic."

Loki smiled. "You're starting to get it, but that will kill the grass and could burn down your house. What else is there?"

Jake knelt down and felt the grass. "In essence, we want the grass to only be a certain length. So we could either stunt its growth at that length or reverse the growth to the proper length. Is that an enchantment?"

"Actually," Loki said. "That's still necromancy. Necromancy isn't only zombies, it's the magic to take life force or create it, fully or partially. But, yes, that's an option. And that can become very beneficial."

"How so?"

"Well, you are pulling life force from the grass to slow its growth. You can pull that energy out and store it to use later."

"So, you keep the grass short, and you create a bio-battery at the same time." Esmy reflected on it. "Neat."

"Find something big we can draw on, not directly on the grass, and I'll show you some rune magic."

They went into the garage. Esmy returned dragging a large sheet of plywood, Jake came back shaking two cans of blue spray paint. They brought it to the middle of the yard.

"OK, so, there are some things you have to define for your spell to work as expected. You need to define the target, which can be the area of effect or a specific single target. In our case, it's an area of effect." Loki sprayed a set of four circles with arcs sweeping outward to the edges of the yard. Inside of them, he scrawled a series of runes, shaking the ball around in the can as he went.

"Technically, you can use any symbols you want as long

as they hold to a defined lexicon. Meaning, you can't write any random chicken scratch and expect it to do what you want. Your symbols have to be consistent to your dictionary. I'm using old Celtic runes here." Loki pointed to the runes he was writing. "The runes here are defining the directional boundary, in my case meters from each center to the fence."

He sprayed a larger circle around the four smaller ones. "Now we bind those together." He wrote some runes inside this circle. "And these runes are to specify the grass is the target, now we have to specify what will be done to the target."

Loki drew another circle and wrote a few more runes inside of this one. "This draws the life force out of the grass, which will shrink it for now and continue to chew the life force while the grass attempts to grow." He drew one more and wrote another series of runes around the edge of the inside of the circle. "This final one will bind the energy to a target. We put something in the center, and it will store the energy into that target." He sprayed a series of arrows connecting the various points and circles together to show the direction of normal flows.

"What do we use for a battery?" asked Esmy.

"Certain crystals and gems will do it. Of course, you pop a car battery in the center too, and it would charge it with the right conversion runes. You'll need something stable enough though in case the power generated is more than the target can handle."

Loki fished in his pocket and found a chunk of pinkish quartz. "This should work well enough for our test run." He dropped it in the middle of the target circle. "Now we need to give the spell a little juice to start the magic. You can invest some personal energy with your will, which will tax you but may be an easy alternative once you learn it. For now, your two choices are to imbue it with a power source like we are creating or with a drop or two of your own blood."

Jake nodded. "So this is like starting the kindling to catch the bigger logs in the fire."

"That's a good enough analogy."

Esmy disagreed. "It seems more mathematical than that though like E equals MC squared. Our energy output to our crystal will be equivalent to mass times a constant squared. In this case, the mass would be the amount of grass affected, and the constant would be the blood multiplied per blade of grass."

"That's a much more scientific approach to the idea. I like to think there's more art to it, but essentially it can come down to that. Go ahead and try it out, see what happens."

Esmy stepped forward to the sheet of plywood. She took a pocket knife out and stabbed the end of her thumb and felt the tip of the blade slide through layers of skin. She pressed her thumb and drained a few drops of blood on the circles and runes. The paint glowed. Briefly, the grass started to make a thrumming noise. A few minutes later the grass retracted to a shorter length and looked like it was freshly mowed. The crystal on the sheet of plywood glowed green.

A voice from over the fence called over, "That's a new way to do it, wanna take care of mine next?"

Loki, Esmy, and Jake turned suddenly to see Billy staring over the fence at them.

Esmy called over, "Hey Billy, how much did you catch of all that?"

"Just the end, coolest shit I'd seen in ages," Billy replied. "Your magician buddy want to do that for the kegger tonight?"

They realized they lucked out and Esmy decided to keep the conversation casual. "Wasn't the kegger last night, something come up?"

"Gator had another heart attack. We postponed going to see how he was doing down at the hospital."

"Who's gator?" asked Jake.

"Gator's Froggy's dad lives over past Winthrop and Main."

Esmy asked over, "Wasn't serious, was it?"

Billy laughed, and another laugh joined him, an older female laugh. This time the woman's voice responded, "I was over there to pick him up on account of he hadn't been feeling too well recently. He said he had to go drop a deuce. Five minutes later I'm calling the ambulance 'cause he went pushing too hard. I told that jackass not to blow an O-Ring, and he goes and does just that."

Billy called over again, "How about it, you all want to come over for some drinking tonight? Don't have to put on the magic show if you don't want to."

"Sorry Billy," Esmy responded first. "I've got a lot I wanted to catch up on this weekend. I'll probably be working on some stuff late tonight."

"Not really my kind of thing Billy, and I need to go check on someone tonight too," replied Jake.

"How about you mister, we're always happy for a new face."

Loki pondered it over for a moment, "I haven't had a good night out drinking for the hell of it in I don't know how long. Esmy, if you don't mind, I'll take Billy here up on his hospitality."

Esmy shook her head. "Have fun, I'll be here. Come back through the gate between the two fences tonight, I'll leave the back door open for you. Billy, this is Loki by the way. He's kind of a ... relative. So best behavior, OK?"

Billy nodded. "Got it, no felonies and try to work around the misdemeanors."

"You two keep practicing from the books and try not to conjure anything crazy. Don't summon anything that wants to strike a deal, that's always a rookie mistake."

Loki headed through the gate. "Billy, what do you have that can hold the most liquid?"

"I got an old hundred-gallon fish tank in the shed."

Esmy and Jake headed back into the house, with the sounds of Loki and Billy discussing brewing something in the old fish tank.

CHAPTER 11

KYLE

Kyle turned the corner of Jackson onto Franklin Street. The corner met the end of a shopping area that was still walkable from either downtown or the college campus. Looking up and down the roads on one corner he saw the 24-hour gym sitting opposite a liquor store. A third corner of the intersection featured a restaurant decorated in the colors of the Italian flag and called itself "Mamma Mia's Pizzeria."

Kyle pulled into a strip mall on the last corner of the intersection. He passed the CPA's office on end furthest from the corner and parked in front of a small gaming shop called the Elf's Quiver. Kyle looked up to his right as he shifted to park. Over half of the strip mall contained blackened windows with neon signs for a strip club called The Double V. The large sign above the entrance featured a cartoonish Viking woman that winked and flashed a "V" with her fingers.

He hopped out of the van and looked to make sure the mural of his van faced out so it could be seen from all corners. He grabbed a small backpack from his front seat and strolled toward the front door of the Elf's Quiver.

Kyle walked over to a girl sitting on the bench between

the game shop and the strip club. She was too skinny in Kyle's opinion, pale and wore a lot of makeup to cover up some gnarly pimple scars from her youth. Her bleach-blonde hair had purple streaks. She wore a short white fur coat closed, knee-high red boots with high heels and a pair of red, pleather shorts that barely covered her.

Kyle sat down next to her for a minute. "How's your bony ass doin 'Chablis?"

She blew out a puff of smoke and tapped the ash out of the end of her cigarette. "I made rent last night and should score enough to cover my car by next week. Can't complain. Anything new on you?"

"Oh, y'know, same ol 'same ol 'for me, eh. I got pulled over by a deputy yesterday," he replied.

Chablis nodded to the van. "Anything to do with Merlin giving it to Twilight Sparkle over there?"

"Yeah, some people really got no appreciation for art. What's going on over at Mamma Mia's?" Kyle pointed to a tent with a bunch of kids in uniform waving poster boards.

Chablis puffed out another cloud of menthol smoke. "Girl Scouts, they're out trying to sell cookies I guess."

"No shit? Near here?"

"No shit Kyle. They tried setting up first in front of the Fitness Forum, but the manager ran them off. Mamma Mia's let them set up though, even gave them coupons to hand out with cookie sales."

Kyle looked around the area. "Man, between the game shop, the Double V and that liquor store, you'd expect it'd be too much sin for parents to let their kids around. Guess those fuckers know no bounds, eh."

Chablis stamped out her cigarette on the bench arm. "I gotta go over there; those assholes got me craving the damned little peanut butter cookies like they're fucking meth now. You coming with?"

Kyle looked over at the Girl Scout tent again. "I probably shouldn't, cookies were my big trouble spot when I was a kid."

She looked back at Kyle. "So you were a fatty as a kid Canuck? I wouldn't have guessed by the look of you now."

"Yeah, I had some issues, pushing three hundred for a while. My uncle, Alphonse, big fella too. Real tragedy, he was chaperoning a school field trip because my parents were both working, eh."

"Hey, what doesn't kill you, right? So walk over with me, you don't have to get anything, test your will."

They started across the street together. "So what happened to Alphonse that made it a tragedy?"

"Oh, the field trip went to a farm, they were harvesting wheat. They were showing us how a grain thresher worked, when Uncle Al fell in, eh. He wanted it to seem like he would fall, but he lost balance. His last words were, 'Hey kids, check this out.' We all did, he just flew everywhere. Real tragic, right in front of all the kids."

Chablis stopped to wait for the crosswalk and stared with a cocked eyebrow at Kyle. "Jesus, what the fuck man. How did that make you lose weight though?"

"Oh, Uncle Al would eat donuts and cookies for breakfast a lot. The thresher didn't get all of him, it kind of chewed through most of him, but the bones, they like caused the machine to clog or somethin'. Anyway, it opened his belly and sprayed everything over all of us. Really ruined a lot of sweets for me for a while. "

They crossed the street getting close to the tent. Kyle continued his story, still very deadpan and calm-voiced. "I couldn't even look at a Tim Hortons right for ages after that. Real tragic, all over the kids and all."

At the tent, Dolores and Sam sat at a folding table while Sofia and three other uniformed girl scouts held signs trying to wave in cars. Dolores caught the tail end of Kyle's discussion and decided to use that as a start to broker a sale. "If you like Tim Horton's, you should really buy some cookies, we have recipes on our official website for Girl Scout cookie donuts!"

Chablis ignored Dolores, she walked towards Sam

knowing that this other woman must be crazy to compare anything to Tim Horton's to a Canadian. "I'll take a box of the peanut butter ones and a box of thin mints." She pulled a wad of single dollar bills from her pocket and peeled nine bills off.

Kyle scoffed. "Lady, have you ever had a Tim Horton's donut? I wouldn't degrade them with anything from this pile of over artificially sweetened and flavored nastiness. That's like saying your eight-year-old can improve the Mona Lisa, y'know."

Dolores scowled at him, Sofia nearby started a game of patty-cake with another scout at that very moment. Their rhyme could be heard very clearly, "Mamma Mia's, Pizzeria, had a little diarrhea!"

She tried to ignore Sofia's annoying rhyme as it repeated. "You seem to really know fine art there, mister, isn't that your van over there?" Dolores nodded to Kyle's painted van. "The disgusting one with the bestiality? How can you drive that thing in public?"

"Really?" Kyle started to sound angry. "You're gonna try to play a morality card when you set up shop with kids basically between a liquor shop and a strip club, eh? What's that about, mom of the year?"

Sam stepped closer to Dolores, sensing the argument heating up. "Dolly, we've made a lot of sales today, maybe we should pack it in for the day."

"Sam, we are fine, if this gentleman and his little friend would take their monstrosity over there and leave."

Kyle scoffed loud enough to be heard over the children's rhyming which now changed to a chant of "poo poo, pee pee, diarrhea goes a whee whee."

"My little friend, lady, happens to be a nice working mom trying to make ends meet."

Chablis pulled Kyle's jacket a bit. "Kiddo, let it go, these fights aren't worth it, let's just go back. I got my cookies, c'mon." She gave another tug, and he finally gave way.

He turned back to her and started to head back across the street. Sam started to pack up while the girls were all chanting, "pee caca with a dash of wa wa makes me go a ga ga."

When they got back at the bench in front of the Double V, Chablis opened up a box of the cookies. "I can't believe she was getting you that worked up man."

She offered Kyle a cookie. "No thanks, don't want to start that again. I can never eat only one. If I start, I'll be down the whole box."

Chablis shrugged her shoulders and took a bite. With half a mouth full of thin mint she asked again, "Really man, I get the whole thing with self-control, but you were starting to go apeshit on the woman. What the fuck was that about?"

This time Kyle shrugged. "Got worked up about the cookie crap, she insulted Tim Hortons, eh. She started to get on your case and the van. That piled up and I kind of lost my shit there."

They nodded back and forth for a moment watching the girl scouts packing up across the street. Kyle noted the message on the board that the manager put out front. It changed weekly; last week announced the amateur busty cheeks competition. He read the sign aloud "Hump Day Wednesday! No Cover 5-8PM. Corn Hole Tournament! Thursdays at 6PM, Weekly Trophies! Saturday Night Live: DJ Dirty Stache and the Inappropriate Boners!"

"What's up with that, eh? Cornhole? I didn't think Dave even allowed guys touching?"

Chablis gave him the quintessential expression of "what the hell are you talking about" while munching another cookie.

"Cornhole. Isn't that like, y'know, butt stuff, eh?"

Chablis laughed so hard it made her spit cookie crumb all over the bench. "No, no. You thought we'd have like an anal orgy in the parking lot?"

"So, that's not what corn hole is?"

"No, it's this game a lot of folks play. Basically bean bags and boards. You try to toss the beanbag onto the board or through the hole or something."

"Why don't they call it beanbags?"

"Probably want it to sound pervy, but I'm pretty sure the

bags are usually full of field corn, not beans, but it feels like beans. You want to know more, join the damn tournament?"

"Who's DJ Dirty Stache and the Inappropriate Boners?"

"Local band, the Inappropriate Boners kind of suck, but Dirty Stache can lay down some good beats to dance to."

She checked the time on her phone. "Ah shit, it's been fun, but my first dance in 15 minutes. See you later."

"Yeah, later Chablis."

Kyle turned away and headed into his game shop, turning back to get one last glance at the girl scouts packing away.

CHAPTER 12

ESMY

When Loki left in the early afternoon with Billy for what sounded like some lively and recreational drinking, Esmy continued reading and studying the large volume of magical reference material on her tablet in the screened-in porch. When she was reading through the section regarding how to brew potions and the various botanical ingredients that combine for them, she could hear choruses of raucous laughter came from over the fence.

While reading the reference sections regarding runic languages, a series of random explosions occurred from the yard past the fence. She smelled the strange clouds of colorful smoke wafting across the block. She read on though, paying close attention to runic logic gates, selectivity for spell-work and appreciating the chart and multi-colored drawing depicting directionality and importance for rune scribing.

The afternoon and evening carried on in this fashion. She broke for dinner late and came back to reading, hearing the party still continuing over the fence line. Esmy was really starting to get a full appreciation of what her abilities were with using runes for spell casting.

Around midnight, Esmy heard something strange: silence. She looked at the clock on her tablet and decided midnight was awfully early for Billy's keggers to taper off. Especially with the cacophony of noise from the porch earlier in the evening.

Esmy went back into the house and called out, "Jake, you around?"

"In here," a voice called from the living room. Esmy went into the living room, it was sparsely decorated with older furniture she and Jake had picked up at some second-hand shops. Overstuffed chairs and a long, old grey couch. The TV hanging on the wall that hadn't been used in nearly a week now. A stone fireplace sat at one end of the room, with a large picture window looking out at the street on the opposite end.

Jake was sitting cross-legged on the grey couch with his copy of the vast magical reference in front of him. He'd been apparently studying it all day as well, a highlighter was tucked behind one ear, and he held a pen in his left hand. "Esmy, do you know what I find extremely weird about this whole book?"

She rolled her eyes and said with as deadpan a voice she could muster, "Besides that, it can make mystical clones of itself, attune itself into electrical devices and that it was given to us by an actual member of mythology?"

He looked up from his copy of the book. "Well yeah, besides all of that."

"What is weird, Jake?"

"For all of the reference it gives, and the history it offers for the explanation of the spells and sources, there is literally no history or reference to how the various magical beings and worlds interact with each other or with our world. Sure it goes over what each being is, what it can do and how to kill it. No description of political turmoil in vampires, if the fey tries to screw over Egyptians, if werewolves have hereditary gambling addictions. Nothing like that."

Esmy mulled that over, she had done a quick glance over the section regarding species to find humans. She expected to see a simple entry reading, "Mostly Harmless." She was quite happy to see it was a bit more expanded than that and detailed how interbreeding with some other beings may have led to some disease outbreaks and ailments. The section had many listings, confirming at least vampires existed, but it showed far more. Fairies, were-beasts, elves, dwarves, etc. But Jake was right, they each had what the species were and a brief history of their realms, but no description of how they met each other. No great wars or treaties mentioned, no interactions in this so-called great realm of Midgard that Loki made Earth out to be, merely objective reference materials.

Esmy grimaced. "Well, that's about as weird as what I noticed."

Jake cocked an eyebrow. "And what did you notice?"

"Listen," she said.

Jake sat and listened for a moment. "I don't hear anything."

She gave him a glance, darting her eyes to the rear property line.

Jake got the hint. "Oh shit, I don't hear anything. What time is it?" He knocked the book off and tried to stand up. "Ahh, needles, pins and needles." He slapped his legs a few times to get feeling.

"Past midnight, when's the last time you remember one of Billy's keggers wrapping up before three?" Esmy asked Jake.

Jake stopped a moment and seemed to regain his feeling in his legs. "Uh, that time Cooter lost the tip of his middle finger back in June."

Esmy nodded. "Yeah, that's what I thought too. How about we go check on them. It's probably time to get our ancestor back to bed, and you can ask him about the missing history while we're at it. By the way, I thought you were going to check on someone earlier, forget to leave?"

"Nah, I called her, she's doing ok, just needing some time to rest."

They headed out back to the fence, crossing through the

gate. Jake and Esmy found a wasteland of passed out bikers across the backyard of Billy's house. The light of the gibbous moon shone brightly to help illuminate a yard dimly lit by old party lights hung around the fence line and some fading tiki torches. Jake tripped over a prone smaller biker and stumbled back to his feet.

They approached closer to Billy's deck where they found a large aquarium on the ground with a bubbling foul-smelling, brownish liquid. Billy was slumped over on the table snoring. Across from Billy sat an old woman hanging onto a glass groggily, one eye open and was drooling.

Next to her sat Loki, with his back to the fence, so he didn't see the twins. They overheard what he was saying. "This might be one of the rottenest things I've done since I killed Baldur." He was slurring his speech. "Honestly, the whole Baldur thing was a party joke gone wrong. I mean, here you got a guy that they say can't be killed by anything and they're all surprised when I says, 'oh really? 'Couldn't take a joke that lot."

Esmy started to move forward to step onto the deck steps, but Jake pulled her back. He motioned her to stop and be quiet for a moment. They continued to listen.

"I told those kids that I didn't know their great-grandmother was pregnant." He took a deep drink of whatever the foul liquid was in the fish tank. "I mean, my last kids were a massive wolf, a serpent that can destroy ships and the daughter that became ruler of the underworld. One of them is already dead too, killed by Thor a few centuries ago. Poof! Gone."

Loki dropped his glass and started sobbing. "I knew she'd have the baby. I knew what would happen though, most humans can survive birthing a baby with an Asgardian, not a Jotun though, that's rare to survive that birth."

Billy's mom tried to raise her arm, but dropped it and managed to only squawk out, "What's a Jotun?"

"It's basically a frost giant, believe it or not, I am a giant."

Her open eye tracked lazily over Loki. "You don't look so big."

"Some say I was a runt, but I'm really good at shapeshifting. I prefer a smaller size."

Esmy walked forward, Jake tried to pull her back again. She broke free from him and ascended the steps.

Loki turned to see who was coming. "Oh, hey, Esmeralda, how long you been there?" He saw Jake come up behind her and saw a flash of anger on Jake's face. "Oh, long enough to hear me droning on, well shit."

Esmy put a hand on his shoulder. "Loki, how about we get you back to the house, the party is pretty much over here."

Loki looked around the yard littered with the passed-out bodies of the bikers. Suddenly, Billy's mom turned and barfed. She sat up and barfed again. After a few more intervals she finally sat back in her chair and wiped her chin with the sleeve of her pink sweater.

"I don't know what that swill you made was, but nothing tied onto me like that since I tried to go one for one through a bottle of Rumple Minz with Billy's fourth daddy."

Billy's mom looked back down at the ground, Esmy wondered if she might be in for a final round of puking. Instead, she looked back at them and said, "Shit, I puked on his boots. He'll kill me if he finds out I did that one. If he asks, it weren't me, OK?"

Esmy made a zipper motion across her mouth. Loki replied, "Your secret is safe with us Darla."

The old woman slapped the table. "I've told you I don't know how many times tonight, the name is Shirley."

Loki gave a wolfish grin. "Surely, you're joking?"

She promptly flipped him off. "Like I haven't heard that one a million times. You kids get this ass home OK, I'm going up to bed.

Esmy and Jake led Loki across the yard of snoring men and women, some still clad in jeans and leathers. A few were in states of undress, with a whole segment of naked bikers in a far corner of the yard that Esmy hadn't seen before. She was secretly glad they were all passed out.

For as tall and giant of a man as Loki appeared, he wasn't hard to lead. They got him in the house and laid him down on the long, grey sofa in the living room. Jake grabbed his copy of the book while Esmy returned from the kitchen with a large bottle of water that she sat next to Loki.

When they were all settled, Loki planted a foot on the floor and rubbed his temples. He spoke quietly, "I guess you know now, I am a massive douche."

The twins looked at each other and back at Loki. Jake broke the silence first. "I don't expect that being self-deprecating will really help you much on this one. Why did you leave her?"

"You heard me, I found out she was pregnant. I knew the kind of woman she was, she'd have the child, and the kid may live or may not, but what kind of father would I ever be?" Loki covered his eyes with his palm. "I loved Beatrice with every ounce of my being. I couldn't watch her die, especially by choice because I was too weak to refuse her love."

Jake got more heated. "You could have stayed, helped raise your daughter though. Our grandma still today doesn't know her father, and our mom doesn't have any idea you are her grandfather either."

Loki sat up and drank some of the water. "Have you ever read any of the mythology?"

"Yes," Jake shot back belligerently. He chewed about it for a moment. "The history is a bit muddy though because accounts were written down much later than the oral versions. How much of it is true?"

Loki drained half of the water bottle. "Some of it. Most of it. Except for Ragnarok. So you get it, I don't have a great track record for progeny."

They were quiet for a moment. Jake still looked angry, but Esmy spoke finally, "It's quite sad, really. You were so worried about it, but Grandma came out to be a wonderful, kind person. You could have been a great part of our family. She has your eyes by the way."

Loki peeled at the plastic label on the water bottle.

"Maybe, but it's also hard to explain some things about myself to humans though. I can't see it being an easy conversation with her parents that, not only did I get Bea pregnant, but she has a one in two hundred seventeen chance of surviving the birth. Or that I'm a giant from another world, that I have one of the deepest wells of magical knowledge in the universe. See what I mean? Not exactly Sunday dinner kind of topics."

Jake looked puzzled at Loki. "So why now? What changed?"

Loki shrugged. "I had some things to attend to on Midgard, decided I'd hunt up some folks, see how things turned out."

Jake squinted at Loki, he leaned forward and pointed a finger to punctuate his words. "No, that's not right. You mentioned to Esmy you'd been back on Earth some in the 1980's, so you've been here before again and not bothered to find your daughter, our mom or us until now. Something drove you to find us. What was it?"

Esmy looked over at Jake. "Jake, maybe we should chill about this and talk about it in the morning."

Jake shook his head and stood up. "No, we need to figure this out tonight. We can't sleep under the same roof as this maniac if we can't trust him, and I'm pretty far from that right now."

Loki looked up at him. "You sure? It's a bit of a long story."

Jake crossed his arms. "Give us the straight facts on it, no window dressing."

"Well, it started back in September. I went to meet a guy in Indianapolis. He wanted me to meet him at the TGI Fridays down near the canal. If it were me, I'd have preferred like St Elmo's or something, but this guy won some gift cards at the convention."

Jake stopped him. "Wait what convention?"

"It was some kind of comic con or game convention, something like that. Those things get blurry. I mean, when I walked into the damn Fridays, there was a table of five ladies dressed as Harley Quinn. The one dressed as a crossover Incredible Hulk Harley, ugh, break me off a piece of that."

Esmy laughed, she said, "Eww... you're our great grandpa, ew ew ew."

Loki continued, "There were a bunch of others too, some Avengers, and this cool group dressed as the entire company of Thorin Oakenshield. Guys even had a Gandalf and Bilbo. Bunch of princesses and weird game characters. Now the big burly dudes dressed in drag as the Powerpuff Girls, I thought were cool, but some folks didn't like that one as much."

Jake pinched the bridge of his nose. "Wrong details. That literally tells me nothing, who's the guy you were meeting?"

Loki took another slurp of water. "Oh, Seth."

Esmy cocked an eyebrow. "Seth who?"

"Seth," replied Loki. "Egyptian Seth."

"I don't know any Egyptians," Esmy said puzzled.

Jake sat back down, his mouth agape. "You mean Seth, the Egyptian god of desert, storms, chaos, and violence. That Seth?"

Loki rolled his eyes. "Yep, that's him. Really a bit of a drama queen and micromanager, for all the crap with tradition he tries to hold onto, he goes to these conventions with cosplay contests and tries to win random crap. Leaves his regular head on and dresses up in his old battle gear."

Esmy looked to Jake for more explanation. "Black fur on a head that's like a cross between a dog and an aardvark. The rest of his body is supposed to seem human, but if it's war dress for ancient Egypt, he'll still be showing some skin."

"Anyway," Loki continues, "I get there, and Seth already has a corner booth, a couple of glasses of water, and he's brooding like he got some bad news from his proctologist. I sat down and ordered three pints of Osiris pale ale."

Jake bent over laughing at that, Esmy looked confused. "What did I miss here?"

Jake and Loki looked at Esmy dumbfounded. "Do you remember anything about Egyptian mythology Esmeralda?"

She rolled her eyes at the name. "We studied a whole

month about it in third grade and again in world history our sophomore year of high school. Seth and Osiris were brothers."

"OK, so what?"

Jake continued, "Seth grew jealous of him and got Osiris killed. It took two or three times to really do the job, but even after all that Isis supposedly was able to get enough use out of Osiris to have his son, Horus."

"OK, so you guys are really passive aggressive jerks to each other. Gotcha."

"So, after that, I got on him for walking around with the damned head that makes him look like a fennec fox until he finally put on at least a human face."

Jake stopped him this time. "Wait, he was walking around as like a jackal or something, and no one said anything? And he can shapeshift without anyone flipping out?"

"Yeah, he said some assholes mistook him for Anubis, but yeah, it went unnoticed as excellent cosplay. And, yeah, most people probably looking at him even in the middle of shifting would just explain it away as something they never saw. Trick of the light, swamp gas off Venus, whatever. A human brain is remarkably well suited to excessive and endless skepticism. Funny how damned religious they can be."

"Well," Esmy began, "was Seth being at least as much an ass to you?"

Loki laughed. "Oh yeah, in spades. He saw some kid wearing a shirt for something called 'My Little Pony' and asked if he should introduce me as the first Brony ever. I don't know what the hell a 'Brony' is, but I knew what he was getting at."

Esmy smiled. "This one I get!" She looked confused. "How were you the first brony though?"

Loki looked down and folded his hands together. "I'm guessing Jake knows this story."

Jake cleared his throat. "A wall needed to be rebuilt around part of Asgard once, and a man claimed he could do the task by himself with his horse in a short time, but wanted the goddess Freya as payment. No one believed he would complete the task, so Loki convinced them to let him try so he could complete at least some, if not most of the work for them."

"So, how does that make him a brony?"

"Well, the guy was really a giant in disguise and was able to build the wall quickly. He was getting close to having the wall complete, and the gods demanded that Loki fix the situation so that Freya would be safe. Now, the giant was able to build the wall on his own, but he needed the horse to help him haul the rock back from a quarry. So, Loki here rigged the contest by leading the horse away."

"So, he stole a horse?"

Loki interrupted, "No, if I stole the horse, a great stallion, that would have been clearly cheating, and we'd have forfeited the wager."

Esmy looked confused. "I don't get it, what did you do?"

Jake chuckled lightly. Loki shot him an expression of mild annoyance, and he stifled a laugh. "Our great grandfather here has a known ability for shapeshifting. He took a form of an attractive mare and led the stallion away into the forest. The giant was unmasked, and Thor supposedly killed him. If the story is accurate, Loki came back some months later with a young eight-legged horse that he gifted to Odin."

She looked between the two of them, Loki reddened slightly. "You can become a horse and get pregnant?"

"It's not a story I'm proud of," Loki said rubbing his temples, "and usually I like to bring a lot of pain to people that discuss it, but yes, there are risks to any ... enterprise."

Esmy paused and stared at him for a few moments. Finally, she inhaled. "OK, well those are all fascinating details, but what did you two actually meet about?"

"Well, it used to be in the old days a lot of us stuck to certain areas and didn't go around the world. A lot of that changed a few hundred years ago, most of us that can have real bodies on your planet got together and signed a treaty of sorts. A kind of armistice. We don't get involved with human affairs if possible, and we maintain a peace agreement between the realms to avoid any of the odd wars and bloodshed of the past."

Jake looked slightly shocked at that. "How in the hell did you all manage that?"

Loki gave him a kind of dumbfounded smirk. "It was pretty easy, you humans put your faith in us and our tales, we needed to give you something bigger and better."

Esmy caught on and shook her head. "No, you didn't, tell me you didn't. I thought you were actually joking about faking the crucifixion, but to fake it to cover for a supernatural cold war?"

"We created a greater narrative, something that could be followed easily, require minimal faith and be simple to tell. We tried to make it easy and more peaceful, something to give folks an example to live with each other. We made it all up and acted it out, put some writers to it and pushed the storyline. Thor was onboard so much he allowed himself to take on the crucifixion. It was fake though, magic can make much better special effects than Hollywood can even manage."

Loki spread his hands palms up. "We needed to massage the narrative later on, but he hung on that cross for about six hours. We made it look good with some magic, he wasn't in any real danger. I kept trying to tell him he needed to wrap it up and 'die, 'but he had to draw it out. Kept saying that 'Father hung himself for nine days, I can push one up here. 'I think he finally got bored too. We hid out in a cave for a few days. Someone rolled the rock away, and we took off."

Esmy stared in disbelief, Jake looked shocked. Loki continued, "Believe it or not, but the point is, it gave us all a way to get put out of the way and be more conspicuous about trade and moving around. Now suddenly we can all interact, and it starts to get even more muddled."

"Alright," Jake interrupted. "So you caused about the last couple millennia of holy wars. What's that got to do with anything?"

"Well," Loki said, "Seth spends a lot of time stateside and was keeping company with Pan and some pixies out in the Bay area. Pan had just gotten back from visiting with an Inuit god Pinga up north. Pinga usually runs around with Olifat. Now, Olifat had some business over in Africa not too long ago and popped over to see Bes through the Nile. A long time ago, Horus died in battle here on Earth somewhere, but his body was never recovered. So, while visiting Bes, Olifat hears that there are new leads on the body, which he tells to Pinga, Pinga tells to Pan, and Pan lets slip to Seth."

Jake stares at Esmy for a moment and starts connecting dots in the air with his finger. Finally, he looks at Loki and says, "what?"

Loki pauses for a moment and lays back down on the couch. After he closes his eyes he starts again, "Every Time there's a war between humans, it gives some of the realms a good excuse to have a little skirmish of their own. Horus was killed in one of those battles. They may have found the remains of Horus. Supposedly, Isis is running down the lead herself and trying to make a claim on the body."

Esmy at this point is starting to feel more comfortable being confused. "So, dead body? What's the big deal?"

"Oh, crap, I get it," says Jake. "If Horus was dead, the de facto king of their monarchy was Seth wasn't it?"

Loki nodded.

"If Horus is found, Isis could do what?" Jake asked. "Bring him back to life?"

"Well, it didn't work like that with Osiris, but they think she can do the same thing and take his seed to make another child that can contest Seth's rule as she did with Horus."

Esmy understood now. "So they're in a race to find a supernatural sperm donor."

Loki nodded. "To put it bluntly."

"How does that put you here though?" asked Jake.

"The lead," Loki explained, "is that the remains were collected on an expedition and made their way to a special collection held by Baldur College's School of Preternatural Sciences."

He continued, "I owe Seth for some strings he pulled to have me freed after that misunderstanding with me killing Baldur. Unfortunately, it's not a small debt. To gain my freedom, he brokered a lot with Odin and managed to gain my complete obedience. I get a decade or two off now and then, but otherwise, I'm just his errand boy. He decided it was a twist of fate since the college was named for the same person I'd killed. I'm mainly supposed to help confirm the remains are on the campus, get a location of where they are and steal the vital bits if possible before Isis can claim the body. If I do that, my debt contract might finally be fulfilled, and I may be free of my obligations."

Esmy quirked an eyebrow. "You have to loot a dead god's cock and balls to repay a debt?"

"Truth is often stranger than fiction."

"What happens if either side actually gets the remains?" asked Jake. "They've both been searching for quite a while, right?"

Loki rubbed at his temple. "Probably, if either got his body, it would end a long-standing cold war and ignite a new war. If Seth gets the body, he'll claim full reign and try to start a new empire. If Isis gets them, she'll create a new heir which will ignite a new war. Either case could expose our narrative and destroy the secrecy."

They sat quietly absorbing this all. Jake and Esmy heard Loki sigh and start snoring. Esmy and Jake looked at each other and then at a clock on the wall, it was past two in the morning. Esmy stood up and waved Jake to follow her to the kitchen, he did.

She whispered to Jake, "Well?"

"Well, what? We should give him the boot," Jake replied.

Esmy tapped her teeth with her index finger thinking. "I don't know, I've gotten to like him."

Jake's eyes widened. "Esmy, the man is a known trickster, he has a whole mythology shaped around his ability to lie and steal. On top of that, he's the slave of an Egyptian chaos god! You can't trust him."

"I know, but I think he's not as one dimensional as all of the stories make him out to be. Loki seems to be genuinely different than all that. Besides, we heard only stories. Most of them leaving out the last couple thousand years."

"Maybe a couple thousand more years of scams."

"Besides, if his debt has made him a slave of this god Seth, maybe it would be good for us to help him out. He IS family after all."

"Family? He bailed on our family?"

"Which may have been the best move for all of us. Think it through, how well do you think Loki could have played family being on the hook for an Egyptian war god? And how do you know that whatever contract binding his slavery wouldn't also give Seth power or rights over any children Loki fathers?"

Jake flustered to find an argument. "Point taken."

"This weekend has been more insightful and exciting than just about anything I've ever known. I'd like to keep him around to learn some more." Esmy yawned. "But it's damn late; we can discuss it more another time. I'm beat."

"Alright. But I don't want this to end with an 'I told you so.' It may be our last words given his history." Jake stormed off to bed.

Esmy muttered, "Drama queen." She shut off the downstairs lights and put a blanket over the sleeping form of Loki on the couch before heading up to bed herself.

CHAPTER 13

SETH

Seth sat in silence filling out the crossword in the paper and eating at the kitchen table while Julia sat quietly. Caesar made a slight whimper.

"Controversial Chinese protein source, three letters," Seth read aloud. He gazed down at the whimpering Caesar. "Dog." He scratched down the answer and continued.

Julia took a cautious sip of coffee.

"Must you be so damned loud with your slurping?"

Her hand trembled, spilling blotches of coffee on the table. "Any plans for today?"

"Not that it is any of your concern, but I think I will explore the town a bit today, maybe enlist some more help."

"Would you like me to come with you, show you around the town?"

Seth was wearing a light brown turtleneck shirt and grey pants. He turned and put a hand on Julia's shoulder.

"Julia, I have roamed this planet on and off for over six thousand years. I have been worshiped as a god of destruction, war, chaos, famine, and the desert. I think I will be fine roaming around a small town in Indiana." His eyes flared with a scarlet flame, and his voice increased to an intensity to cow Julia.

With that, he scratched Brutus behind his floppy ear and walked out.

Seth wandered away from the house, walking briskly in the crisp autumn breeze of the Sunday morning.

He crossed the campus, walking up the main walking path between the academic buildings only once so as not to draw suspicion. He stopped briefly at a small building known as the Wellhouse. It had no well, but he remembered Julia calling it the Wellhouse. She wasn't sure why it had been called that either, as she noted, there was no well. There was some minor amount of graffiti on the inside roof. It mainly seemed to be a small brick structure with an archway opening on each side and a cement seat in each corner of inside.

He moved on past the old Bastard and headed off campus. Seth continued his stroll through town and after some time found himself at the corner of Jackson and Franklin streets. A pair of men clad in denim and leather jackets were loading equipment into a black van. A tall man in a white Adidas tracksuit sat watching them on a bench smoking a cigarette. He wore dark sunglasses, had a blonde mullet and a thin whiskered blonde mustache. A short dwarf of a woman sat next to him, in leather pants with a purple mohawk, green eye, and lip makeup. She wore a lot of piercings in her ears, eyebrow, nose, and lip.

As he came closer to the group, Seth heard them having a debate. One of the men was moving an amp into the van while the other sat down on the tailgate. The one on the tailgate wore a flannel shirt under his leather jacket. Sweat beaded on his bald head.

The sweating man spoke, "I'm telling you, we need to get some recordings done and get a demo to some people. We could get a record deal."

The smoking man took a drag and puffed out some smoke. "People? What people?"

"Y'know, people in the record business. Like, studio execs and shit."

The girl responded now, "And do you know any studio execs? I don't know anybody."

"Nah man, but somebody has got to know somebody right? Like one of those six degrees of Kevin Bacon things and shit. I mean, the dude at the college when I went there said if you want to get somewhere, you gotta network. I think he meant like hitting Facebook and LinkedIn or something, but we gotta know somebody that knows somebody."

"Meh, I like playing our gigs," the girl responded. "Besides, what song would we demo?"

The other man in the van hopped out and sat next to the bald one on the tailgate, it appeared they were twins aside from the baldness. "Dude, we should make a demo of 'Copperhead'!"

The girl scoffed and gave a face of disgust.

The smoking man took another drag. "You mean the song where the chorus you wrote is 'My dick is like a copperhead, let it poison you, baby, My dick is like a copperhead. Copperhead water rattler, copperhead water rattler, copperhead."

The twins on the tailgate laughed and nodded. "Yeah, but you make it sound so weak. You gotta add the feeling and the thrust!" With that, the bald one imitated playing the guitar and thrusting his pelvis.

Seth approached them. "Excuse me; am I to understand you folks are musicians?"

The whole group turned and looked at him. The bald one answered first. "Yeah man, we're DJ Dirty Stache and the Inappropriate Boners!"

Seth pointed at the smoking man with the mullet on the bench. "I am guessing you are DJ Dirty Stache?"

He snuffed the cigarette on the bench and nodded.

"And the rest of you are the Inappropriate Boners?"

The twins smiled and yelled, "Hell yeah." The dwarf girl on the bench rolled her eyes.

Seth saw her disapproval. "Are you not a 'boner'?"

She scoffed. "Yeah, I guess I am. I'm the drummer, these yahoos," she pointed at the twins, "wouldn't accept any other name, so I rolled with it. Who are you?"

Seth leaned on the van door. "My name is Seth, and I know few guys out west area a recording studio."

The two men high-fived and yelled, "Wicked!"

Seth looked back at the dwarf. "Are they twins?"

She shook her head. "Irish twins, Carl and Luke." She pointed at the bald one first and the brother with hair.

Carl waved. "I'm the big bro, lil 'Luke here has another nine months before his hair will disappear like mine!"

Luke punched him in the shoulder. "Nuh-uh dude, different dads, mine still had all his hair last I checked."

Seth pointed at the dwarf. "And your name is?"

"Bernice," she replied.

"Really? Bernice? You have these two guys and a guy going by DJ Dirty Stache, and you just go by Bernice?"

She shrugged her shoulders. "I get enough with being a dwarf drummer."

"OK, well, one point I think you can work on is your song."

Carl looked offended. "Dude we slaved over copperhead, that shit's golden!"

"No no," Seth responded. "It has got some powerful and phallic metaphors, excellent for singing at parties. But it is technically wrong. It is not poisonous."

Luke jumped towards Seth. "Dude, that is completely accurate. I have a book about snakes that I read the shit out of and the copperhead water rattler is totally poisonous!"

"No." Seth put up a hand. "It is venomous."

Carl patted his brother on the shoulder. "What's the difference man, it can still kill you."

"Yes, but let us put it this way, you sound dumb."

Bernice and DJ Dirty Stache laughed at that.

Seth stood back off the van. "Here is an easy way to remember. If you bite something and it kills you, it was poisonous. If something bites you and kills you, it was venomous."

The two brothers looked at each other and nodded to one

another. Carl asked, "OK, so like snakes are venomous because they bite you?"

"Yes," replied Seth.

Luke asked, "But like that Asian blowfish thingy is poisonous because you bite it and it kills you?"

"Yes Todd, Fugu is poisonous," replied Seth.

"Dude, his name's Luke," replied Carl.

"Luke, Todd whatever." Seth waved his hand to dismiss the difference. "Point is: I can scratch your back if you can scratch mine."

"Wait," Bernice started, "you can get us a record deal?"

"I can help you get on the right path. You get me a demo tape by the end of next week, and I will put it in the right hands. I've helped advance some careers in my days."

"Like who?"

"Well, Bernice, there was some help I gave to Mitt Romney, Donald Trump, Manuel Noriega, should I go on?"

"That's all political, what have you done in the music industry?"

"I was responsible for helping launch many musical careers. Most notably Limp Bizkit, Nickelback, and the Justin Bieber."

"That's one fucked up resume, mister."

DJ Dirty Stache spoke for the first time, his voice had a Slavic accent, "And vat do ve have to do for you?"

Seth panned his head to look directly at the man in the tracksuit. "I am trying to procure something in town, and I might end up needing some muscle to help me out. I have not seen any gangs for hire, but you all would do well I think."

"Woah man," Luke said. "That depends on what we're doing. I can't steal anything. I'm still on probation for that arson thing back last summer."

"Arson?" asked Seth.

"Yeah," Luke replied. "Carl and I got bored last summer, so we got a gallon of gas and burned down this old abandoned church out east of town."

Seth raised an eyebrow. "If it was an abandoned church in the country, how did you get caught?"

Bernice answered, "Tweedle dee there," she pointed to Carl, "told the gas station clerk when he paid for the gas."

Seth turned his quizzical gaze to Luke. "You guys paid for the gas that you used to commit arson? Why did you not steal it?"

Bernice fell down laughing. "That's the exact same thing the judge asked, and tweedle dum said..." She snorted some more laughter. "He told the judge, 'we didn't want to do anything illegal'!" Dirty Stache started laughing at that too, the brothers hung their heads a bit defeated.

"So yeah," Luke responded, "we can't do any thieving."

"That is fine," Seth said. "I can take care of that part, or my associate will. I mainly need a little back up for driving and protection."

"Oh, right on," replied Carl. "We can totally bust heads."

Bernice just rolled her eyes again.

"Now, I need some proof of your commitment." Seth waived for them all to join them by the back of the van.

He sat down on the tailgate. Seth closed his eyes; he opened his right-hand palm up in front of him. After a few seconds, a giant black scorpion filled his hand. He opened his eyes and looked at the arachnid, petting it gingerly with one finger across its bulbous stinger.

"Prove your commitment to me; take a single sting from a pet of mine to show me you have no fear."

They all took a step back. Carl gave him a disgusted look. "Is it uh.."

"Venomous?" Seth answered himself. "Yes, most scorpions are. The venom will not kill you though. In fact, it may be quite the opposite effect for you."

"Ewww," Bernice replied. "I think I might be OK with small gigs over this."

DJ Dirty Stache chuckled. "Just this?" He rolled up his sleeve and presented the skin of his left forearm.

Seth smiled, he put the scorpion forward and tapped its back gently. The black scorpion chittered, in a flash, the stinger struck out. A tiny dot laid bare on Dirty Stache's arm, then welled with a drop of blood. He started open and closing his fist. DJ Dirty Stache stumbled back and sat down on the bench again. His body started convulsing. Bernice ran over to him.

"Dude, are you OK? Do we need to get you to the fucking hospital?"

He shook his head. "No, that is the fucking best, oh shit, that was better ..." He zoned out and fell asleep.

"Satisfied? You will not die; I just need you to prove you can be fearless and face down any danger for me."

They all nodded and started to circle around him again.

"Here," Seth said. "How about you all hop in the van for this? I do not think having everyone passed out in broad daylight would be favorable with the local constabulary."

"Huh?" asked Carl.

"He means the cops dingus," Bernice replied.

They all hopped in the van. One at a time, they took their sting, gradually moaning and falling into a deep sleep. When all three were passed out, Seth brought the scorpion level to his eyes. He blew a soft breath across the black shell, and it disappeared from his hand.

Seth climbed out of the van and shut the back doors leaving the brothers and the dwarf woman sleeping inside. He surveyed the scene again to see if anyone had noticed what had happened. Cars passed by as the lights changed at the intersection.

He noticed across the street a pair of women setting up a tent outside of Mamma Mia's Pizzeria and a pair of small uniformed children. He crossed the street to investigate.

Seth approached to see a full figured, tall white woman pulling up the side poles of the tent while a slender woman with a skin tone of deep caramel was unloading boxes onto a table. The two playing children were discussing boys they seemed to like from school. One girl had a light chocolate tone of skin and straight black hair; the other had large glasses and curly bright red hair. Seth had a good idea about the one child, but couldn't see a resemblance of the ginger child to either woman.

"Hi," Dolores called out cheerily when she saw him approach. "Can we interest you in some girl scout cookies?"

Seth cracked a broad smile. "Do you have the thin mints?"

CHAPTER 14

ESMY

Late Monday afternoon, Esmy returned home from the campus and work. She carried her laptop and tablet in her messenger bag slung over one shoulder, the other shoulder she hauled a thin red metal broom with black bristles with a plastic bag dangling from the end of the broom.

She avoided walking through the front door and headed for the backyard instead. She shut the gate behind her and set the broom down next to a lawn chair. Esmy sat in the lawn chair and opened her tablet. From the inside cover of the tablet, she peeled out a half dozen stacked yellow post-it notes. She started sticking them to the arm of the lawn chair.

She pulled the bag to her lap and pulled out a battery powered handheld rotary tool and a pair of small engraving bits. She opened the packages. Esmy packed a fresh set of batteries into the device and set one of the bits into the tools chuck. She laid the broom across the arms of the lawn chair. From the bag, she removed a pair of safety glasses and a roll of duct tape. Esmy peeled two strips of duct tape from the roll, trying to strap the broom to the arms of the chair.

She popped on the safety glasses and hit the button on the

rotary tool to check the speed of the bit. She looked through the post-it notes a few times. Finally, Esmy started to carve intricate rune symbols down the length of the red painted aluminum broom.

After about an hour, the gate creaked, and Esmy looked up to see Jake come into the backyard. He sat down at the picnic table a few feet away and set his bag down on the table. "Got a new project?"

"Yeah, I was trying to come up with a fun, practical application of a lot of this at the office today, and I kept coming back to the classic idea of a witch's broom."

Jake scoffed. "You're kidding, right? You're going to go whooshing through the night?"

Esmy smiled, looking slightly demented in the safety glasses with her wavy brown hair pulled back into a tangle of a bun. "Can't you hear me cackling across the sky already?"

Jake considered it for a moment and nodded. "Actually, yes, I could see you cackling, right before you crash into somebody's house."

"You have no faith, my fine brother. How was work?"

Jake slumped his shoulders and stared up at the clouds above. "Ugh, boring today, the usual getting everything set for the fall break. I will never understand this campus. Every other college gives two days for fall break, Baldur does three, and always right at the end of October."

"No kidding, they always make sure that there are somehow at least days around Halloween to make the break. This two-day school week is making my normal schedule weird and boring. But at least I've got this to keep my focus."

Esmy blew some metal flakes from her lap and started reviewing the engravings against a series of the post-it notes.

Jake gave her a curious glance. "Hey, I got a question for you."

"Shoot," Esmy replied.

"Bang," said Jake without hesitation.

She threw the roll of duct tape at him, and Jake leaned to

dodge.

"OK seriously," Jake started, "have you have any weird dreams lately? I had a really strange one last night. For some reason, I was hiding out in a rainforest, and you suddenly came through the underbrush to where I was hiding."

"That's kind of odd," Esmy replied without looking up from her work.

"By itself that's odd," said Jake. "But you went on to inform me that not only were dinosaurs real and we were being hunted by a Tyrannosaurus Rex, but you also knew how to kill one."

She looked up at that. "That can be beneficial knowledge! Do you remember what I said?"

"Yeah, you told me, 'Jake it is a little-known fact that common household rat poison can be used to kill a T-Rex. However, the delivery system is really tricky. You have to use a whole coffee can of the stuff and send it in as a suppository.'"

Esmy gave Jake a horrified expression. "What the fuck man? How could you even manage to pull that kind of thing off? The thing would smell you before you could get close enough to even search for a butt hole. You may need to see a shrink Jake, if you keep having dreams where I tell you it's a good idea to hunt dinosaurs by fisting them with rat poison."

"Like I said," replied Jake. "It was a weird dream. I woke up pretty soon after that, it didn't seem like we were going to test out your interesting concept."

She shook her head and looked down at her engravings again. "Actually, I did have a strange one too."

"Oh?"

"Yeah, I was around 11 or 12 again and got home from school. You remember those two dogs we had? Freckles and Scotty?"

"Yeah, the little terriers Mom liked."

"Well, I got home, and the dogs were lying on the dining table unconscious. They were on old newspapers, it seemed like there was a lot of blood and both dogs heads were shaved with stitches and staples across both animals skulls."

Esmy looked up at Jake who she could see now was wearing a similar horrified expression to her own from Jake's dream.

"When I walked into the kitchen, I found Dad washing stuff in the sink. He was wearing that ratty red BBQ apron he kept and some really thick black rubber gloves."

"Mom really hated that apron," Jake interrupted. "I'm pretty sure she burned it last year finally."

"Anyway, I ask Dad what he's doing, and he informs me that he took a day off work to swap the dogs 'brains. I started yelling at him for doing something like that in my dream, and you know what his response actually was?"

Jake pondered for a second. "I'll bite. What did Dad say?"

"He looked me square in the eye and said, 'Well, Esmeralda, at least I put papers down for an easy to clean up'"

Jake laughed, Esmy started chuckling. "Just like when we used to carve pumpkins! How he always got on us to put down old papers first, so we weren't dumping seeds and pumpkin guts on the table."

Esmy nodded. "And that's where the dream ended. Strange one for sure."

She set down the tool and began to peel off the duct tape from the broom and armrests. Jake walked over behind her to take a peek at what she carved into the metal of the broomstick. He looked over the scribbled post-it notes with the runes and back to the ones on the broom.

"They look pretty good, what will you use to power the enchantment?"

"Well, you read through the parts about powering spells and enchantments yet?"

"I skimmed it."

Esmy nodded. "The gist of it is that with this kind of long-term enchanted item there are a few approaches. In my view, I've got two choices, really. I can seal the enchantments with some of my blood to link it to myself and my will. The upside there is it's tied to only me so it can't be stolen. The downside is it taxes me directly, and I don't know how long I'd be able to keep going."

Jake nodded at the idea. "So what's the other option?"

Esmy fished in her pocket. "With this." She held up the piece of glowing green quartz they infused with the energy harvested from the yard.

Jake stared at it. "Hmm." He watched as she placed it along a pair of engravings near the top of the broomstick. Esmy peeled off a long strip of duct tape and wound it around the broomstick and gemstone. "Will that actually work?" he asked.

"Well, from what I have read it's a maybe. The theory seems reasonable enough, it's simply energy transference. The energy we pulled from the grass should power the spells engraved into the broom."

"What spells are engraved into it?"

"Well, I put a few spells on there. Levitation for when I need to hang in the air and gain some altitude. There's a spell for speed to give me propulsion and a reverse direction set I found. I'm not entirely sure, but that may give me whiplash."

Jake gave her an extremely skeptical glare. "Will this actually work?"

"Only one way to find out," she replied. Esmy stood up and gave the broom a few taps on the ground, apparently making sure it was, in fact, still a broom.

She walked into the garage and rummaged around for a few moments. A minute later she came back with an old bicycle helmet. Esmy strapped the helmet on and straddled the broom.

"Hey, if this doesn't work, you did remember to mark me as your beneficiary for your life insurance right?"

"Har-har smartass, you'll see in a moment." Esmy looked down the length of the engravings on the red metal and pressed lightly on a rune she knew would activate the connection between her other spells and the stone. The carvings around the other runes suddenly started to glow with a soft green light; she felt a gentle thrum of vibration shooting up and down the metal broomstick.

"See, it's activated and starting to run!"

Esmy put her thumb down on the rune to begin levitating. Surprisingly, she started levitating, and her feet lifted from the ground. She gave the runes for forwarding momentum a small tap and began to move forward slowly. Leaning, she was able to gain enough control to circle around the yard. She cackled merrily as she made it back around Jake.

Jake smiled. "OK, so you can travel at a walking pace. Any idea what the range of that thing will be and what kind of speed you can accomplish with the energy you harvested?"

She hit a rune to make the broom stop and levitate again. She sat in the air a foot off the ground; she leaned back and rubbed her chin. "I was white boarding it a bit at work today when I got bored."

"Nothing to do today at the office?"

Esmy shook her head. "I've got some crap tasks until fall break starts Tuesday evening, getting staff ready to be off. After that, I can actually work on my long-term projects uninterrupted. Like today, Dr. Neidermeier got her laptop clogged up with malware again. I swear there were more unnecessary things installed on there than some of the freshmen machines I've seen."

"So, a lot of time to kill?"

"Most of the time, I have to set up a few scanners to run, so set it and come back later. Gave me time to run some numbers. Given the size of yard and an average yield of energy against the average use of energy to propel my weight, the crystal should last for about two thousand miles, depending on my speed."

Jake nodded. He pointed at the broom. "Did your equations include anything about that?"

She looked at the end of the broom. Where the crystal was taped to the broomstick, the duct tape began to melt and bubble. A big bubble of duct tape popped, and the broom shot out from under Esmy firing straight up into the clouds. She fell hard onto the ground. She considered for a moment about what was happening, looked at the sky and rolled away to under the picnic table.

"Take cover!"

Jake ran for the garage and made it inside the doorway. They both peered out from their hiding spots. Nothing happened. Jake started to edge his way out of the garage when they both heard what sounded like a bomb being dropped.

The broom dove straight down and hit the ground with such force that it buried itself the whole length of the broomstick up to the bristles. Dirt spewed making a massive pit. The hole glowed green, shifting colors of light to pink and blue, then back to green. The twins came out from their hiding spots and started to approach the buried broom. At about that time, Loki appeared at the back door.

"What's going on?" asked Loki. "I heard someone yell about take cover and it sounded like a bomb went off."

They looked at Loki. He was wearing a pair of sweatpants and an old t-shirt with a logo of a pentagram and an eye that read "Miskatonic Astronomy Club." They looked at the broom. He tracked their gaze and looked at the glowing hole and broom bristles.

Loki chuckled. "Is that what I think it is?"

"That depends," replied Esmy. "If you think it's a broom I picked up at the supermarket on the way home to make into a flying broomstick, then yes, it was."

He stopped laughing when he saw the worried expression on Jake's face. "Oh, you're serious?" He stepped forward from the back step and looked at the glowing hole closer.

"Esmy, why is the hole glowing?"

Esmy blew a stray lock of hair from her face. "Well, there's a power source still connected to the broomstick and the enchantments may have a bug in them."

"Power source? What power source?"

Esmy became tight-lipped. Jake answered for her. "It was the gem we stored the energy from the lawn last weekend."

"Both of you need to get in the house now!" Loki yelled, "Hurry!"

They all ran into the house, through the patio and inside. Loki ran to the breakfast nook off the back of the kitchen to peer out to the backyard. The hole was still glowing cycling colors of light, cycling colors faster and faster. Esmy and Jake crowded next to Loki.

"What's going to happen?" asked Esmy.

"Wait."

They didn't have to wait for long. About half a minute later the cycling light stopped entirely. The bristles smoked for a few short seconds, then a plume of fire erupted from the hole. It shot over ten feet in the air and only lasted about 20 seconds.

When it stopped, Loki stood up, looked calmly at Esmy and said, "That, Esmeralda Hansen, is why."

"Don't say it," Esmy interrupted. "Don't you fucking say it."

"That is why real witches do NOT ride Rubbermaid."

Esmy sighed heavily. "OK, fine, good feedback. Still, it was reasonably successful at first. Any notes for future reference?"

"You took an energy source that was storing the gathered life force of over a thousand individual plants and strapped it to an untested string of enchantments. That's the kind of batshit crazy I'd expect from myself. I'm not used to worrying about the outcome actually hurting someone."

Esmy nodded softly. "So start smaller?"

"Two points to take away here," Loki started. "First, yes, please start small. Before you rope a power stone like that onto the enchantment, seal it with a blood bond to your will and test it with something you can throttle easier first. Worst case scenario, you'll pass out, but it's highly unlikely you'll die or kill your brother."

"OK, I need to find a way to black box these things better. The other point?"

"There are dwarves in Svartalfheim, a realm not too hard to cross to from Midgard," Loki began. "Some of them are master craftsmen, and it has taken them decades, some centuries to master working metals and ores with enchantment to produce some of the most astounding magical treasures you'll ever see. Treasures like Mjollnir. That is how you enchant metal, not by carving and engraving into the metal."

She sunk down onto a seat and folded her hands. Loki saw her shoulders slump looking depressed. "If you want to make a flying broomstick, Esmy, you need to understand why they used to be made out of broomsticks."

She considered it, but Jake seemed to catch on quicker. "They were easy to conceal. You start keeping odd things around that are specific for enchantments, people tend to notice it more. But in those days, most brooms were handmade from wood. So nobody really would question anyone having a broom."

"That's one excellent reason for it," Loki said to Jake. "Another is that it's made from wood. Depending on the kind of tree you start with, the age of the branch or whole tree you are making the broomstick from and how long it's been since it's been separated, you can lock that power into the broomstick and not have to power it from yourself or a separate power source like the crystal. By changing out the bristles on a regular basis with new pine needles or other elements, you can maintain a renewable energy source as well."

Esmy sat up and smiled. "So, I was on the right track, I just used the wrong materials?"

Loki bobbed his head a bit. "Yeah, that's a way to put it."

Jake took a seat across from Esmy, and Loki sat down between them. "Anything else exciting happen to you today?" Jake asked Loki.

"I finally woke up this morning, and you two must have already been off to work. I spent the day browsing the internet to catch up on things since the last time I was here in the eighties."

Jake shut his eyes and winced. "You tried to get all that from the internet?"

"Yeah. There's a ton of great info on there. Some stuff I hadn't heard for a long time, some stuff was pretty new to me. Like I learned about rule 34."

Jake put his face in his hands, Esmy laughed. "Rule 34?

You learned about rule 34?"

"Yes, apparently it's something about if you wonder about certain kinds of porn, it's likely you can already find it online."

Esmy kept laughing. "No, we are well aware. I imagine you learning about it and trying to think of weirder porn than is already online."

"Well, I must admit that most of it was already there," Loki replied.

"Most?"

Esmy jumped back in before Loki could expand on what he couldn't find. "What about the other rule, 'anything is a dildo if you are brave enough'?"

Loki rolled his eyes. "Hells bells, Esmy, that's not new. You should see some of the stuff that used to be used for a dildo before the industrial revolution."

Esmy tightened her lips and made a zipper imitation across them. "Nope, don't need to know more. We're all good, I'm already sorry I brought it up. What are you up to tomorrow?"

Loki shrugged.

"Want to come by campus? I could use some distraction, work is boring right now, and I got something I needed to bounce off you."

"Sure," said Loki. "I should probably try some embedded learning there anyway, and I can swing by your office in the afternoon."

"Oh, I was working on Dr. Neidermeier's laptop today and found some strange symbols scanned in from a book. I couldn't understand it, and it didn't seem familiar. I've still got her laptop at my desk though; can you take a peek at it for me? I didn't know she was in the Preternatural Sciences department, but it doesn't appear to be normal math or algebra kind of symbols."

Loki furrowed his brow. "Yeah, you never know. Could be a lot of things. By the way, do either of you have a way to watch something called 'The Iron Chef'? I saw some clips on the YouTube site today and wanted to study this cooking battle more. It's too intriguing to pass up."

Jake stood up. "Yeah, follow me. I'll introduce you to the world of modern cooking shows. It's a lot more than Julia Child, and the Cajun Cook used to be. When you're ready, I'll show you Epic Meal Time, those guys make some stuff they probably would kill for in Asgard."

Loki followed Jake into the living room, Esmy stayed back in the breakfast nook for some time, staring at the darkened hole in the yard that was her first attempt at a flying broom. She thought about what Loki said regarding wood and brooms. She remembered there was a large white ash tree in the park; it survived a lightning strike from an early summer storm. It split part way, but the near century-old tree survived and was still blooming new leaves. It was definitely an idea to ponder as she stared at the dark hole.

CHAPTER 15

SETH

Seth entered the staff dining room ahead of Julia. He collected a plate of salad, primarily lettuce leaves, when Dr. Neidermeier spoke up behind him. "The talk today seemed to go a lot better today than it did yesterday."

He finished piling his plate and poured a thin line of vinegar across the leaves while Julia took a piece of roasted chicken breast and some quartered red skin potatoes. "Yes," Seth said as they found an empty table to a side of the room. "It was roughly the same lecture, but the tone of the questions and overall reception seemed a lot more open."

They both seated themselves at the table and just unfolded napkins when Dr. Jeffords strode toward their table. "You folks mind if we join you?" he asked. Professor Mull stepped around Dr. Jeffords into view, carrying two massive plates of food. The two looked like quite an odd couple in the setting.

Dr. Neidermeier looked at Seth, who just gestured his hand out and said, "Yes, please, the more, the merrier."
While the two situated themselves, Seth leaned over to Julia. "Who are these two bozos?"

"The creepy one with the chest hair and gaudy gold

medallion is Dr. Jeffords," she whispered. "And the dwarf Colonel Sanders in the loud Hawaiian shirt is Professor Mull."

"I mean, maybe you should give us a more formal introduction, even if they are dressed like degenerates you could show a little respect to faculty."

Seth nodded and sat back upright, he smiled congenially at them.

Dr. Jeffords sat down while Professor Mull hopped gingerly onto his chair. As the pair set, Julia introduced them to Seth. "Derrick, this is Dr. Jeffords and Professor Mull. I was happy you gentlemen were able to attend Dr. Boule's lecture, did you enjoy it?"

Dr. Jeffords was already mid-bite of his beef Manhattan. Professor Mull had taken a large bite of a drumstick which didn't stop him from responding. "It was quite fascinating Dr. Boule," he said, chewing the chicken intermittently and waving the bone towards Julia. "I am always a little skeptical going into these guest lectures, but I left this one thinking, 'now here is a frood that can really store some grain!'"

Seth gave a quizzical look across the table to the dwarf. Dr. Jeffords swallowed and jumped in. "I'll have to apologize for my colleague. Mull doesn't have the best of manners at the worst of times, and I fear he's got the worst of manners at any time."

Jeffords wiped his mouth with his napkin and continued. "What Mull means, is that we were surprised by your lecture. The depth, knowledge, and reasoning were thoroughly sound. The last lecturer in the matter of Egyptian Mathematics was pretty poor. He basically made a lecture of translating hieroglyphics for equations and some examples of the scrolls encountered in the Nile valley."

Seth furrowed his brow. "Tsk tsk tsk, that is just awful. An hour or two is a short time to devote to the subject, but to bore the students with something they would have encountered in third grade is just condescending to them."

"Now, now," Mull spoke up, dangling a dripping spoon of mashed potatoes. "To be fair, most of our guest lecturers are here for the general student body. It's not often we receive such a distinguished guest that is able to ignore skepticism."

"I was more proud of our students today," Julia commented. "Better than the reaction from the math majors and general student body on Monday. I was surprised by their incredulity."

Jeffords again wiped his lips and wagged a finger at Julia. "Now, there is the major difference in opinions. You have to understand what separates them, the two student bodies."

Julia scoffed. "The difference between the muggles and the magi?"

Mull scowled at her as he shoveled a spoonful of mashed potatoes into his mouth.

"It's not as stark as that," replied Jeffords. "Looking at it from that perspective dooms most people to a lifetime of being an outsider. You could consider it as the oppressed and the liberated, but even that may not be an apt enough description for it."

She frowned at the rebuffing. "Enlighten us then, Dr. Jeffords. What is a good way to describe it?"

Jeffords picked up his fork and a slice of bread that set off from the side of his plate. "Let's say my place setting here represents our little world. The two pieces of bread you see here are our student body as a whole. The piece over here in my hand, white and untouched by anything, is most of our students, like the ones Dr. Boule addressed Monday."
Julia nodded her head thoughtfully.

"Now, let's pretend our Preternatural Sciences students are this other piece already in the gravy of the beef Manhattan. Essentially, both started out the same, but the PS students been exposed to a lifetime of the unknown, how to handle it, how to mold it and understand it. They've soaked up the rich, meaty juices of the world outside and became more flavorful for it. Follow me so far?"

"Not sure I see where you're going with the beef, but continue."

"We'll get there. Now, at both lectures, Dr. Boule presented a theory that the ancient kingdoms of Egypt didn't span just back a few thousand years like common archaeological theory tells us in most textbooks. He presented an alternate theory that the way the Egyptians built the Great Pyramid of Khufu and the change of how we see mathematics in their culture in the later kingdoms that their society spanned back much further. Possibly tens of thousands of years. On my plate, our students that already accepted some of the rich globulant universe outside of itself were more receptive to Dr. Boule's theory."

"Our general student body over here," Jeffords continued, holding up the clean bread. "Responded with skepticism as they have not known the flavor explosion of the meat and gravy. That was their general reaction, but you caught a few students." Jeffords tore off a part of the bread and dipped it across his plate. He held the newly soaked chunk in his other hand. "A few of the students allowed themselves to open up to his theory of advanced ancients in the Age of Osiris."

Seth winced at the term but nodded.

"These students…" Jeffords wiggled the bread in his fingers, shaking some gravy onto the tablecloth. "They now know the salty flavor explosion of the beef. They could stop here, or they could continue to take on more gravy until they become saturated. They can begin to embrace the umami! When you first started teaching here Dr. Neidermeier, you were bread. Now, you are semi-saturated. I'm sure you've read some of the books in your predecessor's library, maybe you've tried out some of his work for yourself. Each day, you may become more of a flavor explosion."

Seth cleared his throat. "That is quite a colorful metaphor, Dr. Jeffords. Can I assume that you believe me to be part of your Manhattan as well?"

Mull shook a drumstick in his direction. "If you spent as much time in some of the circles I think you have to posit a theory like the Age of Osiris, then it's a good bet you are part of the Manhattan. Depending on the years you were in Egypt, you may have even met the shade of our Professor Emeritus Crowley."

Seth's expression turned grim. "Aleister teaches here?"

Jeffords chuckled. "He becomes corporeal enough to teach every third year or so. He'll be back on campus next semester."

"Good, we parted on some unfortunate terms," Seth said, stabbing a final piece of lettuce.

Seth folded his napkin over his plate and sat back in his seat. "Tell me, Professor," he said addressing Mull. "Do you accept my theories on the ancients of the Nile valley?"

Mull nodded. "Aye, it does track. I do know from some of our studies and interactions that it's more likely than not."

"What exactly do you teach here Professor Mull?" asked Seth.

Mull smiled brightly behind his whiskers. "Languages and linguistics, with specializations in ancient and dead languages."

"So you've spent some time studying over near the pyramids as well, then?"

"A long time ago," responded Mull. "I was able at one time to get a rubbing and some photographs myself of the inventory stela near the Sphinx."

Seth rolled his eyes, "there are a lot of people that consider the inventory stela as a hoax. What would be your professional opinion Professor?"

Mull discarded the last of his chicken bones onto his empty plate and settled back into his seat. "That's the tricky bit. People point to it as a hoax because of what it claims, but some of the claims don't make sense of how a pharaoh would normally act."

"What do you mean by that, how would a pharaoh normally act?" asked Julia.

Mull scoffed. "They'd lie their ass off. Most of the time, it's tricky to trust some of the claims because they'd claim they did or built something they may not have. But in this case, the inventory stela lists off some things that Khufu did build, like the Temple of Isis and some statues. When it comes to the Great Pyramid though, it only says that Khufu discovered it, it was already there."

"But people consider it a forgery, do they not Professor Mull?"

"Aye, they do. There's a good reason for that too, linguistically speaking. But it raises some good questions. There are no records of how the Great Pyramid was built. The rest of the pyramids weren't built to the same exactness as that one nor any as big. Also, they conjecture it to be a burial tomb for Khufu, but there was little there about Khufu aside from a small statue and his tomb. If this was his epic undertaking, shouldn't he have more carvings on the walls about him constructing it? Shouldn't he have more statues of himself inside the burial chambers?"

Seth and Julia nodded.

"I suggest that pyramid was built much earlier by some precursor to the Egyptian civilization we know of today. I'm not entirely sure what its purpose was," continued Mull, "but I am certain it was related to the Age of Osiris. The beings that the Egyptians reference as gods, I believe we have misunderstood. They are not gods, but extra-dimensional beings."

Seth gave a sly grin. "That is quite the theory, Professor Mull. Is there any proof?"

"Jer," started Jeffords. "I think it's time we should be going."

"Ah, proof you want, Dr. Boule? I met one of them, watched him die and carted his corpse halfway around the world for him."

Jeffords cut him off, "Jer, come on, you sound crazy saying that, and we really need to get going, you have a one o'clock class."

Mull looked at the time and hustled off his chair, Jeffords grabbed their plates, and they headed off to leave.

After they left, Dr. Neidermeier looked at Seth. "You don't think they actually meant, you know, do you?"

"I do. That little man witnessed my nephew die and brought his body back to this campus. He was right about a few other things as well."

"The pyramids?"

"Yes, what he referred to as the Age of Osiris, was an age when my people did come across the dimensional divide. We built the great pyramid after teaching the humans we found at the time how to read the stars, understand the magnetic poles of planets. We taught them a lot. The pyramid itself was a station."

"Like a train station?"

"Yes. It was our Grand Central Station stop for this planet. Khufu ended up installing his tomb for lack of other ideas what it was for. If it were not for Horus, it would have still been operational, and my kind would have ruled humanity."

"What do you mean by that, Seth?"

"It is a long story for another time. For now, we know the remains are somewhere on this campus. Now we just need to find it and destroy it."

"Destroy it? Do we have to do that? Won't just having seen a corpse be proof enough that Horus is dead and you can claim your throne?"

Seth narrowed his eyes at Julia, "proof alone is not enough. I need proof and to destroy enough so they cannot pull the same stunt they did with Osiris. I will make sure there is nothing left to make more of him this time.

CHAPTER 16

LOKI

Loki woke up late Tuesday morning. He looked at the screen from the DVR, the timestamp he paused on was from four in the morning. Loki regretted his binge session of Iron Chef. After a quick shower, he cleared the mirror and stared at himself in the mirror. He guessed Seth was possibly somewhere nearby now. Loki also realized that, though he's created allies with his relatives, there was too much unknown at the campus to risk his real face.

He stared at each of his features in the mirror: thick raven dark hair, pale skin, icy blue eyes. His slender face came to cliff-like edges at his cheeks and chin. The starkest things Loki saw when he stared into his own reflection were always his lips though. Centuries of random drips of acidic burns left permanent scars. He got used to the minor concentration he needed to fill them in. Loki took a deep breath, and the scars filled out once more.

The easy part was over, now he needed a disguise. Loki closed his eyes. He reached back into his mind, browsing through centuries of faces and people he met. He picked a face, matched his height to the face. He finally projected some clothes onto the character. When he opened his eyes, the mirror reflected an elderly man, receded gray hair and mustache, shorter in stature wearing a brown tweed suit and wire spectacles.

"Hmm.... you would be less recognizable Dr. Jung," Loki said to his reflection in a thick Swiss accent. "You are a bit dated though; I don't believe this will work out."

Loki closed his eyes again and remembered more fresh faces and figures. He continued forward in his memories to a mall food court in Baltimore. He pushed his body to change and shift with the new persona.

When Loki opened his eyes, the reflection staring back was drastically different. He was no longer an elderly Swiss man but now looked like a 19-year-old girl. A short razored pixie cut of black hair fell across her forehead. She wore a grey t-shirt that fit snugly across her chest, stretching the words that read "Vote Beeblebrox, Two Heads are better than one!" The jeans fit loosely over her legs and followed into heavy combat boots. Loki looked down at her arms to study the tattoos, a pair of ravens in flight around a tree on her right arm, on her left a silhouette of a planet with a single ring encircled with the words 'don't panic. 'She looked into the eyes, still glacial blue, and followed the rounded nose down to a ring that went through one nostril.

"Hello Megan," he said to his reflection. Loki pursed her lips. "No, you don't seem like a Megan, perhaps Sheila? Kelly? No, Kalli, we'll call you Kalli."

Loki turned around staring at the mirror for a minute. "Yes, nice ass, Kalli." He grabbed the tablet Esmy loaned him and shoved it next to a grey hoodie into a backpack while heading out the door.

Kalli walked to campus, she remembered the way to the college. When she got to school, she decided to wander to the center to see if there is a map. The campus consisted of what appeared to be a dozen buildings laid out around a set of walkways and grassy knolls in the middle.

She saw a small brick building with no apparent use and

wondered if it was an information posting area. Kalli walked through it and found it was merely what it looked like, a small brick building with four open arches and some benches inside, but nothing else.

A small group of five students were sitting together under a tree nearby. She stopped next to them. "Hey, can you guys tell me, what is this building?" Kalli hooked her thumb to point at the small brick structure.

A tall, older looking student wearing jeans and a red flannel shirt looked over at her and the building. "Oh, that's the Wellhouse."

Kalli cocked an eyebrow. "But there's no well," she said.

"Yeah, I'm pretty sure it's decorative," he replied. "You new to campus? I thought all the students knew that was the Wellhouse."

"Oh, I'm visiting," Kalli invented quickly as Loki realized he hadn't considered being questioned. "I didn't set up a tour. I'm kind of related to some folks that work here and was looking for them. I'm Kalli by the way."

"I'm Kyle, nice to meet ya," replied the student. "All of these guys are new students this year too, if you want to join us to get an impression of student life."

Kalli looked around at the group of students. They looked fresh-eyed and naive. A little idea gnawed at Loki sitting behind the façade of Kalli: that it might be funny to screw with them a bit. "Sure," she said. "I've got a few minutes to kill. Is this a class?"

"Kind of, at Baldur, the administration has this idea that if new students get a better chance of success if they take mentor sessions with an upperclassman."

"Cool."

"Today we are discussing some new trends at colleges, like safe spaces and trigger warnings. Safe spaces are areas at the college where anyone can be sure they can express ideas without discrimination, criticism, or fear of emotional harm. The trigger warnings are getting some clear warning that something you are going to use or discuss may be disturbing."

A plump young man with shaggy dreadlocks in a grungy green hoodie sat across from Kyle. "I was saying they're probably a good idea."

"Right," Kyle continued as Kalli sat down to join the group. "Rasta Pat was telling us about his thoughts."

Kalli put her and up. "Isn't calling him Rasta Pat a little discriminating?"

"No," Rasta Pat cut in sarcastically. "It's my nickname and what I like to be called, thank you very much."

Kalli pursed her lips and nodded her head to that.

"So anyway, like I was saying, my dad's this bag of dicks that would always tell me I was full of shit, pardon my French."

Kalli spoke up, "It's OK, that wasn't French."

Rasta Pat gaped at her open-mouthed. "Anyway, he was always arguing with me and telling me like I wouldn't amount to anything and I needed to get a job. I just wanted him to actually listen and be proud that I had ideas, but he always said everything I did was crap. So like, I need uh safe spaces so I can fully express myself."

Kyle nodded. "Suuure, Rasta Pat, that's a great observation, but can you give us an elaboration. Let's pretend this is a safe space, what was something you would tell your dad about that he didn't understand?"

"OK, like one time, I read this article I was trying to tell him about. I checked it out too at a local lake, and it was right. So, this dude said the government was dumping chemicals into our water supplies, like lakes and rivers. Anyway, these chemicals are turning frogs gay, dude. I mean, don't get me wrong, I've got no problems with gay folks, but like, I'm straight. I want to know that if I'm going to be gay, it's like my choice and not because of something the quote-unquote establishment dumped into my water supply. And that's why I always drink pure filtered bottled water."

The entire group was now staring at Pat waiting for someone to speak. Loki made sure Kalli caught the opportunity. "So, your dad called you crazy for believing that the government was putting chemicals into the water to turn frogs gay? Did you observe any gay frog-sex happening at a local pond?"

"See," Pat screamed pointing at Kalli. "This is the crap I'm talking about, and why I need a safe space, you guys are totally discriminating my idea here."

"No, Kalli here is asking if you had anything verifiable outside of an article that you read on the internet. Were there any scientific studies to support it or did you actually see that kind of thing happening?"

"That's the discriminating part, duh! How can I feel good about myself and my ideas if they are being questioned all the time?"

"Well," Kyle continued, "that's not productive. You won't learn anything if someone doesn't ask you to prove it. I could claim that we're turning frogs gay, but I don't have any proof. Now, there are verifiable studies that in some species of frogs, if there isn't enough gender diversity, the frog can release a chemical reaction to cause a change of sex. So they may appear to be gay frogs if given a pool of only males, but in actuality, some of them caused their own change to become female."

Rasta Pat scoffed and crossed his arms. "Typical, you guys are just like my effing dad."

"Now, a good example of a trigger warning would be if I told you this session was going to include violent content, and you might hear depictions of rape and/or murder. Now, I don't have any stories, involving rape and murder, but I can share an experience of rape and dismemberment, eh."

The group all looked over at Kyle with mouths agape.

"So, I was about seven," he started. "And my Uncle Al took me to a circus traveling through the province. He was acquaintances with a guy, Gary, that was a clown with them. Well, we weren't aware that he got fired the night before and apparently really upset about the whole thing."

Kalli cocked an eyebrow, looking around the circle, she could see everyone else getting curious too.

"Anyway, Gary decided he'd ruin the whole circus

experience for everyone by giving a lion enough horse tranquilizers to make him passive and woozy. He planned to sneak into the cage and have sex with the lion to ruin the whole show, would even take the keys into the cage with him so no one would stop it."

"Dude, what the actual fuck man?" asked a girl in the group.

"Yeah, we're pretty sure he drank a bit too much, y'know Canadian beer is about as strong as moonshine. Anyway, clowns aren't known to be good veterinarians, and Gary didn't seem to know out how much to give the lion. Things were going to his plan at first. He'd got in the cage, full clown gear and makeup on. The lion was really docile. He exposed himself and started thrusting into the lion, honking this bicycle horn on his belt with every thrust, honk honk honk honk."

Kalli looked around the group again. Everyone seemed really shocked in horror. Loki was more intrigued than horrified but did his best to make Kalli match their expressions.

"Long story short, all the tamers were looking for a way to get him out of the cage, I guess the tranquilizers wore off. The lion came back to his senses and started mauling Gary. Took a big paw across his neck and slashed open his jugular. They were hosting a local children's hospital cancer unit too, so all these young kids were in the front row. Blood sprayed across them. Yeah, he died, real tragic, right in front of the kids and all."

Kyle looked around the circle and saw the looks of horror. "And that's a good example of a trigger warning. I warned you about the topic would include rape and dismemberment in case it would cause you emotional trauma. So, Kalli, did that story trigger anything emotionally from your past that made you uncomfortable or traumatized?"

She shrugged her shoulders. "Well, your trigger warning didn't tell me the story would be about bestiality."

Kyle nodded. "Sure sure, I should have mentioned bestiality. Is that something traumatizing in your past? You don't need to discuss it if you are uncomfortable."

"Well," Kalli started, as Loki felt a pang to want to really screw with them. "I never met my real family, I was a bit of an orphan, and my real family decided I was too small, so they gave me up. I had kind of an adopted family, and my life with them was a bit bumpy and hectic."

"Sure," Kyle nodded. "We can all sympathize, family issues."

"We needed to fix a wall around where we lived, and this contractor offered to get it done quickly, but his prices were really high. Now, we lived in a very rural area so the contractor would need to use horses to move the rocks for the wall. My family didn't like the price he quoted, but I got them all to agree to a contract. The contractor only got to use one big horse, and if he didn't complete the job in a brief time, we wouldn't pay him."

Everyone nodded along.

"We got close to the deadline, and the guy moved really fast. It looked like he was actually going to finish it on time, but my family didn't want to pay his price. So, they said I caused the mess, and I needed to fix it or else they'd kick me out. Long story short, I made myself seem like a mare in heat and lured the builder's horse away where it raped me in the woods. I can still sense his hot breath on my neck, the braying, and the hoof beats if I close my eyes. But the builder didn't finish the wall, so he didn't get paid."

Rasta Pat looked disgusted. "What was the price that would make any family find it reasonable to let a horse rape a kid?"

"Oh, if he finished the wall, he would force my adopted aunt into marriage and servitude far away. She was gorgeous and said she'd kill me before she'd be married off like that."

They looked dumbfounded at Kalli.

"So, trigger warning I guess," she said softly, smiling slightly

"Where the fuck did you come from?" asked a girl sitting nearby.

"Ummm, Montana?"

A tall, broad-shouldered older man in a brown tweed suit walked through the Wellhouse. "That was quite an enlightening story and a fantastic example of trigger warnings young lady. All of those were great reasons we don't observe them much here at Baldur."

Kyle jumped up and offered his hand to the man. "Dr. Longfellow! I didn't expect you to sit in with us today."

He shook Kyle's hand and stepped beside him. "I wasn't, just passing by and overheard from the Wellhouse. Now, I can see the reasonable expectation of a trigger warning so it wouldn't cause a relapse of emotional trauma such as in young Kalli here, but it sounds like it helped her deal with the trauma as well. And let's face it, students, safe spaces may let you express ideas, but some ideas should be challenged. Such as this notion of chemicals making frogs gay."

Longfellow chuckled and continued staring directly into Rasta Pat's eyes coldly. "It's been a while since I'd heard anything so ridiculous, and that is something easily challenged academically."

The group nodded, except Rasta Pat who scowled at Dr. Longfellow. A pair of ravens in the tree above them cawed conspiratorially.

"Now Kyle..." Longfellow broke off his stare at Pat and looked up to the ravens. "I'm interested in your visitor here. Do you mind if I borrow young Kalli here?"

"Sure, thanks for your input, Dr. Longfellow."

"Thank you, Kyle, follow me miss, let's go find somewhere more comfortable to talk."

Kalli followed him along the narrow walkways from the Wellhouse to the back entrance of the Old Bastard. "Excuse me, Dr. Longfellow," Kalli said, walking faster to keep up with his long strides. "But I've never been to campus, where are you taking me?"

He turned to her. They stood near the mahogany staircase. He punched a button to call the elevator behind him. "Forgive the sudden interruption, but I find it in my best interest to personally meet new students and in some cases prospective students as well."

The elevator doors opened with an off-tone ding, and Dr. Longfellow motioned for Kalli to enter. He followed her into the elevator. He licked his finger and touched the button labeled B2. Kalli saw a slight pink glow in the button at his touch. The doors shut and dinged back open again swiftly. "Down here," Dr. Longfellow said. "There's a nice boardroom we can discuss your career privately."

Kalli followed him into a room, the chandelier lighting as they entered. Dr. Longfellow stepped off to the side and watched her enter. Kalli turned to peer through the room, stopping cold at the sight of the giant serpent head on the wall opposite them.

Kalli sat down in a near chair. She looked back and forth between the head and Dr. Longfellow. "How? Do you know what that is? Who are you?" She asked all three questions rapidly.

Dr. Longfellow sat next to her. "If I told you, you wouldn't believe me. I figured this might be the only thing I could show you to make you believe me. Look at me again, Loki."

Loki stared at him through Kalli's eyes. "Magni? Magni the Strong… is that really you? How?"

He chuckled. "Which do you want first, about me or your son up there," he said nodding at the serpent head.

Kalli shifted back into Loki, who now sat in the chair almost a foot taller. He was staring at Magni and rubbing his chin. "I heard rumors someone killed him, but was it you that killed Jormungundr?"

"Not only me, it took all three of us, Modi, myself, and Thrud. It was how we all learned how to wield father's great hammer on our own. You remember it, right?"

"I didn't mean to scare you when I pulled you down here," Magni said. "But I saw Huginn and Muninn in the tree when I overheard you tell that story. I figured out who you were and needed to chat, but not near the ravens. It's good to see you, Uncle, but why are you here?"

Loki gnawed for a moment. "I've spent lifetimes of deceit

as a means to my ends. Right now, those ends forced me to come here too. Would you trust an honest answer anymore?"

Magni sharpened his glare onto Loki. "Dad wouldn't have. You were like a brother to him, and he wouldn't trust you any further than Mom could throw you. On the other hand, the All-Father would always give you enough rope, so to speak."

"How is your dad? I haven't seen Thor in a long time."

"Dead," replied Magni.

"Oh," Loki responded, appearing genuinely saddened by the news. "I'm sorry to hear that."

"That's why we took Mjollnir to kill the serpent over there. Modi has it for now, but I got his favorite goats."

"Grinder and Snarler are still running around? You learned the trick right?"

"Yes, but I usually don't resort to killing them, at least not often. We found ways to take blood between the two of them to feed the chupacabra."

"Why do you have a chupacabra, Magni?"

Magni flashed a devilish grin that made Loki slightly jealous.

"So, your honest answer, why are you here, Uncle?"

Loki gave him the story of Seth he told to Esmy and Jake. He continued to tell him about Esmy and Jake, how they were related and what they were learning from him. He managed to get it all in about twenty minutes.

When he'd finished, Magni didn't appear shocked. "The twins are quite full of surprises aren't they?"

Loki was shocked by that response. "That's all you have to say? I tell you that an Egyptian God of Chaos and War still has me under his thumb, is planning to steal something from you, possibly attack your college and you don't care?"

"Oh, I care, but it's not wholly unexpected. Hell, I remember Detroit. I'm surprised it's taken this long," replied Magni.

Loki stared at him, mouth agape.

"Hey?" asked Magni. "Have you talked to Esmeralda and

Jake about my staff members? Or given a poke around yourself?"

"Some brief conversation," replied Loki.

"Well, to fill you in, your descendants came here to work and very recently discovered our Preternatural Sciences department. I'm guessing someone working in that area may be talking to Seth and letting on about the remains. Anyway, the twins caught on enough that I may admit them as part-time students. Especially after your... intercession."

"So, you became a teacher?" asked Loki.

"Yes and no," replied Magni. "I'm an organizer. I got most of these people together to mold the young minds with talent or to bring talent to moldy young minds. Your pick."

Loki smiled at that idea.

"Oh, I do get to teach one course now. Basic Hand to Hand Combat with Deities, Demigods, and the Supernatural."

"Of course you would," replied Loki. "Isn't that a little unfair to the humans though?"

Magni bobbed his head considering the point. "Perhaps, but I took over the course this week. It's usually taught by our PE instructor."

"What happened to the original instructor?"

Magni sighed and rolled his eyes. "Bureaucracy. He's being investigated for unnatural relations with a sasquatch."

Loki rolled his eyes. "Heard about it."

"Yeah, some students saw him blowing a sasquatch. It may have been a minor. We have to deal with it more modernly though; it's not the fourteenth century anymore."

"Yes, I was there, saw the whole thing go down first hand."

"You know what I've never found out?"

"Magni, I swear on my remaining children, if you ask if a bigfoot's dick is normal or a red rocket kind."

Magni held up his hands and stopped him there. "Hey, no harm in wondering."

Loki unfolded his hands and sighed. "Well nephew, you got my story and who else is here. What would you do to me?"

"You've got to keep playing your part uncle," replied

Magni. "I couldn't expect you to welch on your deal with Seth. But, I have an inkling you're tired of playing the servant. I'm sure if the right moment were to assert itself, you'll find an interesting way to resolve the matter. In the meantime, we must wait for our enemy to reveal himself."

"Why?"

"You've got to clear your debt with him still. If you position yourself against him, he'll call for you to be put back into your prison."

Loki shivered, remembering his old confines.

"Plus, he is under the impression he has the element of surprise right now. The only thing he can really surprise me with will be how much force he'll bring and when. I can guess the when will be tomorrow, likely evening. If you can discover what kind of force he'll possess aside from himself, it will help us defend the campus better. Still, I'm not worried."

"Have you fought someone like Seth before?"

"Not Seth directly, but folks like him. Most of the campus will be cleared out by tonight for Samhain Break, or as the normal students like to call it, Fall Break. We learned quite a long time ago how dangerous some of our studies can be, so the buildings are more protected than you'd expect. The protective spells will keep them from taking on too much damage. So, there's no concern for students and my campus should be pretty safe."

Loki nodded.

"Also, I have a vampire here to help me with defenses. He can be quite persuasive. Plus, you are going to get the twins to help fight him."

Loki blinked. "What? I'm not going to let them anywhere near that. They aren't ready, they just learned about our world last week."

"Trials by fire are pretty decisive. Besides, you must have something in mind for them if you brought yourself into their lives. You couldn't have simply wanted to a family reunion."

Loki sunk into his seat and sighed.

"You did? You actually only got in touch with them to get to know them?"

Loki shrugged. "I was never a big family man, but I really loved their great-grandmother. I owe it to her to be a part of their lives now that I know of them."

"You'd better be preparing them pretty heavily tonight. Tomorrow, those two enter a battlefield, and I can't guarantee what will happen. If we all survive, we need to sit down and talk about what influence you should have on your family moving forward." Magni gave a foretelling nod to the giant serpent head. "We don't need any repeats after all."

Loki scowled at Magni. "Fine. It looks like I've got quite a lot of work to do tonight. If you'll excuse me, I was supposed to meet Esmy today for some more lessons." He blinked his eyes, and he shapeshifted back to Kalli.

Magni stood up to walk out with her. "Good, any luck we'll only deal with Seth. I hope he doesn't bring Apep along. We don't need another incident like Detroit." They both shuddered.

"By the way," Kalli started as she walked to the door. "Is there a metal colander in the staff kitchen?"

CHAPTER 17

LOKI

Loki walked out of the Old Bastard as Kalli. He sighed deeply, and wandered off, pondering his next moves. He stopped a random student. "Can you tell me where I would find a metal colander?"

The student, a plump girl with frizzy blonde hair, looked at Kalli strangely and pointed down the campus walkways to the dining halls.

Kalli walked the neat cement pathway around the manicured lawn with odd patches slightly lighter than the rest. She looked out at those patches and wondered what became of the students that created the spots, laying in the sun on sunnier days. Were they ordinary students with regular majors? Were they the sort that studied in Magni's Preternatural Sciences department?

For that matter, Kalli wondered, could you tell them apart? Would some students hover more surreptitiously over their books than others to hide arcane and supernatural lore from the passersby? He wondered if the entrance test was to see if the pupil could make a dusty old tome look like an average calculus textbook.

Loki had learned now of two professors in that department, Magni, and a supposed vampire. Would the rest of the professors be notable in their nature as well? Were there specters and demigods on staff, wondered Kalli. For that matter, if there were vampire staff, would there be vampire students, werewolf undergrads, and changeling co-eds. The possibilities seemed too curious to ignore it all.

Kalli approached a pair of brick dorms connected by a glass hallway in the middle. The names on the buildings read Huginn Hall on the left and Muninn Hall on the right. It all seemed so obvious now. The way the college was named, some of the architecture even resembled buildings he'd seen built in the newer ages of Asgard. Here were more drastic cries of how evident the influence was over the campus. Two dorms, literally named for Odin's raven patrol, Huginn and Muninn, Thought and Passion. It was pretty obvious which was which, too. Though they were joined in the middle, Huginn Hall was a utilitarian rectangular three-story brick building. Muninn Hall was more artistry to the architecture. It was mostly the same brick and also three stories, but with peaked roofs and granite steps leading up to the front entry.

Ominously, two large black birds cawed from a tree overhead near the dorm at that exact moment. They caught Kalli's attention, and she stared angrily at them to intimating to buzz off and leave well enough alone. She followed the direction they were leaning and their gaze. In a parking lot behind Muninn Hall, several students were loading onto buses with several middle-aged and older people. Kalli walked along the side of the building to get closer.

As she got closer, it all seemed normal, students putting duffle bags and luggage under a charter bus and getting names checked off some official looking clipboard as they load onto the bus and get situated. She listened. Loki understood the real value of listening wasn't in merely hearing something, but really paying attention to it and using it to fill in all of the gaps of missing information.

So, Kalli pretended to stop to read an email on the tablet from her backpack. She picked up on a conversation that did help to fill in some new information. Kalli scanned and saw a wispy blonde girl talking to a white-haired dwarf with a snow-white mustache and goatee. Kalli could hardly believe it was an actual dwarf, but it was apparently easily passing himself off as a human midget.

"I meant to ask Professor Mull," said the wispy blonde, "but why are we taking a bus? Wouldn't it be cheaper, easier and quicker for us to cast a gateway spell and all walk through to a known point?"

The dwarf raised his eyebrows at the girl. "Good question, Hyacinth. There are a few issues with that idea. First, a number of your classmates outside of our department know you are traveling and would expect to see you leaving like this."

The girl seemed to nod in agreement with that initial assessment.

"Secondly, we would generate a noticeable disturbance in the campus electrical system if we made a gateway sustained long enough for us to all travel through. Instead, we will take the bus to a large wooded estate nearby owned by an alumnus. They graciously allow us use for such cases. There we will be able to make a gateway big enough to transport the bus and everyone in it without anyone the wiser."

"But won't we be pretty noticeable in Louisiana if a big charter bus drives out of nowhere?"

The dwarf chuckled. "We're not that careless. Your itinerary says we'll be studying for two days with a bayou Vodun and taking a two-day tour of New Orleans itself. The Vodun is a friend of Dr. Longfellow. She's made sure to ward off her land from visitors for the night so we will be able to drive right through and be at her doorstep. No one will ever be the wiser. Most of the teaching staff is with us as well, except Dr. Longfellow and Mr. Mordido of course, in case we hit any problems."

Kalli stowed the tablet back in her backpack as the

dwarf and Hyacinth were boarding the bus and finishing the conversation. It was an enlightening exchange though, knowing what they were doing and getting a gauge of some of the staff. Also, finding out there were apparently many friends and well-off alumni. Kalli slung the backpack on again and continued to walk around the dorm back to the central walking paths.

She started down the path between the dorm and the library and stopped short. A small open-air wrought iron gazebo sat between the dorm and the library. A wrought iron bench wrapped around the inside of the gazebo where Kalli saw a person with the same human head that she'd last seen Seth using and some abnormally large woman that looked like an undersized ogre. She turned back and went back behind the dorm.

Seth and the woman hadn't been looking in her direction, so she was reasonably sure that she hadn't been seen as Kalli. She stood with her back pressed against the wall of the building for a few minutes to process through the situation. Given the gravity of the case now, and knowing how many more players were suddenly in the game, it stood to reason that she needed to get some information. Kalli also decided that it would be best to keep this form from Seth.

She looked around, the bus pulled away; most of the parking lots were more sparse than usual as well. She slinked along the wall to a tall hedge and knelt behind it to gain some more cover. In a brief moment of concentrated will, her form shifted back to Loki, tall with short black hair and glacial blue eyes. He stood again wearing jeans and a heavy dark red hoodie. He pulled the hood up and walked around the corner.

Loki approached the gazebo, Seth and the woman he didn't recognize were sitting close together talking in hushed voices. He walked into the iron enclosure and took a seat next to Seth. He raised his head so his face could be seen and said with a grin, "Hi, I'm a prospective student visiting, are you both professors here?"

The olive-skinned bald man spoke, "No, I am Dr. Boule, a

visiting lecturer, but this is Dr. Julia Neidermeier. She is a math professor and also teaches in the Preternatural Sciences." He turned his head to whisper to Julia, "This man knows me well, Julia. I hold his debt, and he is working to my ends. Please meet Loki."

She leaned forward and asked, "Loki, is that your first name or last?"

Loki raised his head, so his grin gave way to his icy blue eyes. "Madam, it is my only name."

She chewed that over for a moment. "You are surely joking? You mean you are—"

Seth cut her off. "Julia, do not be obtuse. You have seen all sorts of things now and have been friendly with an ancient god for months. Can you really be surprised to meet another or that I would be using another."

She sat back and crossed her arms feeling a bit chastised by that statement.

"A bit of information sharing is in order," Loki said. "What have you found out and what are you planning?"
Seth recounted some of his conversations and what Julia was digging up, as well as the campus situation and what professors were expected to do in defense of the school.

Loki listened to everything Seth was saying, but his mind was in two places. He always knew Seth to be an entitled, pretentious prick, but the way he was going over everything and talking about how horribly defended the campus was made Loki really take notice of that fact more. Loki also contemplated his reunited family. He brought them into this, what could he do now?

"And that is everything I have discovered so far," finished Seth. "Your turn, what have you been up to?"

Loki leaned lazily onto one knee. "Well, you've got suspicions and innuendos that the remains are here. I got confirmation. I've been slouching around campus in and out of places for a couple of weeks now," Loki lied easily. "And found out they are here and where they are."

Julia cocked an eyebrow. "But this is the first I've seen you anywhere on campus. I'm sure I would have recognized you if you'd been hanging around."

Seth scoffed and chuckled. "Julia, that is exactly why I called Loki into help me. He is the most accomplished shapeshifter I have ever known, mortal or immortal." Loki almost beamed with pride at that statement.

Seth continued his praise. "He once even took the form of an old crone to simply ensure against the resurrection of his own adopted brother. I am not surprised a novice such as you would take no notice of his skill." Loki grimaced at the grim reminders of his past transgressions.

"Yes," sneered Loki. "I'm not new to being incognito as it were."

"Anyway the body is secured in a series of underground vaults guarded by more than you have heard. You only expect there to be the vampire and the old man, but there are beasts guarding chambers below and other security measures."

Seth sighed. "That settles it, from what Julia has found out, Isis is likely coming to make her claim Friday. We have to move soon."

Loki waved a hand. "Don't rush it, that's always your problem. We have time. By your own account, the rest of the faculty and student body will be gone by tonight. Let's wait out anything until later in the week."

"No, the sooner, the better," countered Seth harshly.
"Patience good doctor. I need a little more time to suss out the rest of the security, these aren't measures you can blast through. I have a plan."

"You have a plan?" Seth asked incredulously.

"Yes, I have a plan. Look, you've got some goons right?"

"Yes, some band I took on in town here."

"Great, they don't have to be great fighters or anything, I need you and them to cause a distraction, make some noise. Think you guys can handle that?"

"Easily."

"If I can do anything," Julia said, "anything at all, let me know. I am yours to do with as you please."

Seth smiled. "I have just the thing in mind."

"Great," said Loki. "You stir up some mess while it's the old man and the vampire on guard duty. While their attention is turned, I can break through the vaults and the chupacabras to get what you need. I'm not sure I can get the whole corpse though. You only need the…" Loki tried to find a way to phrase it delicately. "Only the naughty bits, right?"

"I need all reproductive organs. The rest of Horus' body is useless, and Isis can do as she wishes," said Seth. "For all I care you can destroy them as long as I see you do it. I need the confirmation."

"Great, good to know," said Loki. "Listen, I've got some more prep work to do on my end. How about we agree that you launch your attack sometime after nightfall Thursday?"

"Tomorrow," shot back Seth. "We act soon."

Loki frowned. "That puts me in a bit of a rush, but I suppose it's doable tomorrow night."

"Afternoon. The afternoon is the latest we should wait. I want to keep the vampire out of the fight if possible."

"You and I both know that vampires aren't as affected by the sun as the humans are led to believe," replied Loki. "I need time. It's not so damned simple, late afternoon at the least, close to dusk, say around six?"

Seth nodded. "Five. You better deliver on your promise, Loki. How long will you need?"

Loki bobbed his head. "If I get it right the first time, between thirty minutes and an hour. Less if I get lucky."

Seth nodded again. Loki stood up. "Til tomorrow." He headed off, leaving them still sitting in the gazebo.

He walked past the library and turned the corner to another walkway that led to the rear of the dining hall. Behind a dumpster, he shifted once more back into Kalli. Kalli strode to a set of stairs by the loading dock and sat down to weigh the option that lay ahead.

Kalli noticed a back door near the loading dock was open. She strolled through it. Loki learned over the millennia that all you had to do was be confident about where you were, and people wouldn't question why you were there. To Loki, Kalli was now a student that worked in the dining hall kitchens part-time. She strolled through to check the work schedules.

She found no work schedule but did see a delivery schedule. She read the meat delivery invoice, "three sides of veal, sixty-five pounds of ostrich meat and one whole bison." It was dated to be delivered Friday.

Kalli walked through some of the food prep areas. She found what she was looking for on a shelf almost immediately. She picked up the stainless-steel metal colander and stashed it in her backpack, checking that no one was watching her. The kitchen was oddly empty though. She dug through a few utensil areas and found another useful tool, a handheld Bernzomatic torch. She stashed this in her bag as well.

She walked through the rest of the kitchen, still finding no one. Kalli finally saw most of the kitchen staff standing outside the serving counters. They were lined up and watching a group of about a dozen students packing up some totes and folding a pair of tables.

Kalli sidled up to a tall older man wearing a grease-stained cook's apron. White hair peeked out from under a Fightin 'Goats baseball cap. His bespectacled eyes were staring at the students packing things away.

"What's going on here?" she asked him.

"It's the vegan club," responded the geriatric fry cook. "They protest our serving any meat every day. Handing out leaflets about meat is murder, breakfast, lunch, and dinner. They're always here like they hold a constant vigil."

"And now they're watch has ended," Kalli joked.

"They'll be back, they're packing up to protest somewhere else over the break. Probably a Chick-Fil-A or something. Maybe they'll at least take Sunday off if that's the case." He stared at them silently again. "They've always been such a fixture, we all come out to see them off when they do pack it in."

Kalli gave him a sideways glance. "Really? Why? Wouldn't you be happy to be rid of them?"

The man finally turned to look at her for a second. "You must be new. We hated them at first, but over time we all came to kind of give them a kind of respect."

"Oh. Why?"

"They really kind of stuck with it, years go by, students come and go, but they've held constant protest like clockwork. They talk to folks that'll listen, they hand out leaflets, but they won't knock the food out of your hands. We'd even started offering some vegan options to accommodate them some. Margie over there," he pointed at a large raven-haired woman in a floral apron, "she makes a killer vegan 'chicken 'parm made with garbanzo bean."

"Hmmm," agreed Kalli. An idea ticked in her head and Loki smiled widely from the back of her mind.

Kalli thanked the man for his information and headed past everyone to outside the dining hall. She found the rest of the vegan club loading the items into a minivan, led by a short sophomore with long dreadlocks wearing an old army jacket. She approached her.

"Excuse me," Kalli said. "Do you lead this group?"

The girl crossed her arms defensively. "Yeah, I'm Angie."

"Kalli," she responded. "Where are you headed?"

"It's break, so they aren't serving students," Angie replied. "We thought we'd go picket a food court down in Indy somewhere. They won't be cooking any meat here for almost a week."

"Oh, but you are wrong there," Kalli said and detailed the expected delivery. "Given all of that, it sounds like they are preparing for a special occasion. It's time to up your game here."

Kalli walked away back towards the other side of campus once more. She heard Angie ordering her club to unload to the lawns and find some tents. "We'll be camping out between here and the loading docks for the whole break," she announced to them.

CHAPTER 18

ESMY AND LOKI

Kalli went down the steps of the stairwell in the Old Bastard. She wandered into the basement, the sign next to the stairwell and elevator listed department and rooms. The only department listed was Campus Information Technology. Some computer labs were registered, a few offices, she found Esmeralda Hansen and started to search for her office.

A few minutes of roaming aimlessly later, Kalli found a small set of cubicles. One displayed the nameplate he was looking for and the voice of a woman cursing silently. Kalli knocked softly on the side of the cubicle and peered in. Esmy was staring at a computer screen, looking utterly bored. She appeared to be wearing a pair of grey slacks and a blue blouse, with her curly dark hair pulled back into a ponytail.

Esmy turned around with a headset on and saw Kalli. She stared at her for a second. "Hey, got a connection issue?"

"No Esmy, it's me," Kalli said.

"Yes, it's you," responded Esmy. "And could you tell me who is you? Or is that who you is? Nevermind, who are you?"

Kalli let Loki's face flash across her own.

"Oh, it's you. Of course. And what should I call you

though?"

"Kalli, I go by Kalli today," Loki responded changing his face back.

"So," continued Kalli, "what were you cursing at before I stopped in?"

"Oh, that laptop I told you about. Dr. Neidermeier brought it in because it slowed down so much that it was barely usable. I've barely been able to get into the OS enough to even start to see what's going on and I've been at it two days now. Here take a peek at these though."

She passed a small stack of yellow sticky notes to Kalli. Kalli thumbed through them as Esmy was restarting the laptop in front of them and holding down a set of keys again. The machine made a few beep noises and prompted a stark text interface instead of the rich and smooth graphical one of Esmy's other devices. Kalli drew in a sharp breath as she looked at the last of the stack.

"Esmy, you need to shred these immediately. You didn't read them aloud, right?"

"No, they seem like old Egyptian hieroglyphics. I hadn't read that chapter yet. Jake could probably read them with what he's read from history books, but its doodles to me."

Kalli sat back in the chair. "Destroy them, now."

Esmy shoved the small stack of post-its through a cross shredder near her desk. "OK, now want to tell me what they were?"

"Well, your Dr. Neidermeier was into some nasty things. Some I recognized, some I didn't. Parts of that stack were the conjurations to say to summon Seth, commonly known as the ancient Egyptian god of chaos, war, the desert and destruction. The rest were notes on summoning Apep, a chaos demon, and massive serpent. We've got enough issues with Seth walking among us, we don't want Apep here."

Esmy turned from the screen. "Wait, Seth, the war and chaos one is here?"

"Yeah, I need to talk to you and Jake about that tonight,

but it can wait, I hate repeating myself."

Esmy nodded and turned back to the screen. "Well, you don't sound too worried, so I'm guessing I shouldn't be either."

Kalli rolled her eyes. "Esmy, he's still considered a god by a lot of Earthly standards. He is technically an immortal and does fight very dirty. But, he also uses a lot of misdirection and side effect to his fighting. He rarely gets into a direct fight."

"Apep though?"

Kalli whistled. "Apep will fuck you up. That's the long and the short of it. He would be hard to escape, no talking, he wouldn't warn you. You'd just be dead. Hell, they even made spells to recite to protect the dead; Apep was considered an eater of souls and could reach you in an afterlife."

"Shit, will Seth call him up?"

"No, nobody wants him brought up. Nobody."

The laptop made a chirp and winked to darkness.

"Well, shit," Esmy said.

She flipped it upside down, pushed a small switch and slid out the laptop's hard drive.

"What is that?"

"You've never seen a computer hard drive?"

Kalli shook her head. "I never got into understanding over-complicated human technology."

"It's the hard drive. It holds all of the information and programs the computer runs." Esmy popped the drive into a sled bay that sat on a pile of papers behind a monitor on her messy desk. She shook a can of Pringles and tossed it into a trash can. "When it gets this bad, I have to start running scans and analysis tools against the drive from a different machine."

"So that rectangle is necessary?"

"Very, it's an interesting piece of technology. This is one of the solid state ones, so it's a bit more stable, but the older ones were basically like extremely tiny high-speed record players on crack. This one works on chips that store the data, so not as prone to corruption so easily."

"How much can that drive hold?"

"This one is a half terabyte drive, so if we were talking books. Let's say your average book was about 300 pages, one gig could hold over three thousand books, if it's only text. In half a terabyte or five hundred gigs, that comes out to about one and two-thirds million books, less if there are images."

Kalli looked awestruck. "That's a pretty magic rectangle. And you walk around with these devices in about everything."

"Sure, some have more or less data. But it is fragile; you can destroy it with too much electricity, water or even dropping it. On top of that, they can get infected with viruses."

"But, they don't live do they?"

"Not in a biological sense, the viruses are malicious programs meant to destroy, hijack or spy on the device. This one's got some nasty hooks too. I'm set, we can let it scan and go take a walk, and I need some fresh coffee anyway."

They got up, Kalli tossed her backpack on, and Esmy picked up her phone from beside her keyboard. They headed back for the stairwell. As they passed Jesus's office, he called out to them.

"Hey Esmy, come in here for a sec."

They entered the darkened office. Jesus sat behind his desk, bathed in the light from a pair of LCD monitors in front of him. He didn't seem to have ever looked up from them.

Jesus spoke up as they entered. "If you and your friend are heading up campus to the student union, can you hit the science building? That Kyle kid over there with the van is having issues with the WiFi again."

Kalli stared across the office. "So you're the vampire?"

Jesus looked up at that comment. The door shut abruptly behind Kalli and made Esmy jump.

"Wait," said Esmy. "You really are a vampire?"

"Your friend here has a big mouth," Jesus said to Esmy and turned to face Kalli. "Who are you?"

"I'm an old friend of the family," responded Kalli.

Jesus got up from his chair and walked around to stand near Kalli. Kalli could finally see that he was wearing a green polo shirt and khakis. His dark hair was parted at the side, and he looked like he should be in a board meeting or heading to some executive retreat.

"I see, so this is Loki."

Esmy stared back and forth at both of them. "I have so many questions right now."

"I only have the one," said Kalli.

"Dr. Longfellow told me you were here Loki. It doesn't take too many guesses to figure it out when you blurt out something like that. Go on Esmy, I'm used to this series."

"I always joked about it, but you really are one?"

"Yeah," replied Jesus. "Bloodsucking, mostly immortal beast of the night. Well, that's not really true. We got some... bad press."

"Bad press? You make it sound like there have been a few centuries of PR mistakes," said Esmy. "So, I mean, what's it like? Can you go out in sunlight? Do you get a handicapped spot, so you don't have to walk as far in sunlight from your car? Can you turn into a bat? Do you want to suck my blood? Do you want to suck everyone's blood? Are you ancient? Did you kill Bram Stoker?"

"Ha, that sunlight thing, best misdirection ever." Jesus chuckled. "Esmy, if we couldn't go out in sunlight, what would make moonlight any better? It's the reflection of the sun's own light from the opposite side of the planet."

Esmy nodded at that explanation.

"Well, it kind of does. We don't go tanning because our skin has about the same UV resistance as an Irish maiden. We tend to wear a lot of sunscreen. Ironic, I get it, dark-skinned Hispanic that now can't walk in the summer daylight without burning."

Jesus pondered the questions for a moment. "Let's see, yes, I can turn into a bat, but I could do that and many other animals before I turned. No, I don't want to suck your blood, I've seen your diet. Besides, you're off limits. I want to suck everyone's blood like you want to eat every ounce of food in a restaurant. I eat, it's not an addiction. I turned in 1893, so I'm not that ancient, especially next to your new friend. And Stoker was killed by syphilis."

"So, can you eat normal food?" Esmy asked.

"Yeah, it doesn't do anything for me. I get no nutrition from it, and it really costs me more energy to process it than I get from the food. But I do love a good hot dog or brat with some semi-coagulated blood on it at times. It's mostly for the mouth-feel."

Esmy nodded. "Huh, that's interesting. Did you get turned by some spooky dark stranger that drained all your blood?"

"Ugh, that whole thing." Jesus rolled his eyes. "No, I banged a nun."

Kalli chuckled at that. "Wait, you are telling us vampirism is a sexually transmitted disease?"

Jesus shrugged. "I don't see why you're surprised. I'm sure you'd seen vampires before and are familiar with the whole situation."

"Yeah, the traditional way of passing blood between the vampire and the progeny, not the uh, well, the erotic passage of fluids," replied Kalli.

"You know, I really have no idea if she was a vampire. The town I grew up in was extremely catholic, and Sister Sara Marie was a very devout woman. She was also a beautiful woman, with such a vast..." Jesus cupped his hands to his chest. "Eh, habit."

Esmy frowned at him. "But you turned into a vampire after that right? So she must have been a vampire too. Otherwise, how would you be one?"

"She never seemed like it or anything. The next day when I started to change, she vanished, gone forever. I assume she was a vampire, but there's a part of me that always wondered," Jesus trailed off.

Kalli picked up the train of thought. "Wondered if the sin of your seduction made some vengeful God curse you to walk the Earth as a vampire?"

He nodded without really responding to Kalli. "You're taking this pretty well."

"Jesus," Esmy shut her eyes and pinched the bridge of her nose. "We've got a secret wizarding school, my great-grandfather is apparently a Norse trickster god, I managed to transition a magic tome into a magic e-book, I tried to make a magic broomstick but just blew up part of my yard, the PE teacher supposedly has same-sex interspecies relations with Sasquatches, and apparently we have an Egyptian god of chaos running around. Finding out my boss is a vampire is one of the more tame discoveries in the last week."

Jesus looked over at Kalli. "Shit, are you serious? Dr. Longfellow mentioned we might see a hit this week, but is it Seth or Apep? Please tell me it's not Apep, I remember what happened in Detroit."

Esmy raised an eyebrow. "What happened in Detroit?"

Kalli waived her hands. "Nevermind, it's Seth, not Apep, that I know of, but it looks like Dr. Neidermeier is working with him and discovered the scripture to summon Apep."

"Shit," responded Jesus. "I always thought that lady was up to something. She got into the board too quickly, she's just too damned creepy, and that's from a vampire."

Something seemed to click in Jesus. "Wait, he is your and Jake's great-grandfather?"

Esmy gave a tight-lipped smile. "Yep, I can only imagine what the next family reunion is going to be like now."

Jesus laughed. "You know, I remember Dr. Longfellow telling me there was something special about your family when you two hired on, I didn't suspect it was divine ancestry."

Kalli raised an eyebrow. "That's curious because it was news to him that I was related at all. We need to have a talk about that this weekend with your Dr. Longfellow."

"If we live that long." Suddenly Esmy looked up at Jesus. "Oh crap, no offense, since, y'know."

Jesus laughed at that comment. "You folks get so damn funny when you're uncomfortable. Anyway, bio department, go find Kyle and see what's up with that whole WiFi issue."

"Fine, fine bloodsucking slave driver."

"Keep in mind I still consider vampirism a non-reversible medical condition," yelled Jesus back at them while they walked away.

They left the building and headed down a set of walkways, this time of the opposite side of the lawns from the dorms and the library. Between the Old Bastard and Miller Hall were an apartment-style dorm, the small Wellhouse and a set of parking lots.

As they passed the parking lot, Kalli gave a double take. "Esmy, tell me, is that van over there painted with a mural of a wizard having some very comical sex with a unicorn?"

Esmy turned to study the van, and they both stopped. "Yes, it appears so, and it does answer an old question."

Kalli didn't turn from staring at the van. "And what question is that, Esmeralda?"

"If a wizard's staff does have a knob on the end."

She started walking again, and Kalli stepped back into motion, too. They entered Miller Hall and headed for the second floor. Most of the offices and classrooms were dark. There was one lit door down the wing. They led down towards that door, hearing voices as they approached. As they neared, the conversation began to coalesce.

"Come on, Kyle, I need this grade to pass at least one class, or my dad's going to stop paying for my tuition. He said I gotta pass at least one class!"

"Pat," they heard Kyle's voice this time. "I'd like to help you out, but you dug your own grave with this one. I'm not your admission counselor, so I really don't care who is paying your bills. Dr. Gene, your professor for Bio 101, gave some pretty simple assignments I was to be grading. Out of 27 people, 26 managed to turn them in. You couldn't even turn in the sketch of a cicada on time."

"Dude, there aren't any cicadas out there. I looked."

"Pat," Kyle started to say.

"And for the last time, it's Rasta Pat! God, why can't anyone take my choice as a Rastafarian seriously?"

"OK," Kyle sounded pained to say it. "Rasta Pat, cicadas do hibernate for seventeen years, but this is their waking year, they are literally everywhere. Creepy little red-eyed things flying around, making that terrible screeching sound from the trees all the time. Recognize that?"

"Oh, those things. I totally could have gotten that done, but like I told you before, my car broke down, it made this gnarly grinding sound that needed to get fixed." They heard Pat complain.

"You could tell me that two nuns and the pope were dancing naked around your car in the light of the full moon while slashing your tires." Kyle made an audible sigh. "But while that would be an interesting story, it still wouldn't change your grade. Maybe you just weren't meant for college."

They heard Pat shout back at Kyle. "Maybe you were just meant to get bent!" Pat stormed out of the room and headed past them down the stairs. Esmy and Kalli looked back at one another, shrugged and headed into the room.

Kalli started wandering the room. It was a biology lab with tall tables able to sit four stools. The walls were covered with various expert taxidermy specimens. Kalli gravitated towards a far wall with a large glass case housing the new wasps' nest. Esmy introduced herself. "Hi, Kyle, is it? I'm Esmy from IT Services. You put in an issue about the WiFi here?"

Kyle looked at both of them. "Oh yeah, it worked itself out, and I'm about to head out anyway." Kalli was staring at the hive and tapping on the glass. "Hey, your friend shouldn't be tapping on that? I don't want to get the hive worked up."

"Magnificent fear-inducing little insects aren't they? Tell me, did you collect this hive?" asked Kalli

"Yeah, outside of town, got pulled over on the way back too, the sheriff got a real knob on about my van."

"You drive that van with the magnificent piece of art on the side we saw parked outside?"

Esmy made air quotes with her fingers, saying "art."

"Now Esmy, many people judged Van Gogh's painting as horrible in his day too, but time is the true judge, and everyone is entitled to their own opinion of what is art," said Kalli. "I find the depiction on this young man's van to be inspired."

Kyle smiled broadly at that statement. "Thank you. You are the first person to really agree that it is a genuine piece of art and not some trashy porn scene."

"Trashy porn? How else do you expect to see a wizard celebrating the birth of a homunculus?"

Kyle was beside himself now. "Whoa, I may be in love."

"You want to get involved with me, Kyle?"

"Yeah, that's a pretty bad idea, things aren't quite what they seem," added Esmy.

"Oh, she may be a year or two younger than me, but it's not like I'm robbing the cradle here."

Kalli turned back to Esmy. "Esmeralda, we have a learning opportunity here, and Kyle could be a valuable resource later on. So, if you don't mind, I'd like to share a few things."

Esmy rolled her eyes at the use of her full name. "Go ahead and reveal thyself or whatever."

In the blink of an eye, Kalli shifted, and where she once stood, Loki stood, over a foot taller than Kalli, lean and short-haired again. The clothes changed shape with him, so he was still wearing a t-shirt and loose fit blue jeans.

Kyle stared wide-eyed. "What the actual fuck?"

"Kyle, meet Loki, trickster God of Asgard and apparently my great-grandfather." Esmy shrugged her shoulders and put her hands in her pockets. "So, you're right, you wouldn't have been robbing the cradle, but he probably would have been. He's a few thousand years older than you." Kyle looked back and forth between the two of them. "You guys are really serious?"

Loki put a hand on Kyle's shoulder. "Yes, I am much older than I appear, but you probably should forget me being related to anyone, it always gets people in trouble."

Loki opened the backpack he'd been carrying around as

Kalli. He pulled out a metal colander, a small belt, and the Bernzomatic blow torch.

"Now Esmy, do you have your copy of the tome?" asked Loki.

"Yeah, one sec." Esmy tugged a small, slender zipper down the side of her grey slacks; it unzipped further down than the seam showed. She reached in and started fishing around.

After a few moments, she was half bent over with her arm shoved into the pocket up to half past her elbow. "Esmeralda, did you enchant your pants?"

She stood up straight and put her hands on her hips. "You've gone about masquerading as a woman, but have you ever bought women's clothes? The damned things never have pockets! So, yes, I enchanted a hidden closet worth of space basically into my slacks. Problem is, my tablet fell under something. One of you will have to fetch it if we need it."

Loki grimaced. "Kyle, you'd better take on this task, I'm related, and so it feels wrong to go feeling around her trousers."

Kyle walked over and was about to reach into the pocket when Loki spoke up again. "Never mind, I can remember enough of it to wing it." He walked over to a dry erase board and wrote a series of twelve words.

"OK, Kyle, I assume you've done some work with this hive correct? Have you seen the queen?"

"Yeah, right after we relocated it into the lab, I found her and made sure she was settled."

"Excellent. Esmy, what we are doing is a man in the middle enchantment. Normally, it only takes two people, but we want to create an artifact, so it will require the will and effort of three."

He motioned them all to come to a table nearest to the hive. Loki placed the items in front of him on the table and turned to face them. "Kyle, I want you to focus everything in your mind on that queen. Everything you can about her, what she looks like, where she may be, what she's doing. Anything. Esmy, you are going to put your left hand on Kyle's shoulder and your right on mine, and you will continue to recite the phrase on the whiteboard until I tell you to stop," Loki explained. "I will be pushing that enchantment onto this colander using my own will and this cute little blow torch. Everyone understands what they are doing?"

Esmy cocked an eyebrow. "You said using manufactured items was a bad idea?"

"It is a bad idea for you," Loki answered. "However, I have apprenticed with the Svartalves, dwarves and some other artificers over the last four millennia. This is pretty simple for me."

They formed a small triangle. Esmy reached up to touch both of their shoulders.

"OK, Kyle, focus on the queen. Esmy when you are ready, start reciting."

Esmy stared at the board and took a deep breath. She began reciting the twelve words. She stopped only between each recitation to take a breath and started again. Loki ignited the torch. He started spinning the colander in one hand while applying the torch flame with the other. He closed his eyes while Esmy continued chanting.

After a few minutes, the incantation Esmy was reciting started to glow red in a cursive slanting script around the edge of the colander. A moment later, Loki slowed the spinning strainer and killed the torch.

"OK, Esmy, you can stop," announced Loki. She stopped chanting and took her hand away from Loki and Kyle's shoulders.

Loki turned Kyle to face him. He tied the belt loosely around the handles on the side of the colander and placed it on top of Kyle's head, slinging the strap under his chin.

"Now, if you would Kyle, please tighten the belt down to where it is comfortable but that the colander doesn't slip from your head."

He did so. "OK, I look like a complete goon. Now what?"

"Now focus on the queen again and gently nudge an idea

of what you would want a swarm of wasps to do. Let's say, you want the whole hive to swarm to the left side of the enclosure."

Kyle looked at him like he was nuts, but he turned to view the glass cage. He pictured the queen and focused on the entire colony of wasps swarming to the left side. Slowly, wasps began to filter out of the hive. Gradually, they kept filtering out and at a faster rate. They formed an evil cluster of buzzing malevolence on the left side of the cage.

"That's pretty damned wicked," Kyle said. "Will they do anything I want?"

"Yep, have fun with it, I have one thing you must agree to," replied Loki.

"Anything, this is super awesome."

"If anyone asks you where you got this power or artifact, you must lie." Loki extended his hand to Kyle.

Kyle shook his hand. "Sure."

"The pact is sealed," Loki said ominously and turned back to Esmy. By the time he'd spun around he was transformed back to Kalli. "Ready to head off when you are Esmy."

They left the building while Kyle was opening the enclosure, seemingly having fun watching the wasps move around the lab to his direction, flying in intricate formations.

CHAPTER 19

KYLE

Kyle played around the lab a bit more. He learned how to command the hive to swarm, to scatter. He gave more subtle thoughts to bend them and watched as they split and took formations to their flight patterns. Kyle found a small box and set it up on a lab table. He tightened the slipping strap on the colander. Kyle concentrated the wasps into a tight cloud slipping around each other smoothly in the air. With a shift of concentration, they darted through the room, surrounding the box, he shifted focus again, and they darted across perforating the box repeatedly.

Kyle made a slight mental effort, and the colony flew back to their cage, and he closed the opening behind them. He sat down at one of the lab tables and unstrapped the colander, gently placing it in front of him. The hive resumed a typical pattern, seeming random to the average human eye.

He always wanted to believe magic was real, but Kyle never expected to get proof not only shown, but handed to him so directly. Yet, here it was. A gift from some stranger

Kyle wondered what he should do with this impressive, yet limited power. He went to the chalkboard in the classroom and started jotting down an idealist. He wrote, "study the hive, how it would interact with other hives." He jotted down, "get better insight than anyone into the dynamics of a hive mind with these insects." Kyle looked at the box he'd used for target practice. It was a Girl Scout cookie box. That gave him an idea. He drew a picture on the board of the little Girl Scout icon and crossed it out with a dramatic slash of the chalk.

He walked out to his van and found an old loose-fitting rust colored hoodie. Kyle jogged back up to the Biology lab. He put on the hoodie, strapped the colander back on his hood and slid the hood gently up over the strainer taking care not to knock it off balance. He opened the enclosure door. He made a subtle mental effort, and the colony swarmed together to follow him through the room. He took care to encourage the queen to fly out as well. "If we're going to hit the road guys, I don't want to worry about the helmet having a maximum range and have thousands of you guys lose contact with the queen suddenly. Wait, why am I talking to wasps now?" He stopped for a second to make sure he didn't keep speaking out loud to the wasps.

He walked outside and opened the driver's door to his van. He decided that the van may be too recognizable. With a gentle push of will, the wasps landed and clung to the mural on the van, obscuring most of it. As he started up the van and drove away, he noticed it was taking a minor toll on his concentration to keep the wasps in place and convinced to stay instead of sliding off the side. Though he also realized that it wasn't any more of a driving distraction than holding a cup of coffee in one hand and eating a sandwich with the other while driving with his left knee. He decided this was actually a bit easier, especially with using both hands on the wheel.

As he pulled up to the corner of Jackson and Franklin, he found his target was there and set up to hock as many boxes of sugary evil as possible, but there weren't any customers or kids. It seemed convenient and like a generous gift.

Kyle revved the engine and brought the van up straight over the curb. He braked hard and came to a skidding stop in front of the table obscuring the view from the road. The sudden halt on the loose gravel also kicked up a massive cloud of dust. Kyle was glad for the dust; it blocked his targets from seeing him clumsily fall out of the van.

He gave a gentle nudge of his will, and the swarm came through the cloud of dust behind him as he strode up to the table. When he was clear of the dust and knew the two women could see him, he spoke from inside of the hood. "I only give you this one warning. Pack up your booth and leave this place, never sell your cookies here again, eh!"

Dolores and Sam were actually still waving out some of the dust clouds from their face. They knew something was buzzing and some weird tall guy in jeans and a rust-colored hoodie in front of them. They both stood up to try to peer through the cloud more. Dolores coughed and sputtered, "Wh-what?"

Kyle's vision was obstructed under the hood, so he pulled the hood back, and it completely exposed the colander, but now he spotted them. Dolores stood over a half-foot shorter than Sam, slightly leaner, mocha skin matting under the dust. She was wearing a red shirt with a black North Face vest. Sam was wearing jeans and what appeared to be a purposefully ugly Halloween sweater depicting a witch flying in a night sky. The witch looked a bit stretched out over her bust and Sam was squinting to watch through the dust.

"Look, I don't want to hurt anybody, pack up your stuff and get out of here. I don't want you taking advantage of these folks with that crap anymore."

This time Sam responded, "What's it to you, mister? We aren't hurting anyone."

"I'm not here to argue, pack up or you face the pointed wrath of the Canuck Stinger!" Kyle was particularly proud of that statement, he'd been rehearsing it in his head the entire trip over from the school.

Unfortunately, the ladies laughed.

Kyle lashed out angrily. A massive cloud of wasps whirled

and split around him into two groups. The first group flew straight to the women. Dolores and Sam found themselves surrounded by the fog of wasps hovering one inch around them. "Dolly, what the hell is this? Are these wasps real?"

"Don't move Sam," said Dolores. "I don't know what this creep doing, but I don't think it will last much longer."

"You're right, it won't. I'm about to make sure you won't be slinging these addictive artificially sweetened shit-pucks anymore."

Through the din of buzzing, they made out the sound of boxes tearing, three distinctive pops and loud hissing. They heard the van engine rev again, and the swarm started to dissipate.

From the driver's window of the van, Kyle leaned out and yelled, "And I don't want to catch you sweet bitches pushing this shit around here again, eh!" He sped off, kicking up a smaller cloud of dust and gravel.

Dolores's daughter Sophia and her friend were in the pizzeria to get a drink when the attack occurred but were standing outside the door now staring at the scene. Dolores started to take an inventory of what happened. Every box and every case of cookies was ravaged by the wasps; some dying wasps were still writhing inside of them attempting to escape.

"He fucked up every box of cookies," she shouted waving her hands frantically at Samantha.

"Yup," Sam replied. "And he slashed three of the tires on your Volvo wagon."

Dolores fumed, clenching her fists at her side she shouted, "Godfucking dammit!"

"Dolly, think of the kids," Sam reminded her.

She visibly calmed looking back at the pizzeria. "You're right Sam. Josh cut his trip in China short and got home last night, anyway. I'll call him in a few minutes and get him to pick us and the kiddos up."

Sam was startled by the quick transition. "You gonna be OK, Dolly?"

"Perfectly fine Samantha. Would you be busy tonight, say around midnight? I've got some chores to attend to in a graveyard."

"Sure, Dolly, anything for you after that, but what are we going to do?"

"Did you notice the van?"

"Yeah, but I couldn't make anything out."

"I did, and I saw a motherfucking wizard fucking a motherfucking unicorn, and I'm about to get me some motherfucking revenge."

CHAPTER 20

ESMY

After work, Loki was still shifted into his Kalli persona. Esmy slung her backpack over her shoulder, and they headed off campus.

"Should we go get your brother before we head back?" asked Kalli.

"Nah, he's got some stuff he wanted to wrap up and something Jake said he needed to pick up on the outskirts of town. He said he'd meet us at home tonight. Besides, I've got a little task for us to work on for now. Follow me."

She led them east away from the college. "Where exactly are we heading?" Kalli asked. She reached over and pulled a banana from a side pocket of Esmy's backpack and cracked it open.

"There's a park not far from campus, I had an idea for some fun and needed your help here."

They continued walking a few more blocks past a variety of homes in the neighborhood surrounding the campus. Crossing another street, the houses stopped. On each side of the road stood high walls of stone and cast iron bars. On one side of the road, the gated area contained a large old cemetery. Esmy headed through the gate of the wall on the opposite side of the street, an old bronze placard at the entrance read Mistletoe Acres Park. Kalli only ate half the banana, she tossed the other half and peel into the road before the park. The area inside was sparsely wooded with gentle hills and well-trimmed pathways.

As they passed through the gates, Kalli's form shifted back to Loki.

"How do you not get sick of doing that? Doesn't the shift hurt or cause side effects like nausea and vomiting or something?"

"It's not a prescription drug Esmy," replied Loki, now lurking a foot taller behind her. "Besides, I've been shifting for thousands of years, you kind of get over the side effects after that long."

She led them over a walking bridge that overlooked a running path below. They stopped at a clearing where stood a massive, thick-covering old ash tree. There was a gap in the center, blackened and smoothed, where the tree got struck by lightning, and a flame burned briefly.

"Esmy, what happened here." Loki eyed the blackened striations.

"This old beauty got struck by lightning in a bad storm earlier in the spring," said Esmy. "They say that the lightning caused a fire to start inside the tree where the lightning struck, but the driving rains put the blaze out within a few minutes, leaving that blackened hole. The parks department thought the strike killed the tree and planned to pull her down in July. But she sprouted new leaves and showed every sign of life."

Loki gave her a flat expression. "Esmy, are we here for what I think?"

She flashed him a rueful grin. Suddenly, Loki understood why so many people hated him over the many centuries he'd turned that same grin their way. There was no longer a shred of doubt in his mind: this was one of his descendants.

"Esmy, can we go home? I really need to chat with you and your brother together about tomorrow."

"Relax, this won't take long, besides you can be less dark and foreboding about whatever you need to tell us and tell me already."

Esmy started fishing around in the deep zippered pocket. She started pulling out items.

"Esmy, I hate having to repeat myself so it would be great if we could get this into the air once and brainstorm the problem." Esmy kept pulling things from the enchanted slacks pocket. Somehow she pulled out a tackle box, a small folding table, a pair of folding chairs and a hatchet. "How much do you have stuffed in your pants, Esmy?"

"Hmm? Oh, some tools and things." She set the chairs up and patted one for Loki to have a seat. Esmy continued to pull out a change of clothes, a helmet and finally, straining, a small anvil with a vice which she placed on the small folding table. She ducked behind a tree and quickly changed. She came back in a pair of jeans and a faded Foo Fighters t-shirt.

"Foo Fighters?"

"Yeah, you heard of them?"

Loki raised an eyebrow. "I'm surprised you'd heard of them. I was one of them nearly seventy-five years ago."

Esmy turned to him and cocked an eyebrow right back at him, the arches seemed to be having an Olympic level high raise competition.

"Dude, this is a band shirt. Foo Fighters is a rock band. What are you talking about? That would've been around World War 2?"

Loki's other eyebrow shot up to meet its partner. "Oh, well, we had a bit of a scuffle too around your World War 2. Air Force pilots would sometimes see unexplained aircraft that moved so fast they seemed like balls of fire and would chase them through some extremely high-speed maneuvers. In truth, foo fighters were people like me. We created some fighter aircraft too." He gave a shrug and a guilty expression. "Sometimes, when I'd need to blow off some steam, I'd go find some mortal pilots and give them a bit of a chase. They called guys like me

'Foo Fighters 'for lack of a better term for us. It was fun to see how far they'd come in the world of flight in about forty years."

Esmy furrowed her brow. "That's kind of a dick move Loki. Those guys were really risking their lives out above battlefields, and you wanted to freak them out a bit? Shit, why didn't you just pop them out and give them a deep anal probing while you were at it."

Loki waved his hands. "No, I was not the guy that did that. I didn't go around for the last forty years abducting loners and probing them. You want to hold someone accountable for that, go find the Roman gods. That was always part of their bag."

Esmy turned away from him, Loki took a seat in one of the lawn chairs and watched her. She slung the hatchet into her belt and started to climb the tree. "Still," she said continuing to climb, "that was kind of a dick move. But the band is pretty damn good, so you ought to check them out." She climbed higher and found a series of branches she could stand on.

"Esmy, I don't think that's a good idea." He was watching her walk a set of branches and grabbing a few to look at sizes.

"Catch me if I fall, but I won't." She kept looking through the branches and finally found one she seemed to like. The branch was about as wide as her arm. She steadied her legs and held onto a nearby larger branch with her left arm. Carefully, Esmy pulled the hatchet from her belt and started hacking through the base of the branch she liked. After a few minutes, it fell to the ground with a thump. She dropped down.

"See? Not dead yet, but thanks for the great-grandfatherly concern." Esmy took the hatchet and sheared off the smaller branches and leaves. Spots of the piece of ash that she held now were blackened from the lightning, taking on a mottled appearance. She cut off the end to leave the chopped branch about five feet long. She took the branch and sat down in the chair next to Loki.

"I can see what you're doing here, making the flying broomstick that you wanted. But you realize, given the lightning and all, this would end up making a great staff."

Esmy started working. She popped on a set of goggles and was using the battery powered Dremel tool she'd brought to start smoothing down the cut ends. "Would that be useful?"

"Sure. Maybe you didn't read this chapter yet, but magic can be insanely hard to do on the fly. That's why it's easier to conjure via runes, circles, patterns, etc. You don't have to fixate with your mind and keep as many things in focus at once. With a proper utensil, like a staff, it can help you to hold the raw power and focus. Like your little power tool, you could do what you are doing by hand, but that tool helps to speed up the process without much difficulty."

"Can't it be both?" Esmy changed bits out to use an engraving bit in the tool.

"I don't see why not." He rolled his eyes to mull over the question. "What exactly are you carving into that stick anyway?"

She stopped working for a moment and handed him a small notebook she'd set on the table. While he read over the notes, she put the stick into the vice on her little table so she wouldn't be carving directly on her lap.

"This is some curious work Esmy. Will this actually work?"

"It kind of did the first time around, went haywire with control at the end."

Loki picked up her pen and scrawled a few extra symbols on the page and handed it back to her. "The idea seems sound, you took a bunch of simpler spells and encapsulated them into one grouping and have another set to control them. I think if you add those," he pointed to his additions, "you'll gain a couple of benefits."

Esmy reviewed the changes on the page. "You've added a focal binding spell; I'm guessing that's to make this a proper staff while I'm not riding." She continued to study the page, everything else was circled, and a small symbol closed the top of the circle. "That encapsulates the whole thing to bind it together. So, if I add some of my blood..."

"The staff or broomstick will bind to you, and you will be the only one able to use it."

She nodded and took the notebook. Esmy crouched over the anvil and started engraving the symbols onto the staff.

"Hey," she said not looking up from the work. "Jake and I are twins, would our blood be close enough to trick it? Could this get confused by how similar we are?"

Loki steepled his fingers. "That's an interesting theory. There is some historical record of magical binding shared with identical twins, not sure about fraternal ones though."

Esmy noticed another symbol Loki scrawled and looked up before she engraved. "What's this one here?"

"Oh, that's definitely necessary," said Loki. "I noticed you added a quick cast for a spell to increase your speed based on your own desperation."

"Yeah, a despair booster. It's kind of like a nitro boost on race cars, but if I'm getting chased and need to get out in a hurry, I hit that, and it gives more power drawn on my own desperation to get out quick."

Loki wagged a long finger at her. "But that won't work. You've engaged it to your own despair, but if you trust it will work reliably, you may not be desperate enough to actually achieve the power needed."

"So, I won't actually be desperate to get away because I'll know that this will propel me ahead?"

"Exactly. That will create a paradox trap. It will enclose the paradox you've created in not knowing whether you are truly desperate or confident in your despair."

She went back to carving. "Interesting, kind of like a catch to get the exception."

"I'm not really sure what that means," said Loki.

"Well..." Esmy sighed and maintained her concentration on the engraving. "When I'm writing a routine in a program, but I think there could be an issue, I surround that block of code with a try and add a catch for errors at the end. Like if my code is supposed to respond to a piece of user data, but the user put in something invalid or nothing at all. The catch will get the exception as the program is running and let me handle the error how I want."

"Very similar," replied Loki pondering the analogy. "However, this catch will keep one of two things from happening, either your speed spell wouldn't have happened at all, or the paradox would have caused you to reach a near infinite speed. You'd probably melt leaving the atmosphere in a few seconds."

Esmy stopped engraving and stared at him. "You're shitting me right?"

"I wish I were kiddo."

She looked back down at the engraving. "Well, this looks basically done. A couple of questions before I test this out. Do I need a power source, like that crystal?"

Loki shook his head. "That was really a nifty idea, but you have enough oomph put into this for it to work on your sheer willpower. Also, you cut the branch yourself from a lightning-struck tree. It's been imbued with some extra kick already."

"Sounds good, what about the staff part of all this. You said I could use part of this to focus magic. Is that something I can only do when it's the only thing going on or can I cast something while flying on this thing?"

"That"—Loki raised a finger—"is a fascinating question. I'm not sure. I'd say give her a go while slow and low to the ground, just in case. Also, I'd start with something simple. Water or conjuration, but no fire or lightning magic while in-flight. That seems like begging to cause problems."

Esmy loosened the vice and removed the long stick. The engravings were very well defined and deeply lain into the wood. She pulled out a pocket knife and made a clean slit along her thumb. Esmy squeezed a few drops of blood into the top engraving and concentrated on the staff. The engravings glowed a deep orange that shifted to a shade of dark emerald green.

She looked up at Loki, he was smiling proudly from his chair. "OK, when I try a spell while using this thing, do I need to know the exact runes or words in my mind?"

Loki tapped his chin. "Here's the funny thing about magic. If you don't have a focus, like your staff, then you need to be pretty exacting with the runes and symbols. Your foci help to create a direct link with your willpower and your mind to the physical world. Sometimes, wizards and witches find it helpful to yell something to propel a spell, much like a bodybuilder is helped by grunting when deadlifting six or seven hundred pounds."

"Well, I guess I'll give it all a shot." Esmy picked up her helmet and mounted the broomstick. "I guess it's a staff for now," she said. "Can't really call it a broom if there are no bristles."

Loki nodded agreement and sat back in the chair.

Esmy closed her eyes and concentrated. The staff began to lift her lightly in the air. She opened her eyes and saw she was about three feet off the ground. Slowly, she started to take a test circuit around a few trees humming something. Esmy began flying higher and faster, doing laps around the trees. She looked down and saw Loki waving her back.

"Were you humming a certain song while you were flying?" Loki asked as she landed roughly.

"Yeah, your little story reminded me of an old song. Why?"

Loki hummed the melody. "Was that it?"

"Yeah, that's it exactly. I thought you never heard Foo Fighters before?"

"I hadn't," Loki said. "I only heard it just now, during your little cruise around the park. Your staff was projecting the song, in stereo."

"I blasted rock music while flying?"

"You didn't mean to broadcast it?"

"No, I was just flying, and that song got stuck in my head while weaving around. I didn't even notice it was playing for everyone."

Loki reached a hand out to touch the staff; he could feel

a charge inside of it. The magic coursing through the staff felt like an amp with a guitar plugged in. There was feedback and the anticipation of what would come next from deep within. "Esmy, I think you made quite a little tool for yourself. Please be careful though, you may cause something worse than some loud music."

She looked at the staff in her hands and nodded gravely.

"Just out of curiosity," Loki said. "Point the staff over at that tree and think of a fine spray of water." He was pointing at an elm tree about ten feet away. It was a younger tree for the park, but still over a foot thick in the trunk.

Esmy lowered the staff in her hands, holding it like a hose and focused her thoughts on a stream of water. The water concentrated into an inch-thick stream with such force and volume that it bore a hole clear through the trunk.
She stopped the stream, and they walked over to inspect the tree. Esmy wiggled a finger through the newly drilled hole. "Now that's pretty frickin 'cool."

Loki furrowed his brow and stared at her. "I know," she said. "Spiderman speech, great power, great responsibility, yadda yadda yadda."

"Well, basically. Two things though. First, if you are broadcasting music simply flying around, you need to really focus, or you'll keep doing that. Kind of ruins any element of surprise if people can hear you coming a mile away."

Esmy nodded. "And the other thing?"

"Was there anything special about your father? Your mother? Grandfather? Anyone in between my getting your great-grandmother pregnant and your birth?" he asked.

Esmy started counting on her fingers. "Well, let's see, dad was a high priest of the pit, and I think grandma married a Polynesian demigod." She broke her straight face and started laughing. "Not that I know of. Hell, you're the first I've known of any of this, why?"

"The amount of raw talent Jake and yourself have shown just in the last week seems unnatural out of people so normal.

There's got to be something we're both missing." Loki shook his head and collected himself. "Are we done? I think we should head back and see if Jake's home yet."

Esmy started packing away the chairs and the table, throwing the anvil back into the pocket of the slacks. "Yeah, he should be home by now."

"You know, the desperation booster was a pretty good idea. Raw emotion is one of the greatest powers you can draw on."

Esmy stood up and gave him an incredulous stare. "So, you can what? Build a drive train on misery and despair?"

Loki flashed a sly grin. "Isn't that how empires are built?"

"Har-har."

"Seriously though, if you wanted to make some upgrades to that crappy old Stanza of yours, have something you can travel in that works and blends in, there's plenty of sources of despair."

She finished packing up her gear and picked up the staff. "Like what? Orphan hearts?"

"You joke, but pound for pound, an orphan heart has more output than a nuclear reactor."

Esmy couldn't believe she would ever have to make this statement aloud. "Loki, I'm not fueling my car off of dead orphan hearts."

They both laughed at the absurdity of it, Esmy more so than Loki. They left the park to head back home, discussing the many sources of despair they could use to fuel a car.

CHAPTER 21

THE INAPPROPRIATE BONERS

It was past closing time at Titan Bakeries. A large garage door rolled up in the rear of the building. A van backed up through the garage door. Bernice closed the door after the van finished backing in.

Carl and Luke began unloading the van. DJ Dirty Stache opened a side door and climbed out holding a laptop case. Bernice turned back to them. She was wearing a white uniform, no makeup and removed all of her piercings. Her previously spiked purple mohawk now lay as a flat mass of purple tangles under a hairnet.

Carl set an amp down next to her and leaned on it laughing.

"What's so funny?"

Carl tried to cut his laughter. "I can't get over it, just how cute you are as a little baker. Did you ever ask your uncle to change the name to Keebler?"

Bernice spun on a heel and punched him in the crotch. Carl doubled over.

Luke set down a pair of guitar cases and patted Carl on the back. "Dude, I told you that shit wasn't funny."

Carl tried to choke out, "fuck off," but was having problems sucking in any air.

"Hey Bernice, you got any more of the Bavarian cream donuts? Those are the bomb."

Bernice shook her head and peeled off the hair net. "Nah, Uncle Jack takes whatever doesn't sell over by First Methodist for the AA meetings."

"Damn, that's too bad." Luke grabbed some more equipment. "I love those things."

Bernice started assembling a drum kit while Luke and Carl finished unloading. DJ Dirty Stache set up a laptop and a small soundboard, and then slipped on a set of studio headphones.

They were about all set up and started a sound check on the guitars and mics. A bright light flashed behind them and suddenly a tall olive-skinned man with a vaguely canine-like head. Dark red eyes stared down the long-curved snout at each of them.

"Whoa, who are you?"

The dog-like creature turned and looked at Carl. He felt his head with his hand absently. "Oh, shit, that is right, you guys never saw me like this before. It is me, Seth."

Dirty Stache took off his sunglasses. "This is vat you normally look like?"

"Yes, I shift back to my normal self when I need to resort to any magical transportation."

Bernice walked around him staring at the snout. "So, teleporting wipes away any enchantments or something?"

"No," replied Seth. "It just gives me a bitch of a headache to try to do both at the same time." He turned around to take in his surroundings. "Why are you all in a garage with a donut truck?" He turned to stare directly at Bernice.

Bernice jumped, scared she'd been caught staring. "It's my Uncle Jack's bakery. He lets us use the garage for practice. The truck is for food fests and doing deliveries to a few local gas stations."

The canine snout gave an eerie smile. "Mild-mannered baker by day and heavy metal drummer by night, eh?"

Bernice nodded uncomfortably.

"Hey friend," said DJ Dirty Stache. "You have any more of those scorpions? I kind of have, a, you know, jonesin 'for some more of it."

Seth shook his head. "Not tonight, I need you sharp tomorrow. You will be fulfilling your end of our arrangement in the afternoon."

"So what are we doing?" asked Carl while he picked up his bass.

"I expect you to be coming to the south side of the college campus at five o'clock to help watch my sides as I try to create a distraction while a compatriot of mine steals something. I expect little resistance, but you must know that we will be against an older skilled warrior and a vampire."

Luke scoffed. "Vampire? Like a Dracula? Like blah-bleh-blah and drinking blood and shit?"

"They are not as simple as that," replied Seth turning to Luke. "Vampires can be tough to kill. The stake nonsense is foolishness, and the myths about sunlight killing them are also a complete falsehood."

"OK, ve have a vampire," said DJ Dirty Stache. "Vat about this varrior. How old?"

"Not known, he could be fifty," said Seth. "He could be five hundred."

"That doesn't sound so bad, we do this, and we get a record deal?" asked Carl.

"Basically, yes. However, do not underestimate these foes. They are skilled, and you are not. If you live, I will make the proper introductions to fulfill your wish."

As he finished speaking, the same light flared up next to the donut truck again. Seth stepped back through the portal and was gone. The light winked back out of existence.

The band all looked around at each other.

"Does anybody else find that all a bit too fucking spooky?"

asked Bernice.

"Man, if it gets us a record deal, I'd crack fifty skulls," said Luke. "Draculas, werewolves, warriors, I don't care if it's a damned mummy. I'll Louisville Slugger some ass to get us somewhere."

DJ Dirty Stache nodded. "dwarf is right, is damn spooky. Fuck it though, he gets us record deal." He put on his sunglasses again. "I'm thirsty, going to get some slushy, you all want slushy? You practice, I go get slushies, and we record when I get back, ya?"

"Yeah, sounds good man," replied Carl.

"I don't have car, can I borrow donut truck, Bernice?" he asked.

"Don't mess it up, or Uncle Jack will send you back to wherever the hell it is you're from in a pine box," Bernice said tossing him the keys.

"Latvia," Dirty Stache replied. "I keep telling you assholes, I come from Latvia, name is Yevgeny. Do you remember, no I am either just this 'Red George 'or a 'DJ Dirty Stache'."

"Shave, and we'll just go back to Red George permanently," said Carl.

DJ Dirty Stache climbed into the donut truck. "Fuck it, I wear your nickname like a badge." He said something loud in a language they didn't understand and flipped them off before driving away.

CHAPTER 22

ESMY

The doorbell rang violently at Jake and Esmy's house. Esmy opened the door to a pair of legs behind a stack of steaming Styrofoam coolers.

From behind the coolers, Jake's voice came out strained. "About damn time, can you take one of these, they're heavy."

Esmy took the top cooler off the stack and strained with the weight of it. "Oof, what the hell is in these?"

She carried it into the living room with Jake following after he kicked the door shut.

Jake set down the rest of the coolers and looked at the living room. Half of the furniture was pushed out of the way. Loki sat on the back on a pushed back sofa chewing on a sharpie and staring at the wall. They had taken down all of the pictures, and the long wall was now covered with diagrams and notes.

"What the hell is this? You guys know those are permanent markers right? I just painted this damn wall last month! One of you is fixing this."

Loki took the marker out of his mouth and looked at the label thoughtfully.

Esmy walked in front of the wall. "Chill Jake, we'll fix it

later. We needed some space to spitball a few ideas."

"You couldn't use some paper or, hell, go find a dry erase board?"

"Well," Loki said. "We were discussing something, and the wall was already here."

"What was so important that you couldn't go for a supply run first? This all looks like a bunch of connected squiggles."

"It's a replacement concept for the Stanza, we were talking about how inefficient and horrible the engine is. The biggest problem with any car is there are too many moving parts and consumables. You've got pumps to deal with steering and fluids, you've got fluids to keep the engine cooled, the engine guzzles gas and oil, and the tires are always wearing down. We wanted to know could we replace most of those core systems and still have a reliable car."

"Wait, you're going to rip the Stanza apart?" Jake stared at them wide-eyed. "Esmeralda, it's a shitty car I agree, but we need it together, not in pieces in the garage."

"Initially," Loki piped in, "we were going to strip down the shitty Stanza. But we didn't know how we'd pick up parts without a car, and there's already so much to rip out of there, we decided it would be better to go pick up a body from a junkyard that's already been pulled apart."

"That's right. We hit up Billy out back. He's got a buddy in his group, Tater, that runs a junkyard out south of town. Tater's got a 68 Chevelle SS that's been stripped already, but the body is still good, we can pick it up this weekend!"

"A Chevelle? Why the hell would you use an old Chevelle?"

"Sturdiness," replied Loki. "They had some Mustang bodies, but they wouldn't have the weight and metal strength to deal with the torque we'd need to handle. The body would probably rattle apart. The Chevelle, Billy has assured me, can handle any engine we pop into it."

Jake looked at the wall closer now and noticed now that it looked a lot like a circuit and systems diagram. It mapped a set of power systems and converters together.

"So you take the engine and other subsystems out of the car and replace it with something that connects to the drive train and transmission to use the wheels to still run?"

Esmy and Loki smiled. "Kind of, we don't really use the wheels though, but they will spin."

Jake turned his head to a side and stared at Esmy like a human owl.

"The wheels have to spin to maintain the appearance of a normal car," said Esmy. "Now the whole thing actually is a kind of hovercraft. When the power systems engage, one spell is a levitation spell that pushes the car a minimal amount into the air. If you didn't bend down, you wouldn't even know it's off the ground, it averages to less than a millimeter."

"How does braking work?"

"That's another great part," chimed in Loki. "We have multiple propulsion systems all over the car to respond to the braking depending on the wheel position."

"Trust me, Jake, we have literally thought of everything with this thing," Esmy said.

"What is this note here?" Jake was pointing at the primary energy prism diagram and some scribbles off to the side.

"Ah, that's our power source brainstorming," said Esmy.

"I thought your goal was to avoid consumables and moving parts. What powers it?"

Loki and Esmy looked at each other, back at Jake and stumbled for words. "Um, well, despair," said Esmy.

"Despair? You intend to run a whole car off of despair Esmeralda Hansen? Where do you intend to find so much despair? Take up a collection before finals every semester?"

Esmy scoffed. "No. We won't be sourcing our fuel from innocent college students, thank you very much. We're going to use drug addicts."

Jake pointed to a paper. "Is that why there's a print out of Indianapolis based rehab clinics pasted to this part of the wall?"

"Well, we don't intend to keep our own drug addicts on-hand," replied Loki. "The goal is to lower costs." He pointed to the ground. "Have you seen the average cost of a drug habit? Meth may be the most affordable for it, but to fuel multiple heroin addictions or even a coke addict is incomprehensible to maintain."

Jake looked at them incredulously. "So you're going to what? Start trolling the rehab clinics and abduct them to power your Chevelle?"

"Addicts seem to be at their worst right when they check into rehab, they're desperate to get clean but also desperate for another fix," explained Esmy. "We go in invisible at night, cast a few small spells and funnel all of that desperation and pain away into a set of energy prisms. It's a win-win, we get a usable fuel, they get ease to their pain. It even dulls the withdrawal."

"You two are insane."

"Look, it's better than Loki's original idea," said Esmy crossing her arms.

"And how much worse was that?"

Loki raised a finger to point at them. "Look, you don't find much more despair than in the heart of an orphan. Not my fault that's one of the greatest places to find it, it just is. One orphan would have powered this thing like a miniature nuke. We're talking sustainable energy for decades from one harvest."

Esmy waved a hand at Loki. "See, the voice of reason here. We get a better car, addicts get an easier time with rehab, and we don't have to kill any orphans!"

Loki started waving his arms around. "Some of the greatest minds in history were orphans, driven by their own horrible situations. Edgar Allen Poe and John Lennon to name a pair, if you bottled their emotions and use them as a battery, imagine the power!"

"Yes," replied Esmy, exasperated. "And some of the best wizards in fiction were orphans too, but we are not harvesting orphan hearts!"

Loki crossed his arms and scoffed. "Oh please, it's not like every orphan is destined for Hogwarts. Nobody will miss one measly little orphan."

The room got quiet for a moment while they all thought through that for a moment. A cooler quaked. Loki looked suspiciously at Jake. "Jake, what do you have in the coolers?"

"Ducks."

Esmy drooped her shoulders. "Ducks?"

"Yes, I picked up a bunch of ducks from a rancher that raises them in the next county," said Jake. "I've got a few more coolers in the car. About thirty-two ducks total."

Another cooler quacked, but the quack was abnormal. It was strained, and a shudder shot through even Loki.

Loki peered into one cooler, lifting the lid an inch before shutting it again quickly. "Jake, were these ducks dead recently?"

Jake avoided their glare and itched his head.

Esmy laughed heartily. "Jake Hansen. You come in here, acting all high and mighty. You chastise us for wanting to harvest some minor human emotions. Meanwhile, you've been spending your night raising voodoo duck zombies? Hypocrite much?"

"Oh, please. It's just a little light necromancy. It took a bit of time, but I found how to sync them all together."

Loki stepped back slowly from coolers. "You have thirty-two zombie ducks?"

"Not yet, only about five." Jake opened a cooler and pulled out a dead duck.

"Jake that one's still dead, it's not quacking or anything," said Esmy.

"Yeah, I take the dead duck." Jake pulled out a box of Ziploc baggies, a pad of paper, a pen and a pocket knife from the cooler. "See, I found a few spells to connect together from the manual." Jake wrote a series of circles and symbols, tore the page off and cut open the belly of the duck.

"These will raise it from the dead, bind it to the others in a squadron for my control and this will bind them to my will," Jake said, piercing the tip of his thumb and smudging some blood on the paper. He sealed the paper into a Ziplock bag and stuffed it into the duck's belly incision.

The duck began to flutter and quack. He picked up a medical stapler from the cooler and stapled the stomach slit shut. The duck flapped up and perched on Jake's shoulder. Its head flopped back and forth sloppily on a broken neck.

"That's fucking creepy Jake." Esmy cringed.

Loki walked over and tapped the duck on the eyeball. It gave a glassy stare and choked out another strained quack.

"Well," said Loki poking the duck's eye again. "I can't say this is a first in necromancy, but it's the first time I've encountered resurrected ducks. Have you tried expanding their portfolio a bit?"

Jake started petting the duck on his shoulder. "Expand the portfolio? Like what?"

"Oh," Esmy said excitedly, she stole the marker from Loki and started scrawling a few things on the wall. "There, add that to one squad of sixteen and this to the other."

"Oh, nice touch Esmy, fire-breathing and ice breathing ducks. Seems like a good combination. Jake, I think this is a great idea, you should do this, and we'll need it."

Jake stopped stroking the duck. "Why would I need weaponized ducks?"

Esmy looked dumbfounded. "What the fuck do you mean, 'why would I need weaponized ducks? 'That's the most ri-fucking-diculous question you could ask. Why the hell wouldn't you weaponize the zombie ducks? Come on Jake, get with the program."

"Actually," interrupted Loki, "we do have a good reason for weaponizing ducks."

Loki recounted his meeting with Magni and his run-in with Seth and Julia.

"Dr. Longfellow, the president of our college," said Jake. "Is actually your nephew and a god of strength?"

"And we're going to be expected to help defend magical artifacts from an Egyptian god of chaos and an unknown number of assailants tomorrow?"

Loki sucked in a breath and nodded. "That's the sum of it.

So hey, weaponized ducks seem like a great idea now right?"

Esmy asked, "Are all Gods obsessed with bigfoot dicks?"

Loki sighed. "I don't know, so far it's two for two this week, but it seems like a low sample size."

CHAPTER 23

ESMY

Not much later, Esmy and Loki heard a knock at the door. They looked at each other in confusion. They stepped away from the wall they'd been sketching battle ideas. Esmy peeked through the window to the backyard; Jake was still working on weaponizing his ducks.

The knock came again, louder this time. It was clearly from the front door now. Loki and Esmy went to the front door together. The door pounded as Esmy turned the handle; Kyle lost his footing mid pound and fell into the entryway. He was still wearing the hoodie and colander.

Loki and Esmy stared at him lying in a lump on the floor. The back door opened and shut, Jake came through in time to find Loki and Esmy helping Kyle up.

"Kyle?" Jake looked puzzled. What's going on here? Why do you have that ridiculous outfit on?"

Kyle tried to tell him about being given the power over wasps by the colander from Loki and Esmy. When he tried to speak though, Kyle found himself compelled to say the most natural lie. "I was larping."

Kyle was surprised with the ease of the lie that he looked

down at himself again.

Jake raised an eyebrow. "Larping?"

"Yeah, it's live-action role-playing. I was supposed to be a warrior mage. This is my plate helm," Kyle said, pointing to the strapped-on colander.

Loki and Esmy fell over laughing. Kyle and Jake stared at them with confusion.

"It's fine, it's nothing," Esmy tried to say through the laughing.

"Care to let me in on the joke?" asked Jake.

"Perhaps you can tell him, Kyle? Oh, wait, no you can't," Esmy choked out before doubling over laughing with Loki again.

After a moment they finally got themselves together.

"Well, first, Esmeralda and I ran into Kyle earlier on campus and did him a favor while I was teaching her a lesson."

Esmy punched Loki in the arm hard. "Part of payment on the favor was that Kyle lies if anyone asked about where he got it."

"It's a compulsion pact," explained Loki. "When he shook my hand, it sealed the pact, and he is compelled to all fiber of his being to honor the pact, even to the pain of death."

"Oh great, now you tell me it includes pain of death. You didn't start off with that clause earlier, eh?"

"Wait," interrupted Jake, "what power? You gave him something?"

Loki and Esmy tried to be sheepish and innocent. "Well," she said. "You remember my first broom experiment?"

"First? You've tried multiple times now?" asked Jake.

"Yeah, I actually have a working model, meant to show you, just made it earlier this evening while you were raising your undead duck army," replied Esmy.

"Wait, you have an undead duck army, Mr. Hansen?"

"Kyle, you can just call me Jake when we aren't on campus," said Jake.

"Anyway," Esmy cut in. "Loki showed me a little lesson on actually creating a magical artifact using existing objects and imbuing them with spells." She pointed at the colander on Kyle's head. "And that's why Kyle is sporting a spaghetti strainer on his noggin."

Jake looked at it fascinated now. "OK, I'll bite. What does it do?"

Loki spoke up, "It links him telepathically to a hive of wasps he captured." Loki looked around. "Kyle since you are still wearing the helmet, does that mean you have the wasps with you?"

"Yeah, they're out on the van. That's actually why I'm here; I've got something that might interest you out in the van. Come take a gander."

"How did you actually find us though?" asked Esmy.

"Oh, that's easy." Kyle smiled. "you guys are actually listed in the white pages."

Jake and Esmy looked dumbfounded at each other. "We don't have a home phone or anything though, there's no reason they'd list us," said Jake.

Kyle shrugged. "Dunno about that, but you were in the book, plain as day. Anyhoo, come on out eh."

They followed Kyle outside to where he'd backed his van up the driveway. The wizard was blocked behind the side of the house, but they were all greeted with the image of the unicorn climaxing as they exited the house.

Jake stopped in his tracks. "That's YOUR van Kyle?"

"Oh yeah, real beaut eh?"

As they got closer, they could hear a faint buzzing. Kyle swarmed the wasps to cover the roof of the van.

Jake just stared at the roof for a moment while Esmy and Loki were following to the rear of the van.

"Yeah, it's pretty cool," said Kyle seeing Jake's amazement. "Check this out."

Almost instantly the whole swarm lifted off from the van and became a cloud. They flew straight up and started performing figure-eights in the front yard.

"Well, that is nifty. Creepy as hell, but nifty."

Loki patted him on the back. "You were stung as a child, weren't you?"

"Nope," cut in Esmy. "And that's most of his problem, scared of anything stingy and bitey."

"Am not," sniffed Jake, but he still didn't take his eyes off of the swarm.

Kyle opened the back doors of the van. "Now don't freak out guys."

They looked in to see an unconscious man with a blonde mullet with a scraggly wisp of a mustache wearing a tracksuit holding a deflated blow-up doll, a Barney the Dinosaur piñata and a whole slushy machine, still full of slushy fluids.

"Kyle, this is a bit fucked up here," said Esmy as they all stared slack-jawed at the contents of the van.

"I don't know Esmy," added Loki. "If we were celebrating Mardi Gras…"

"Kyle," said Jake, staring at the contents. "We have some questions, and I'm not sure this can't affect your on-campus employment."

"OK, well, I know how this looks."

"I don't think you fully appreciate how this looks," said Esmy. "This looks like about three felonies depending on what you've done to that guy and if that's his blow-up doll or yours."

"Why don't you just tell us how these things came to end up in the back of your van, Kyle," Loki said, trying to turn the tone of the conversation.

Kyle began, "Well, I was out with the wasps after you showed me how to use the powers, and first I decided to destroy the Girl Scout cookie stand over by the Double V and the Elf's Quiver."

"I'm sorry," interrupted Esmy, jabbing a finger at him. "You killed some girl scouts with the wasps?"

"No, no, no," shot back Kyle. "I didn't kill anyone. I destroyed their tent, three of the tires on their Volvo and the cookies. The mothers may have gotten a few stings, but the kids weren't even there."

"What's the Double V and the Elf's Quiver?" asked Loki.

"The Elf's Quiver is a gaming shop," answered Jake. "And the Double V is a strip club next door to it."

"Gentlemen's club," Kyle said pointedly.

"Potato Potahto," said Esmy.

"Well," continued Kyle, "after my Girl Scout assault."

Esmy interrupted him again, "Wait, OK, you didn't hurt the Girl Scouts, but why did you even go after them? Sell you some bad thin mints?"

Kyle tried to explain at length his long hatred of the organization. How it made innocent girls and families into unknowing merchants of a cartel dealing in prolonged death by obesity and diabetes one box of high fructose corn syrup filled hockey pucks at a time. After some time and realizing that even a mythic god with unknown magical power was staring at him like he ought to trade a tin foil hat for a straitjacket, he stopped and looked down. "OK, I was a fatty as a kid, and I hold a hell of a grudge."

Collectively they all nodded and sighed.

"After the girl scouts, I wanted to do something nice for the wasps, so I wanted to get a few giant slushies for the hive."

"So, you stole a slushy machine?"

"Not at first. I went into the gas station to just buy a few, but I forgot I was still wearing the helmet. Well, this guy was there," he pointed to the prone disc jockey in the van, "the clerk and this guy started making fun of me for the spaghetti strainer. I kind of lost it and before I could stop myself, the hive was swarming the store, and the clerk was driven out. I got control of the hive again, but this guy just starts babbling on in a Russian accent that I must be some higher follower of Seth, that he's sorry about laughing at me and can he get high on the wasp venom. So I say sure thing, but he has to help me get the slushy machine in my van first. I mean, hell, nobody was around, and the mini-mart probably was insured. After he helped me load the machine, I just uhh, knocked him oot and rolled him into the van."

Loki rubbed his chin and pointed into the van. "What about the blow-up doll and the dinosaur piñata?"

Kyle blushed. "Well, I run a D&D campaign at the Quiver. This was for next week, we were going to do a LARP, and I needed some props, eh."

"So why bring it all here?" asked Esmy.

"I wasn't sure where else to go. I kind of freaked after it was all over, and this guy was babbling about some dude named Seth. I figured you guys might have some idea what the hell it was all about."

"Well, this boy with a van depicting a wizard making epic, sweet love to a unicorn is not wrong," said Loki. "Let's get him somewhere we can talk."

"Dude, it's art. He's not making love to the unicorn, he's celebrating. You said you loved it just today!"

"Oh yes, I do love it. It doesn't change the fact it is a magnificent piece of art of a wizard cornholing a majestic beast."

They took the prone man into the house. Esmy started tying him to a dining chair in the breakfast nook. Kyle convinced them to unload the slushy machine and hook it up inside. When Jake caved to allow it, he stipulated they carry the machine in through the backyard. While trying to wrestle the slushy machine into the back door, they heard a voice from over the fence.

"Damn boys," shouted Billy. "What kind of party is it tonight?"

"Prisoner interrogation," said Loki half-jokingly. "Care to join?"

"Depends on the prisoner," chuckled Billy. "Maybe later though, I promised Ma I'd take her to some movie I'll probably hate."

"Ah, say hi to your mom for us," said Loki trying to act like he was straining under the weight of the machine.

They got the slushy machine inside and hooked up. The man in the tracksuit was starting to come around.

"Ohhh, my fahcking head," said the man. "Vere am I?"

He saw Kyle. "You. You gave me some bad shit man."

"What's your name?" asked Loki first.

"I am Yevgeny. Though people in this hell hole call me by this name of DJ Dirty Stache. Vere am I and who are you people?"

"That's not any of your concern right now," Esmy replied trying to sound intimidating.

"Dah, it is though. I am one tied to chair by vasp man and crazy people. Hey, is that slushy machine?"

They turned to see the slushy fluid starting to reform in the machine. "Yes," Jake said, trying to sound inviting. "Blue raspberry, tell us what we need to know, and you can have some."

"Please," scoffed Yevgeny. "I am not rat to be for slushy whore."

Esmy leaned close to Jake. "You did make it sound like a seductive slushy."

"Never mind the slushy," cut Loki. "You'd like to actually walk away from this alive?" He produced a large kitchen knife.

"You kill me? Here in some kitchen? For what?"

"Wait," said Jake. "No one said we'd kill him."

Kyle spoke up, "Dude, I'm not sure about this. I mean he seems a little whacked out, but do we have to kill him?"

"Guys," interrupted Loki. "What do you imagine we do with prisoners of a potential enemy? Just let them go?" He pointed the knife at Yevgeny. "DJ Dirty Stache here could get back to his gang and tell them who we are, what we can do and what to expect."

"Yevgeny, just call me Yevgeny. I talk to no one. This town has been too fucked up. I go back to Chicago. Normal there."

Loki narrowed his eyes at him. "I don't know Yevgeny. Perhaps I need to cut your tongue out to make sure you don't talk ever again."

Kyle raised his hand.

"Yes Kyle," Loki said, shutting his eyes in frustration. "You don't need to raise your hand, what is it now?"

"Well, he uh, he could just write it out or send an email."

Kyle shuffled his feet and looked down. "Just sayin', it might be gruesome and painful, but not terribly effective."

Esmy hit Kyle in the shoulder hard, rocking the colander off center from his head. "Dude," she whispered loudly. "We're trying to effectively interrogate a prisoner."

"I can hear you," said Yevgeny. "I could have some slushy? You have some vodka, dah."

"Sure, sure, let me get something for you," said Loki. He walked away and poured a slushy into a coffee mug shaped like an owl's head. "Esmy do you have some vodka? In the living room?" Loki winked and nodded his head.

"Uh, sure," she said, catching his drift. "Kyle you stay here to watch the uh, prisoner." She and Loki headed into the living room, with Jake following.

"We don't have any vodka, what are we doing in here?" asked Jake.

"We're not here for Vodka," replied Loki, handing the mug to Jake. "We need to get him talking. Alcohol could help, but this might be more useful than alcohol." Loki reached into the couch cushions and fished around. He pulled out a flask and poured some green liquid into the mug.

Esmy pointed at the flask. "That's not vodka, absinthe?"

"Not specifically," Loki said. "It's the base for what I made at Billy's party the other night. It could have a positive effect on our new friend in there."

"Could?" asked Jake skeptically.

"Or it could kill him." Loki saw them looking pensive. "What? I've never mixed this with blue raspberry slushy before. I doubt it'll harm him permanently."

They returned to the kitchen, where Kyle appeared to be wrapping up a story. Yevgeny looked horrified.

"Yeah, real tragic, right in front of the kids and everything," said Kyle. "The Toronto Forensics Lab techs made them all sit still for like hours to scrape the evidence out of their hair. Really ruined Chuck E. Cheese for all of us."

"Great, you are back, please just get rid of depressing

Canuck," begged Yevgeny.

"Kyle why don't you wait in the other room." Loki put a straw in the mug and brought it closer to Yevgeny. He drank a big slurp.

"I tell you anything you vant, just don't leave me alone with that guy again. I just vant to leave all this and go back to Chicago."

Loki looked at the mug, then at Esmy and shrugged. "OK, you have met a god named Seth?"

"He is god? I don't believe, Latvia was soviet when I was boy, we are all atheist."

"Semantics," said Loki. "Ancient Egyptians worshiped him as one. But you met a guy that calls himself Seth, kind of creepy, seems powerful, can be pretty scary, maybe has a fox head? Bit of an asshole?"

"Dah, I know this man, he told us ve get record deal if ve beat up old man and vampire tomorrow at five in afternoon. As if vampire really exist, but hey, who am I to turn down opportunity. Is like they say in Soviet Russia, do not study horse that is given free in mouth for checking the teeth."

Esmy, Jake, and Loki looked at each other dumbfounded. "Oh," said Jake.Don't look a gift horse in the mouth." Esmy and Loki nodded.

"How many?" asked Jake.

"Without me, just two morons and a dwarf. Don't let her fool you though, dwarf. She is scary one."

"Did he have a bag with him?" asked Loki.

"Bag? I saw no bag. Vat kind of vodka you put in slushy? I am feeling strange."

Loki stepped back. "Strange how? Nauseous? Stabbing pain? Have I turned into a purple cockroach?"

"Purple cock," Yevgeny started to say and suddenly disappeared. His clothes were slumped against the ropes on the chair. Esmy looked into the mug. Jake and Loki stepped forward cautiously to inspect the chair. Inside of the clothes, they found nothing but some strands of burnt blond hair.

Esmy poured the mug contents out in the kitchen sink. "Did we uh, did we blow him up?"

"I don't think so, there would have been more bits around us. That may have teleported him somewhere. I can't be sure if it was on this planet though. But the lack of guts on the walls suggests he wasn't blown up."

"What was that about a bag?" Jake asked Loki.

"Oh, Seth has been known in the past to not do a lot of the fighting on his own. He usually makes other people fight his battles for him and collects trophies afterward," explained Loki. "He had this bag he made from human flesh, and the trophies he usually collected were the fallen warriors 'penises."

Kyle came back in from the other room. "I just overheard that, do you mean this guy literally has a bag of dicks?"

Loki gave a tightly lipped nod yes.

Esmy quirked an eyebrow. "What about females though? I mean, what did he collect from them? Tits?"

Loki looked uncomfortable. "I'm not sure how to explain this. He didn't have too many female opponents, but, he'd do this weird thing where he'd cut out their genitalia and do this thing." Loki paused to pull together a mental image. "It was kind of like making a balloon animal, it's tough to explain."

Esmy held up a hand. "It's OK, that was visual enough for me, and I just threw up a little in my mouth."

"OK," said Jake. "We know Seth is planning to make his move around five tomorrow, he's got at least three thugs, one of them a dwarf."

"And one crazy ostracized math professor," Esmy reminded him.

"And one crazy ostracized math professor," echoed Jake. "What else should we expect from him?"

"He expects my help. I've got a plan, but it will have to rely on them not knowing I'm helping you. Come to the living room."

They all proceeded to the living room where Loki drew out a map with a marker on a clear space of the wall. He explained what he was planning and how he expected everyone to act.

When he was finished, Esmy laughed saying, "That is pretty fucked up. You think you can pull that off?"

"I can, but I know Magni well enough that he will try to control the situation. I need him and the vampire Jesus busy enough for me to do it." Loki pointed at Kyle. "You definitely need to be there too, they'll need help to maintain the confusion, and I can't promise who will target you."

"And you are certain he'll do this?" asked Jake.

"If Seth is anything to me, it's been predictable over the years," said Loki. "My guess is he's made some crazy promises to Dr. Neidermeier too, and she trusts him completely. Hell, he's probably eaten a pet or two of hers by now just to see if she'll notice. She'll be entranced and offer herself for any purpose. The guy loves irony, so he'll probably ask you to pick the method of your own destruction."

"Can I envision a stay-puft marshmallow man?"

"No, Esmy. It needs to be something you can really visualize. Big enough to keep Magni and Jesus occupied, but something you can manage to kill. Can you handle that?"

Jake nodded. "I've been dreaming of something like that since last week."

"Weird response, Jake, but OK. Can you get those ducks re-animated and make sure they can handle the fire and ice like we discussed? Esmy will lend some air support on the broom. We all know our parts now?"

They all nodded.

"Split up and get ready," said Loki. "We'll meet back up tomorrow on campus and hope this doesn't turn into a complete cluster fuck."

CHAPTER 24

DOLORES

By the light of the full harvest moon, the street was as silent as a graveyard. A possum stuck his head out between the bars on the gates of Mistletoe Acres Park. His white face on black fur looked like a skull. He sniffed the autumn air. He was closer now, the scent was stronger here. He squeezed through the bars, wriggling his body to fit his ribs through.

Once free of the old wrought iron fence, he waddled to the edge of the sidewalk and stood on his hindquarters. He swept his paws over his snout and whiskers, cleaning and preening his face. He sniffed the wind again; the object of his desire was only a few feet away. He scurried closer and found his goal. He picked up the half banana. He pulled the peel away with his claws and ate greedily.

The wet chomping and smacking of teeth and banana mush were loud in the dark, silent night. It was loud enough for the small marsupial that he didn't hear the V8 engine of a slate-grey Escalade roar around the corner. His claws still clutched the banana tightly when the bumper impacted with his skull, killing him instantly and sending him rolling in front of the oversized SUV where it lurched to a stop.

Dolores hopped out of the passenger side, jogging to the tailgate while Sam shut off the engine and extracted herself from the driver's seat. Dolores dug through the back. She grabbed a duffel bag and slung it over her shoulder. She walked around to the front of the car; Sam was staring at something in the road while the headlights were still illuminated for the safety timer. Dolores saw the dead possum just before the lights dimmed from the Cadillac.

"Did we just hit that?"

"Yep. I thought we hit a can or something," replied Sam. "Poor little fella, kinda sad all balled up clutching whatever that is."

Dolores walked over and picked up the dead possum by the tail. She gave him a few good shakes to knock the banana loose and shake a small trickle of blood dry. She slung it over her other shoulder; Sam looked mortified.

"What?" Dolores said nodding at her shoulder. "Fresh dead, it will really help the spell."

Sam shivered and pulled her blue North Face jacket shut. She locked the oversized SUV, and the short honk echoed in the night. They crossed the road to find the tall cast iron gates of Mistletoe Green Cemetery shut but not locked. The hinges groaned as Dolores pushed them open wide enough for her to pass through with Sam following.

The cemetery was large, but not massive. It attempted to grow with the town, but the town eventually built around the graveyard. There weren't many graves younger than a half century. Sam followed Dolores across an overgrown path through an older part of the cemetery. She was struggling to keep up with Dolores, who seemed to know every gopher hole and rising root of the graveyard.

"Dolly, when we get wherever it is we are going, what are we doing?" Sam asked. "Are we making some other ouanga thing to tell us where this guy lives?"

Dolores slowed down and looked at a few old graves. They were around one hundred years old with tall, thick old headstones. The profoundly cut engraving of the names and dates faded gently against the stone face from a century of rain, wind, and snow. "We're here," she said back to Sam and dropped the possum between the two headstones.

"So, what do we do now? Get help finding the guy so we can slash his tires?" Sam looked around the graveyard, wringing her hands nervously. "They can kill his swarm, and we can just beat the guy up a bit."

Dolores started to unpack the duffel bag she had been carrying. "Sam, are you a bit nervous? You can wait in the car if you like." She drew from the bag two large boxes of kosher salt, a bottle of rum, a pair of glasses with one lens broken out and placed them on her right. On her left, Dolores pulled out a top hat and three cigars.

"Naw, I ain't nervous, just graveyards give me the heebie-jeebies." A crow fluttered its wings in a tree overhead and made Sam nearly jump out of her skin.

Dolores chuckled and turned around to Sam, she reached up and put her hands on her shoulders. "Sam, it's just a graveyard. Nothing's coming out of the ground tonight, we aren't here to raise the dead, and we're here because we want to put someone in the ground. Now, if a little thing like me can be fine here, you've got nothing to worry about."

Dolores picked up the kosher salt, pulled open the spout and started pouring it onto the ground making a pattern.

"What's that going to be for?" asked Sam.

"This is going to be the veve that will help channel the loa I want to contact for help. Remember that pattern I drew out in Flour in my bedroom last week?"

Sam nodded, watching Dolores drawing on the ground between the graves. A pattern showed a pair of coffins flanking a cross on a pedestal.

"Well, that was the veve for Erzulie, she's partial to flour, so I used flour there. I'm using salt here because it's easier to pour on the ground and holds more significance in a graveyard. We're in the graveyard and drawing this veve to summon Baron

Samedi. He's a powerful loa of death and life."

"You mean life and death?"

"No. He has more power for death, but can cure to maintain your life if he believes you worthwhile," Dolores said, closing the salt.

"Ahh," nodded Sam. "And what's with the rest of this? Why the rum and three cigars?"

"Summoning agents. You want to bring the loa to you, so you need to tempt them. The Baron loves rum, cigars, and tobacco. When you've studied the spirit realms and magical worlds long enough, you'll find that numbers hold a certain significance. Three is one of those numbers, so having three cigars will hold more sway than one. Kind of like if you ask one of the sidhe three questions in a row, they have to answer it truthfully."

"What's the Sidhe?" Sam asked sitting down on a nearby shorter grave marker.

"Pixies, piskies, and the sort, a lot of other races also help to make up the world of the sidhe."

"Wait, fairies are real too?"

Dolores jumped up and waved her hands, she brought a single caramel finger to her lips. "Shhhhh, don't say that, they don't like being referred to as that word, it's like if you were to call my Sofia a mulatto. They get offended."

"Are they here listening or something?"

Dolores backed away and looked around listening for silence. "No, but the realm of the sidhe is one of the closest to ours. The overlap is consistent enough that they have many places and ways to crossover and the veil between is thin enough for them they can listen to our world. They hear places of extreme emotion louder than anywhere else. So, be careful what you say, even in whispers, in graveyards, hospitals, and churches especially."

Dolores went back to setting things on headstones and preparing the ritual.

"OK, I get the liquor and the cigars now, but what's with

the rest of this?"

"The Baron likes top hats." She placed an old worn black felted top hat on a headstone. "The glasses with one lens are a hallmark of gaining his sight between the worlds."

She pulled a large hunting knife from the bag. Dolores cut open the possum, the slit pooled with fresh still warm blood from the animal. She dipped two fingers in and drew a skull in smeared blood over her face.

She wiped the blood on her black shirt. She used the knife to cut the ends of the cigars. Dolores opened the rum and lit a cigar. "Sam, stay back for this part please, just stay over there."

"You do you, Dolly." Sam settled on the tombstone.

Dolores took a big puff of the cigar, letting the smoke roll out slowly. She took a deep pull of the rum. She set the open bottle and the lit cigar in front of the headstone with the top hat. "Baron Samedi," she called to the night. "Ah, I offer you rum to your altar! Ah, I offer you meat to your stone! Ah, smell the heady musk of my tobacco! Come Forth!"

Nothing happened. Sam looked around the cemetery. Dolores started looking around too. She looked around her and started pointing at the various elements. She studied the veve in salt.

Dolores took another long puff of the cigar, letting out more smoke this time. She drew another deep pull of rum. She repeated her call.

Nothing happened again. Dolores looked around tapping her foot impatiently.

"Maybe he's just not that into you," said Sam shrugging her shoulders.

"No, something else is at play here."

Sam pointed and asked, "Is it the possum?"

"No, Sam, it's not the goddamned possum, that would actually have helped."

Dolores looked up at the weeping willow, flowing branches floating on the light breeze above them. She looked down at the veve and kicked it away. Once the ground was clear, she cracked open the spout of her other box of salt. Dolores sketched out this time what looked like a pyramid with a heart above it, crosses connected them and jutted from different angles and lines.

"I'll be right back," she said to Sam, taking her knife with her. She came back a moment later with some long sticks of elm. Dolores arranged them into a small cross in front of the veve. She stood over it and poured some of the rum over the dried wood. She took one more deep drink of the rum herself and tossed the cigar onto the elm cross. It lit brightly into a small fire.

"Grann Brigitte," she called to the fire. "I seek Grann Brigitte tonight, and I offer you rum! I offer you fire! I offer you vengeance!"

The fire danced brightly and shot up from the cross. A shadow rose from the headstone and lifted the top hat.

"Sweet Jesus, Mary, and Joseph," whispered Sam nearby.

The shadow condensed under the top hat and faded to a svelte silhouette of a woman. She wore a lacy white blouse, long flowing crimson skirt and long black silk gloves. Her skin was paler than the moon, and her long red curls were vibrant enough to make her crimson skirt seem faded in comparison.

The shadow chuckled lightly, and it fell on the wind, bringing a sharp chill up Sam's spine. "Don't give me any of your fucking Jesus bullshit Dixie girl! Or you not heard that cross shit was an inside job?"

Dolores gave Sam a pleading look to be quiet, it didn't work. Sam asked very surreptitiously, "What?"

Dolores knelt. "Grann Brigitte, forgive my friend," she started to say.

Brigitte held a hand out. She picked up the bottle of rum with the other. It was still over three-quarters full. She drained it in one swift gulp. When she spoke again, the air felt warmer, as though fire itself were speaking.

"I'm saying, don't go calling your twat idols at me Dixie. They're as false as the tits on a statue! You know nothin', Dixie? Shit, that was an inside job, other gods wanting the confusion."

She looked at Dolores kneeling. "Oh, you. I like you." Brigitte tapped a long twig-like finger on Dolores's head. "You a fucker that knows her rum, good shit, Jamaican shit. None of that American or Puerto Rican rum and good Cuban cigars. My Baron baby, he love a visit from folk like you." She drew a long breath over the smoldering cigar.

"Yes, Grann," Dolores said, standing back up. "I was trying to call on him tonight, but he wouldn't respond."

Brigitte waved a finger. "Tsk tsk tsk, that motherfucker, he been getting called this way and that all week now. It's this fuckin' season. Every year at Carnival is the same, you get a whole crew of fuckers with bad rum, cheap cigars, and papier mache top hats callin 'my Baron off, leavin 'his Grann alone to have to take care of her pleasures on her own."

"Isn't Carnival around Lent?" asked Sam, Dolores gave her another pleading look to shut up.

Brigitte laughed heartily. "Only to your mortal realm pent up ass fingering Catholics. Your Halloween time is our Carnival. Allows me to show up and fuck around a bit in the flesh, especially when some fine bitches call me up with the old dead. Love the bloody skull face and the possum baby, the Baron will be fucking rolling that he had to visit some twat in Alabama over this scene. Now, why you go callin 'your ol 'Grann Brigitte?"

Dolores recounted the attack on her and Sam earlier that day. The details she could remember, she painted vividly for Brigitte.

"Some dumb cunt with a cooking utensil on his head went after you with a swarm of fucking wasps?"

"That's the sum of it," replied Dolores nodding. "Can you help us? Kill the swarm, tell us where he is so we can tool him up a bit?"

"Oh, I want a piece of this fucker on my own, mind if I do a ride along?"

"Possession? What can you do?"

"Oh I can bring down fire on a bitch is what I can do. I can wear your skin suit around and tear that dickless fuckface limb from limb. I can flay him alive with your own fingernails. I knew this guy, creepy Egyptian fucker, taught me this trick for making balloon animals out of genitalia. The trick is to—"

Dolores cut her off. "OK, sounds great, possession could work out. Can you help find him?"

"He's got some protection on him tonight. I don't see the future eunuch anywhere. My sight will wane until midday, but I'll grow stronger on you again with the glooming."

Dolores turned around to Sam. "Go back to the car, call Chris and tell him I'm crashing with you tonight, he'll have to take Sofia tomorrow. I'll meet you back there in a minute."

When Dolores could see Sam get to the edge of the trail towards the cemetery gates, she turned back to Brigitte.

"Temporary possession, right? You get the ride along for the sole purpose of getting to dish out this beat down. I don't want any hidden costs or agendas coming out of this."
Brigitte curled a wry thin smile and leaned in close to Dolores. "Girl, I been waiting ages to stretch my legs and fuck some shit up. Now you gonna let me fuck some shit up?"

CHAPTER 25

ESMY

It was a sunny afternoon. The Wellhouse was flanked to the south by a myriad of elm, ash and hawthorn trees. The leaves shifted almost overnight from a long season of green to wondrous shades of pale yellows, vibrant oranges, and scarlet reds. The grass in the open lawn to the north of the Wellhouse, between it and the Old Bastard, started to fade. It was still streaked with shades of green but was not as vibrant as it in the weeks before. The lawns that only recently had students sprawled out for studying, group discussions, outdoor lectures or just sunbathing were now mostly vacant.

Dr. Longfellow was sitting against a nearby tree, leafing through a copy of the Art of War he brought from his office. In a light brown suit with vest and dark blue necktie, he looked out of place among the rest of the crew surrounding him. Kyle sat with his back against one of the brick archways of the Wellhouse, picking absentmindedly at the grass next to his metal colander helmet resting on the ground nearby. He was wearing the same jeans and hoodie from the day before.

Jake sat across from Jesus in the Wellhouse. Jesus was wearing a black Henley shirt and green cargo pants. Jake attempted to dress casual for the workday in preparation for the upcoming fight. He couldn't stop at just t-shirt and jeans though, he tried to make himself more business casual for what he still considered the workplace with a grey houndstooth sports coat. Jake brought some pieces from old board games around their house and was discussing strategy on the floor of the Wellhouse with Jesus.

Like Dr. Longfellow, Esmy also stuck out like a sore thumb, but for other reasons. She decided that she would likely be riding her broomstick for most of the impending melee. So she raided the college equestrian department for some gear. She lay on her broomstick, hovering a few feet above the ground. She wore a new pair of black riding boots, tight-fitting grey riding pants, a brown shirt and a knee length black coat that dangled over the side of the broom.

Kyle stood up and dusted off the grass from his lap. "I still don't get it," he said. "If we know this guy is going to attack the school, why don't we lay a trap?"

Esmy sighed from her broomstick. "If it looks like we're doing anything out of the ordinary, then he'll scrub and try something else. At least with this, we can attempt to control the chaos."

Kyle mulled that response. "Isn't it kind of suspicious just all of us hanging around out in the open, eh?"

"Like I said a few hundred times now." Esmy sat up on the broom. "Seth knows two actual professors are guarding, he'll be a little surprised by a student and two staff members but will chalk it up to slightly bad intel. We just need to follow the plan, and Loki will get rid of him."

"Why do we trust him anyway?" Kyle asked scoffing. "Won't that ... what are you doing?"

Esmy hopped off her broomstick and was shoving a hand down her riding pants frantically, jabbing around.

"Wedgie," she said, sucking in her breath. "In the front, insanely uncomfortable. Why the hell do they have to be so damned tight?"

She kept leaping back and forth. She stopped suddenly and stared across the lawn. Esmy observed two men, both in denim and black leather jackets. They looked identical except for one having a completely bald head, while the other stood an inch shorter but sported shoulder-length hair.

"Hey, does anyone recognize Tweedledee and Tweedledum over there?"

Jesus and Jake stood up in the Wellhouse to peer over; Dr. Longfellow peeked briefly over the top of his book. Kyle picked up his colander. "I know them, and these two dicks are the Inappropriate Boners."

All four of them collectively turned their gaze now to Kyle, but Jesus was the first to ask, "Ssay what, Kyle?"

"These guys are local idiots. They make up most of a band called 'DJ Dirty Stache and the Inappropriate Boners 'that plays live at a strip club."

"How dumb are we talking?"

"They are on probation for an arson charge from a couple of years ago. They'd burned down an abandoned church out in the county. Got caught on it by a security camera at a gas station where they bought the gas they used."

"That sounds more like bad luck than stupidity though," said Jesus.

"Nah, the judge asked them about it in the trial. 'Why didn't you just steal the gas too if you were going to burn something down?' Carl, the bald one, actually told the judge they would have but didn't want to do anything illegal."

"So, proper morons," said Dr. Longfellow looking back down at his book. "Sounds like round one, you guys take them. I'll wait for the main event fun."

"Yeah, real asshats, I can't stand them, they always call me 'corn fucker'," said Kyle

Dr. Longfellow folded his book down for a moment. "Why corn fucker?"

Everyone raised an eyebrow and met Dr. Longfellow's darting gaze.

"Oh, as in Unicorn Fucker. You're the boy with that van, the one with the comical wizard having conjugal relations with a unicorn, right?"

Kyle nodded, looking down and tight-lipped.

Esmy looked at them on the approach. "Jake, I think this is the start, you might want to get the ducks ready to take off. I'll take off soon. Kyle, think you can handle these two?"

A mischievous grin spread across Kyle's face, and he strapped the colander back onto his head.

CHAPTER 26

LOKI

Loki walked up sullenly to a pair of women standing at the corner of the block where the campus started, in front of the Old Bastard. He wore a green long sleeve shirt and a pair of jeans on, an old faded black baseball cap covered his glacial eyes. The couple he approached was a woman with a brow that could be used to chisel rock and a dwarf-sized girl with a big neon green mohawk, clad in black leathers.

"Who's this?" Loki asked the taller woman.

"This is part of your distraction, this lovely little lady," she said, nodding, "is Bernice. Her band is providing your distraction."

Loki nodded, he kept his hands in his pants pockets. "I guess this might work. Where's our mutual friend of mass destruction?"

"Yes, he should probably be here soon," said Dr. Neidermeier. In a brief puff of smoke, the form of a tall, sleek bronze skinned near-human creature stood beside her. He wore a simple wrap of striped dark blue and gold, with leather sandals on his feet. The head was strange, black fur started at the neck and a face like a mix of a fox and an anteater, with a long snout that curved downward. Tall black furred ears stood high like horns out of a shaggy mane of long fur that flowed down the back of his head.

"Greetings, Loki, are we ready to get this melee started?" the beast asked.

The effect of it trying to enunciate the English words was very disturbing. "Nevermind," Loki said. "Maybe you should have stayed human. Watching you speak is like watching a donkey try to perform Shakespeare."

Seth cocked an eyebrow, which was only noticeable in the dark fur as a great ear also turned sharply.

Bernice was looking at Seth in utter shock.

"Careful Seth, you're making your dwarf nauseous with your real face," Loki added.

Seth turned his attention back. "Beatrice, just keep to your part, and you will get that record deal I promised you and the Inconsiderate Boners."

"Inappropriate Boners, and my name is Bernice," Bernice muttered correcting him softly.

"This is your big distraction?" asked Loki shocked.

"I have a plan; do you have a plan though?" Seth snorted a small puff of steam from his snout. "If you cannot deliver on your promise to me, maybe I will forget your freedom and just drag you back to Odin to clamp you in chains myself. I have worked too hard for this to go wrong now."

Loki sneered from under the cap. "I've got a plan to get you exactly what you deserve. Just make sure they are distracted, shouldn't take more than 30 minutes."

"I believe we can do that, we are heading around to join the others now. Get to work."

Loki walked away down a sidewalk and turned past another building further down the campus block. He looked back briefly to Seth. Julia and Bernice walking around the Old Bastard towards where Esmy and the main battle were already starting to take form. In the sky, he caught a glimpse of a lean figure on a stick fly around the Old Bastard and swoop wide out above the road to circle back to campus. Loki grinned ruefully under the brim of his cap.

CHAPTER 27

DOLORES

Sam sneered at Grann Brigitte possessing her friend. They had been driving around most of the night and now all day looking for the kook that attacked them for Brigitte to lay down the beating. In that time, Brigitte made some bizarre demands. She drank like a fish, but that was only the first annoyance because she appeared to hold her liquor better than a team of Russian sailors.

It was the behavior that was starting to get annoying. During the dull periods she would alternate putting a leg up to rest a dirty boot on the tan dash of the Escalade, then she would take the sharp hunting knife Dolly packed in her duffle and make slim cuts on Dolores's jeans. She drew blood only the first time, a thin line of scarlet welling up across soft caramel skin peeking through the blue denim. Now the jeans looked to have been in tatters for years with cuts and fraying. Her hair was shaken out of its tight bun and was starting to tangle.

The worst part was the language. Brigitte learned how the electric windows worked and would yell at anyone they passed, if not to ask if they'd seen, "some tall skinny cracker of a mother fucker wandering around with a shitty dinged up metal bowl on his head," then to yell at people for not moving across the road. Sam decided to lock the windows when a geriatric pedestrian was crossing, and Brigitte leaned out to yell, "get your fuckin' ass out the road you skinny old bitch, we tryin 'to get fucked up here!"

Sam fielded a couple of calls from Josh as well, which was a challenge with Brigitte clearly yelling obscenities in Dolores's voice. She ignored at least one call now since the last one ended because Brigitte decided to shout, "and if that motherfucker been seeing some whore again, I'll chop his dick off maself! My girl seen the test results he was a hidin'! That boy got him the clap hitting some nasty poon, business trips my freckled Irish ass!" She only stopped to drink more rum.

She pulled the Escalade over a block away from campus. Sam turned to her friend. "Dolly, why don't you brush your hair and we just call it a day, you look like hell."

"Dolores ain't coming back for a while Dixie," Brigitte responded for Dolores. "She called me for revenge, and I'm a gonna stay til she get it." She took another pull of rum; this was close to the end of the second bottle today. "We keep going."

"Keep going until what? We've been searching for hours now, what if we never find this guy?"

"We keep looking til we find somethin 'fucked up. Then we'll be close until then, keep this big bitch of a metal wagon runnin'. That alright by you, Dixie?"

Sam looked back at the road and rested her hand on the shifting knob. "What exactly are we looking for though? What will register as 'fucked up 'for you?"

"You'll know it when you see it." She peered out the windows and caught something on the horizon. "Like that, that's pretty fucked up. How many times you see someone riding a goddamned stick across the fuckin 'sky 'specially in broad daylight. Where that at?"

Sam squinted against the fading daylight. "Looks like it's over the college. It's just a couple of blocks up from here."

Brigitte leaped out of the passenger seat. "You drive too

slow. I'll go on foot, you come get me when it's over, and not a word to that dickless man of hers, you got me, Dixie?"

Brigitte was sprinting off ahead of the oversized SUV, the blade of the large hunting knife glinting in the sun with every other stride. Sam just stared in awe. Her cell rang, the caller ID read, again, "Josh (Dolly's husband)."

"Ah, shit," Sam said out loud before she answered the phone.

CHAPTER 28

THE BATTLE ROYALE

Kyle crossed the lawn quickly with a long stride. He was soon face-to-face with Carl and Luke, standing in the middle of a large open grass area between the walkways that led to the buildings that make up the campus.

Carl and Luke saw Kyle and called out together, "Corn Fucker!"

"Not cool guys, you know I don't like that name," Kyle replied. "What are you doing here anyway? The strip club's on the other side of town."

"You gonna give us a ride in that sweet pedo-van Corn Fucker?" Luke asked sarcastically.

"What's with the chrome dome Corn Fucker," Carl ribbed.

"This helps me with some friends," Kyle replied. "Last chance boys, you might want to clear out."

"What's it to you, Corn Fucker, does it help you get better reception to call your Dracula buddy?" Carl stepping closer to Kyle. He was a few inches shorter than Kyle and had to look up to meet his gaze. What he lacked in height, he was making up for in mass though, compared to Kyle's wiry frame. "You think you and some damn Dracula can stop us, Corn Fucker?"

Kyle made an effort of his will and looked like he might sneeze. "Why don't you meet my friends, I have a few thousand of them."

The buzzing of the swarm became deafening, Kyle stepped back and let the horde create a wall around the pair.

Jake came up behind Kyle and clapped him on the shoulder. "Impressive, but you can keep them under control right?"

Kyle looked over at Jake. "The wasps or the assholes?"

"Well, both. I think we should avoid a fatality if possible, right?"

A voice shouted back from the Wellhouse behind them. "Don't worry about it, just kill them," Dr. Longfellow called out.

"Wouldn't that be wrong?"

Jesus appeared suddenly next to them in a soft puff of smoke. "Why aren't you two killing them?"

Jake sarcastically guessed. "Morals?"

"These two guys came here to cause harm and possible death to any number of people, students included," Jesus said, pointing to the swarm. "Now, what I think Dr. Longfellow is trying to point out is that these are pawns. Seth pushed them into this play to see how we'd react. If you boys react with weakness now, he'll know how to roll you when he shows his face."

A loud, deep laugh came over the sound of the swarm. "They have already made their choice, this pair is too weak of heart to kill anything, I can see it now." They could see Seth, standing on the steps of the rear entrance of the Old Bastard, a mohawked punk dwarf next to his left and a tall woman in a plain dress to his right with a brow-line that could kill a weed whacker. "I doubt the young scarecrow has even seen death take someone in his few years."

Dr. Longfellow approached to join Kyle, Jesus, and Jake. Kyle called back at Seth, "Now there's where you're wrong guy. I first met the cold hands of death with my two brothers when I was three. Our mother died in a car accident."

Seth shot a long tongue from his snout and licked across the long jawline. "Details young man, did you see her body ejected before you, sliced in half against a barbed wire fence, maybe? Blood splatters? Guts and entrails hanging from telephone poles?"

"Actually," Kyle said pushing his helmet up from his eyes, "we all got knocked out. Dad hit an icy patch on a highway, our station wagon spun around and hit a tree off the road. We woke up and mom was gone."

"Exposure then?" Seth was visibly interested now. "Your sweet mother froze, tears freezing on her cheeks as the blood vessels burst in her eyeballs?"

"Nope, the official cause of death was suffocation on cake," Kyle replied, seemingly triumphant.

Everyone turned to stare at Kyle, including Carl and Luke inside of the swarm.

"We were on our way to a cousin's house to celebrate my brother Terry's fifth birthday. Mom was holding the cake, the impact knocked her out, and she landed face first into a four-layer with German chocolate buttercream frosting. Really ruined birthdays for Terry, just darn tragic, had to watch the paramedics trying to scrape handful after handful of cake from her airways."

They all stared at Kyle. Seth's jaw hung open, the tongue almost flopping from the snout, while Julia gasped and held a hand to her mouth.

"Kyle, that's kind of fucked up, you know that right?" asked Jesus.

"Oh sure, sure. But y'know, it definitely makes something like this easier." He looked over to the swarm and flared his nostrils. Immediately the swarm changed flight patterns and descended onto Carl, wasps covered his body, dozens stinging into his eyes and flying in and out of his mouth and nose. In a matter of a few seconds, the swarm lifted to reveal a bloody hunk of a person shaped meat in jeans that just fell over.

Luke looked at what was left of his brother. He charged

towards Kyle screaming, "Corn Fucker!"

He grabbed Kyle by his hoodie but was stopped abruptly when Dr. Longfellow threw a swift jab that caught Luke straight across his face. The force was so great it looked more like he was hit with a sledgehammer. Luke folded and fell onto the ground, his entire right side of his face crumpled in from the impact. His eye wasn't visible, and blood was pouring from his mouth and nose, he started to convulse on the grass.

Bernice gasped, Seth closed his jaw and narrowed his gaze at the older man. "Magni! I thought it was you! How is the Norse man, Magni the Great? How long has it been?"

Magni straightened up to his full height. "I think the last time we met was Detroit, let's not let that happen again. Why are you here Seth?"

"I want Horus."

"His remains aren't yours to have Seth," Magni replied. "You know how next of kin works, and you are a step or two away from getting that claim."

Seth huffed through his long snout. "The throne of my kingdom, my realm, belongs to me. I will not have that whore of a mother of his play me for a fool again. I will burn every bit I can find, even if that means burning your entire beloved college."

"I only see you, one of my staff and a midget with a haircut taller than she is. Why don't we call this and you can just play nice with your sister-in-law, or sister, or whatever you call her? Wait, how is she related now?" Magni chided him. "She was your sister but married your brother, then you killed him, but she's mother to your nephew. Sorry, I get confused when the family tree has branches back to the trunk."

"I will witness you delivered to your Valhalla for your tone, fool!"

"Whatever," Magni replied. He nodded at Julia. "Dr. Neidermeier, this will definitely affect your standing in the department. I'm afraid you might not receive tenure if you continue helping this cretin."

Julia shrugged her shoulders. "I wasn't getting anywhere

in this job anyway, just confusion on top of confusion." She pointed at Seth. "At least he respects me enough to explain it all and help."

Seth turned his gaze and pointed to Jake. "You, the weepy moral one. Choose the way you would like to all die today."

Jake looked shocked. "Um… what?"

"Choose what you would like to kill you, weepy mortal," Seth called again.

"Um … how?"

"It is done. I see your fear from your dream." Seth extended a talon pointed finger and drew a line down in the air. The line he drew shimmered briefly then solidified into a shape and a battle ax dropped from the air. He handed the ax. "Make sure they stay busy for a moment." He put a hand to Julia's head and started to chant a few words.

"What about the wasps?"

Seth spat on her forehead and smeared the glob of mucus across with his thumb. "Now they will not come near you."

Bernice grimaced and rolled her eyes to her forehead. "Dude, that's fucking gross."

She started to charge across the field, but the men on the opposite side of the ground appeared to be indifferent to the threat.

Jake looked back at Jesus and Magni. "Seriously, guys, what is he talking about? I look weepy?"

Bernice made it halfway across the field when something swooped over the library roof flying through the air. Esmy saw the charging midget. She dove the broomstick down increasing to lightning speed. She pulled her right leg back. As she approached the ground, Esmy pulled back the broomstick and swung her leg, connecting to the side of Bernice's shoulder so hard it knocked the dwarf into the air.

Esmy flew off again, hovering over a dorm building. Bernice lay crumpled on the lawn, having landed ten feet away and still clutching the ax in her left hand.   "Motherfucker," she screamed from the grass. She started to attempt to get up.

Unconcerned with Esmy and Bernice, Jesus and Magni looked at one another and back to Jake. Jesus shrugged his shoulder, Magni pursed his lips. "Kind of, you do always have worried eyes."

Kyle pointed to Seth chanting, "Should we do something about that?"

Magni shook his head. "Nah, the buildings are enchanted to resist most attacks. I doubt he'll be able to do much but waste our time."

Bernice made it to her feet and tried to roll her shoulder. The arm lay limply to her side. She looked at the prone forms of what was left of her bandmates ahead of her.   Bernice dropped the ax and threw herself on the ground, ramming her right shoulder hard, it made a loud crack as it popped back into the socket. She stood again, now able to roll her shoulder.

"What does that even mean? Worried eyes," Jake said turning back around. "Holy Moses, what the hell is he doing now?"

They looked back across to Seth, his chanting was growing louder, and Julia was now floating in the air growing and changing shape. Her purple floral print blouse was spreading and folding over her, shifting from fabric to scales and it enveloped her body.

"Guys," Jake whispered back. "I know this is part of the plan, but are we sure about this? Can we handle this thing?"

"Are you kidding," Dr. Longfellow said. "I've wanted to take one of these things on since I dug one up. But I didn't think they were supposed to come in purple."

Bernice started moving across the field again, scanning the skies as she walked.

Esmy saw her starting to move again. She flew up high in the air again and made another arc to dive down at Bernice. This time, she pulled a small water balloon, she formed the thoughts in her head and gave them a gentle push of mental strength as she dove. The balloon in her hand swelled gently with water and suddenly froze into a rock-hard ball.

Bernice saw Esmy swooping down and tried to swing her ax, Esmy pulled up much earlier this time and chucked the frozen balloon instead. It sailed under the ax and made a sickening crack as it shattered Bernice's left kneecap. She curled up on the ground grasping at it yelling, "ahh, fuck fuck fuck fuck."

Jesus sighed. "Are you fucking kidding me, Jake?"

"Dude," Kyle sputtered, seeing Julia growing more, her head distorting into a sizeable reptilian shape.

Jesus slapped Jake upside the back of his head. "You made a fucking Barney?"

"Ow," coughed Jake, rubbing the back of his head. "You guys said a dinosaur; you didn't tell me what color to make it. This will be easier to see, though Esmy will laugh her ass off that damned broom."

The beast was now growing more massive than a house, but Seth wasn't slowing down.

"How much damage can this thing cause? What if he does take out a building?"

Kyle chuckled. "Dude, Mr. Hansen, I've got a magic helmet that lets me control a colony of wasps, you've got a brigade of zombie ducks about to take flight, Jesus is a frickin 'vampire, and I just found out that Dr. Longfellow is a minor Norse god."

"You can call me Magni, Kyle." Magni nodded. "At least during the break and in private company. And I wasn't that minor, I'll have you know my father was Thor."

"See, Mr. Hansen. The son of Thor! I think we can probably handle this. Wait, what do you mean, 'was'?"

"He's dead, not important now," answered Magni. "What is important is who's that?"

They let their gaze fall away from the changing form of Julia to a new person running between a pair of dormitories to their left. She moved with a long stride, elegant like a gazelle and emitted a wail like a banshee. Jesus ran to attempt to intercept her, showing the speed he was hiding with a swift reaction. He was fast, but the charging woman was quicker, she leaped into the air and vanished in a cloud of grey mist. Jesus ran straight through the fog skidding to a stop a few steps later.

Before he could turn around, Dolores already appeared again right next to Kyle. She gave a swift whip slash of the hunting knife. The makeshift strap snapped from the colander on Kyle's head, it came tumbling off. She caught it in another fluid movement that ended in her disappearing again in another puff of grey mist. She appeared again twenty feet to their right. Dolores stood, smiling, dark skin gleaming through the slitted and frayed jeans, the possum blood painted in the shape of a skull chipping from her face in light flakes. She was flipping the colander around in her hands

"Friend of yours, Kyle?" asked Magni.

"She," Kyle started to say, but felt a thin line of scarlet welling and dripping down his neck. "She's a Girl Scout den mother. I, uh, I kind of attacked her and destroyed her cookies."

Jesus, Magni, and Jake all turned to him. Magni said sternly, "Kyle, we will have to sit down for a serious talk about responsible use of magic before the end of the break."

"Your boy might not live that long, old man," Dolores called out in the croaking voice of Grann Brigitte. "I might kill the wee fucker, or I might a just take his fuckin 'eyes and leave him as blind as he is dickless. Aye, my Baron husband loves him some more eyes, pops them like deviled eggs."

"Baron husband?" Magni stared at her, and then it hit him. "Am I having the pleasure of Grann Brigitte in a host body currently?"

"Aye, not so dumb for an old fucker are ya," she replied.

"Tell me," Magni continued, "is there anything we can barter to keep young Kyle here intact? I can assure you he is very sorry, and we will be taking actions, but we have mattered at hand here." He pointed over his shoulder at the growing purple dinosaur, shaping into a fierce Tyrannosaurus. She now stood over fifteen feet tall, with a long tail that seemed to stretch far away from her body.

"Give me the cock-swallowing ass that gave him this

goofer helmet for his wasps then." She dropped the colander on the ground. "I can damn well guess he didn't puzzle this out himself, you make it for him grampa?"

They turned to Kyle. He tried to name Loki but could feel the compulsion of Loki's binding keeping him from speaking the name. Instead, he found himself compelled to lie with the most natural person he could place the blame. He pointed directly at Magni.

Magni furrowed his eyebrows at Kyle. "I'm taking this up with your academic adviser, young man!"

Dolores 'face twisted into a rueful grin. "Trying to pull some wool over ma eyes old man? I'll shove your head up that fuckers arse!" She was pointing across the lawn at Seth.   "Oh that cunt, he owes me his own stones after that shit he put me an 'the Baron through in Detroit. I'm a gonna kick all sorts of ass today!"

Dolores took off across the field, straight towards Magni, howling again like a banshee on the wind.

Julia charged towards the four men now standing in the open. Jake ran back towards the Wellhouse, Kyle dove to try to recover his helmet. Jesus ran to meet the thundering lizard. Jesus was running fast enough at a supernatural speed to dodge the lumbering beast as it tried to snap its great jaws at him.

Jake clambered up the side of the Wellhouse to perch on the roof. He turned to the library, jammed his forefingers into his jaw and whistled loudly. Three large teams of ducks took flight from the library roof in a chorus of horrible retching noises. The ducks were attempting to quack through torn throats and ripped vocal chords. The sound made the dinosaur stumble back and roar in defiance.

Esmy flew back over the Old Bastard, leaning in tightly to the broomstick. She made a sharp turn and skidded to a hovering stop next to the Wellhouse roof.

"What happened to Magni? Who's that?" she asked Jake pointing to Dolores.

"That crazy Canuck made an enemy overnight, she's

possessed by some Voodoo spirit and fighting Magni now."

"Fan-frickin-tastic," said Esmy. "Stick to the plan for now then? Just run interference without Magni?"

"Yeah," Jake said. "What about the psycho-midget though? Is she out for good?"

"I think for a while, I'm pretty sure I destroyed her kneecap with the ice balloon."

Jake nodded at her, he gave a few more sharp whistles, and the ducks split and regrouped mid-flight into two teams, they swept across the sky and divided, each group flying back around buildings on either side of the campus.

"Alright, when I've got its attention, you try to deal some damage," Esmy yelled. She leaned down onto the broomstick and took off fast again.

She swept around the Tyrannosaurus 'head, getting close enough to the eyes to spit into them. The beast roared and swiped at the air. Jake made another whistle, and a group of zombie ducks swooped up from behind a dorm. They dove at the back of the dinosaur spewing a collective blast of molten green fire. Julia was slowed by the colossal body and turned too slowly to swipe at the squadron fire-breathing zombie ducks. She missed all of them, but three went down flapping covered in their own liquid green flame making an even more hideous squawking as they hit the ground in meaty thuds.

Esmy felt something whoosh past her and saw another pair of ducks going down with another couple of thuds. She sped up and climbed some more altitude before looking for the source. Esmy spotted it quickly; Seth apparently started hurling knives at the ducks and anything flying around Julia, now a big purple T-Rex.

She flew down to Kyle, who was finally getting his helmet strapped back on tightly. "Kyle," shouted Esmy. "I think Jake and I can deal with Barney, can you and Jesus double-team Seth?"

Kyle nodded. A swarm of wasps came through the trees and hovered nearby. He ran off past the dinosaur and used a few of the insects to get the vampire's attention.

CHAPTER 29

LOKI

Loki walked around a couple of the buildings to make sure he was out of sight. When he was satisfied that Seth couldn't see him, he took off at a sprint. He knew it was about a quarter mile off campus from the Bosch Fine Arts building to the stables that mark the edge an edge of campus that borders the city limits. Not a long trek, but he was on a tight timetable now.

He sprinted past buildings and dorms, ran down the winding roads that pass the sports complex, football field, and baseball diamond. Passing some more outdoor sports fields, he finally came to the edge of campus. The stables were the oldest building on campus, and one of only a few to never have burned down. The stable structure was older than the Old Bastard itself, and it looked it.

Loki approached it, seeing the old-world design still in use. It was a long building, with large sliding doors on each end of it. The front of the building featured windows for the horses to look through and be fed. The wood, while grayed and weathered, still appeared strong, standing up to nearly two centuries of use. The roof was what really stood out and struck most people as odd. It peaked at the center but didn't stop at the backside of the stables. Instead, the roof continued down into the hillside nearby. What really stuck out was that it wasn't actually roofed with shingles or metal, but was covered with a thick layer of sod.

Inside the stables, Loki could hear the neighs and grunts of the horses, disturbed by his sudden approach and the squeal of the old metal gate as he walked through the fence into the paddock. He heard a short bleat that wasn't coming inside the walls though.

He jogged around the stables to climb the hill. On the other side, he found two massive goats grazing on the rooftop. One was black, the other white and both with long thick horns that twisted up and back around in almost a perfect circle back to their necks.

Loki slowed his pace and approached them gingerly. They both looked up as he approached and he removed his hat. "Hey boys, it's just me." Loki walked close to them; they eyed him suspiciously, still chewing mouthfuls of grass.

He held his hands out placating to each of them to sniff. "That's right, it's just old Loki, you remember me don't you Grinder and Snarler?" The goats took a cautious step forward, and both leaned their heads in to sniff a hand. Grinder snorted and tried to nip a finger on Loki's right hand, but he pulled back just in time. The goats looked at each other, Grinder let out a long, low pitched angry bleat and trod off, one leg limping slightly, to another patch of the roof.

Loki turned his attention to Snarler. "Hey boy," he said, reaching over to itch the immense goat's ears behind the large horns. "I know we don't have the greatest history together, but we have some mutual friends out there." From across campus, the sound of a vast and ancient roar sounded, accompanied by a spooked murder of crows that flew overhead away from the cacophony. Loki and Snarler turned their heads at the same time to the direction of the roar, it came from near where Loki knew Seth would be creating a distraction for his heist. The roar even caught Grinder's attention, he stopped chewing to look.

The goat looked back at Loki again. "Yeah, that's why I'm here," he said. "There's a nasty guy over there," he tried to explain to Snarler. "I need your help. I'm not going to hurt your master, but I will ask you some sacrifice."

Snarler snorted at him. Loki continued, "Look, I know, I can be a dick, but help me out, and I'll square myself with everyone, alright?"

Snarler stood tall enough to look directly into Loki's eyes without having to tilt his head. He nodded down and spit a giant ball of chewed cud directly onto Loki's shoe.

"OK yeah, I deserved that," Loki said.

Snarler sat onto his back legs, craned his neck down and gave a long baleful bleat.

"I really hope that means you agree to help," Loki muttered, climbing onto the broad back of the goat. He dug his hands into the magnificent mane of hair around the neck as Snarler stood.

Loki gave a gentle nudge of his heels into the massive goat's ribs. Snarler took off, he ran up the sloop of the stables roof. At the apex, they leaped, landing far into the paddock with a heavy thump. The beast kept his speed running straight for the fence instead of the gate Loki left open. He leaped again, taking the pair over the fence and landing with another hard thump.

His hooves thundered as they hit pavement and sidewalks, running past the sports fields and complexes at a lightning pace. Loki made a pull on his mane before the main block of campus. Snarler gave a loud snort at him. "No boy." Loki leaned around the horns to see where they were going.   "We don't go to battle, we can't kill our enemy, but we can con him, this way."

He directed the goat around a corner and through a parking lot. They approached the loading docks of the cafeteria. In the loading bay sat a large beige colored tent sporting a large North Face logo, some students sat around in and outside of the tent, some holding signs reading, "Meat is Murder." Loki pulled back on the mane, and they leaped once more, sailing over the students and landing hard on the edge of the loading dock, coming to an abrupt stop.

A short girl with dark dreadlocks wearing an old army jacket clambered out of the tent. "What was that," she yelled.

Loki hopped off of Snarl's muscular back. "Angie, you guys aren't going to want to be there in a few minutes," Loki yelled down, running off and kicking his way into the back door of the cafeteria.

"Who the fuck are you," she yelled at Loki as he ran off. Angie looked around at her small crew of vegan student protesters. "Does anyone know who the fuck that was and how the fuck he knew my name?"

The students pressed in together, all shaking their heads and looking around, unable to find an answer.

As quickly as they all pressed down towards the tent and the closest edge of the bay, Loki ran back out the back doors carrying a large boning knife and another small Bernzomatic torch.

"OK boy," Loki said, patting Snarler on the head. "Here comes the sacrifice part. I need some of your body to make this con work. I promise you won't be gone long and I'll make you whole again."

Snarler huffed and raised an eyebrow at him. "Yes, I will make sure none of your bones get broken. I know, I know it was a bad joke on your brother, but time is wasting here."

Snarler narrowed his eyes at him and spat on his shoe once more. With a flourish, he turned and knelt down towards the edge of the loading dock. The great goat raised his head and looked to the sky. Loki covered Snarler's eyes with his left hand and reached around the massive neck with his right, clutching the long sharp boning knife. He whispered, "thank you" in his ear and made a sharp yank of his arm, leaving a deep slash across Snarler's throat.

Blood spewed from the animal's throat in a great torrent, spraying the gathered students in a spreading shower. The tent was becoming dyed crimson in the blood that still fell in great warm drops as Snarler made a final gurgling and pained bleat. The vegan club stood in stunned silence as the massive goat fell to its side and Loki proceeded to slice off the genitalia in three short strikes of the knife.

Loki sat down on the edge of the loading dock for a moment, holding the goat's penis and connected testicles with one hand. He clicked on the cooking torch with the other and started burning the flesh. He watched the hair curl and burn away, and then made the tissue shrivel down and wrinkle. "That should just about do it, looks close enough to an uncircumcised human cock right," he asked the small group of students and vegans beneath him. The blood started to congeal and dry to their face as they all stood still in shock and awe. One of them fell over and fainted after he asked the question.

"Not my fault," he said to them, shaking the partially charred goat wang in their direction. "I told you lot to move, but you had to stand around and gawk." Loki hopped off the loading dock and walked around the crowd. "Now if you'll excuse me, I have another bloodshed to stop. Go have a goat steak if you want, but don't break any of his bones. He won't like that."

Loki looked up and saw Esmy swoop down over the library. She saw the bloody protesters and the grizzly scene of the goat slaughter. "What happened here?"

"This is all part of the plan," Loki responded.

"And them?" she asked nodding from her broomstick.

"Collateral damage," Loki said. "They'll be fine. What's this look like to you?" He held up Snarler's charred member.

"It looks like a somewhat mummified cock and balls, possibly cooked." She smelled the aroma around Loki. "Gods and balls, that smells horrible."

"Fantastic, everything over there going as planned?" Loki swung around the goat dong.

"Mostly, we had an interloper, but it's handled. Are we ready to wrap it up? We're almost out of daylight."

Loki nodded. "You take down the beasts, and I'll ready the

escape."

Esmy flew off as Loki sprinted away behind buildings.

CHAPTER 30

THE BATTLE ROYALE

Esmy swept a short arc up from the cafeteria loading docks and landed gently on the library rooftop. She walked to an edge and peered out at the scene across the lawns and walkways. She could see Jake was still managing to hold down the sizeable purple Tyrannosaurus that was once Dr. Neidermeier, though it looked like the zombie duck squadrons took on massive casualties. It was now chasing after the last five, and they were barely able to keep her interest.

Near the Wellhouse, Magni was still fighting the possessed Dolores. It appeared as though he was trying not to hurt her, but she wasn't taking the same light-handedness with him. Magni's nose was broken and some scarlet slashes at his shoulders and back where Grann Brigitte connected on some knife play.

Further away from the dinosaur fight was Seth himself. He was maintaining a hold on his concentration to keep Kyle's wasp swarm from getting closer than ten feet while dodging an impressive array of kicks and punches from Jesus. The vampire was moving so fast that Esmy could barely keep track of his movements, yet Seth was parrying and dodging every hit.

The lawn itself lay torn to bits. The grass nearly all trampled to death from the dinosaur chasing around after the dive-bombing zombie ducks as they played cat and mouse. Across that desolate mall, lay the crushed corpses of over twenty undead ducks, freshly re-killed. There were also patches of frost where the ice spewing ducks overshot and singed where the fire-spitters missed their mark. A few small grass fires were still smoldering.

In the middle of all that waste and carnage, Esmy saw the one figure that slipped her mind recently. Bernice lay broken in the middle of the circular lawn. Her battle ax was barely visible under a pair of duck corpses. Limbs poked at obscure angles.

Esmy grabbed a large canister on the edge of the roof. She swung the broomstick back under between her legs and jumped off the side of the building. She kicked again, gripping the broomstick tight with one hand and the canister in the other.

Swooping over to Jake near the Wellhouse, Esmy hovered nearby him and gave a whistle to get his attention. She held up the canister. "It's time, got enough of them left to get the bitch to bend over?"

Jake nodded. He gave a few sharp whistles, and Esmy sped off to get set. She sat hovering over, waiting for the trap to set for the Tyrannosaurus that had once been Dr. Neidermeier. "Shit, I hope this works," she whispered looking down at the canister. The can was an old rusty red gas can. The walls of the can were thin and dented and, aside from the handle on the top, coated very well with petroleum jelly. It was also nearly full of rat poison and gunpowder.

A moment later, the remainder of Jake's zombie ducks gathered in a small group on the walkway. They began making their unworldly quack, sounding as though their vocal chords were soaked in bourbon and scraped with a rusty razor. They quickly got the dinosaur's attention. It turned and bent over to swipe and bite at the ducks.

Once Esmy saw the opening, she flew in fast. She wanted to throw the can and just let go, but she knew she couldn't just expect this to luckily fly where she wanted and be done. At the last second, she made the horrifying decision to go for ramming speed. It worked too well, as she came to an abrupt halt, her arm wedged up the ass of a T-Rex, while she kicked at the broomstick and tried to push against the flank of the beast with her other arm.

The shock of the rusty metal suppository of doom made the shocked dinosaur roar in sudden pain and swing violently side to side, attempting to dislodge Esmy. She sat on her broomstick being whipped around, trying to hold on for dear life.

"Esmeralda!" Jake screamed, "Pringles can!"

Suddenly she remembered the Pringles can problem, her other hand was still holding the handle. She let go and was thrown from the creature's anus with an unexpected pop.

Esmy caught herself and swooped out around back to Jake. "You alright, Esmy?"

"Yeah, I think I'll need a week of showers to wash that off, but I'll live. You got the detonator?"

"Yep." Jake pulled a garage door opener from his pocket. "You think she's too close to Magni?"

"He'll live, just hit it before she tries to crap it out! I'm not pushing that in again!"

Jake hit a button on the remote. A little red light blinked, but nothing else happened. He hit it again and again, still a red light, but nothing else.

"Jake, stop screwing around! Blow the thing and let's get this over with!"

"Damnit, Esmy, I'm trying," he shouted back at her.

The giant purple dinosaur ran into the trees and tried scooting along the ground, acting like the world's largest puppy trying to deal with a severe case of worms. Jake started hitting the remote.

"Dolores," someone shouted from the back steps of the Old Bastard. Esmy swung her attention around while Jake started fiddling with the remote. There was a paunchy pale man with a dark receding hairline and a bushy mustache. "Dolores," he shouted again. "What the hell is going on?' "

He headed down the steps to try to stop her from attacking Magni. This didn't stop her though; she seemed to increase her efforts at the site of the man.

"Who the hell are you," shouted Magni at the man, through grunts of pain while blocking the renewed barrage of attacks.

"I'm Josh, that's my wife you're beating up," he shouted back at Magni. Josh kept circling around them, trying to break up the fight. Dolores turned a shoulder and threw a punch straight up into Josh's nose, breaking it with enough impact to make blood pour like a fountain down his face. She turned back to Magni to continue the attack.

Josh staggered his back to Esmy and Jake. "You bwoke my nose," he yelled, through a splutter of blood. "Dolowes, you bwoke my goddamn nose!"

"Oh, did I mess up your pwetty face," Dolores called over in the sarcastic tone of Grann Brigitte. "Maybe that'll make it just a wee bit harder for you to fuck so many whores on your 'business trips 'ya great slag!"

Jake got the remote backing back into place. He clicked the button again as the T-Rex emerged from the treeline. There was an ominous beep from the remote. As the dinosaur rushed past the twins, an explosion from inside the creature ripped through it with enough force that it completely blew off her left leg. It roared in pain and limped forward, bleeding profusely. Josh turned to the noise behind him, only in time to see the massive beast before it crashed to a stop on top of him.

The sudden, crushing death of her husband dislodged a mental damn in Dolores. She immediately pulled back from her attacks and ran to the dead dinosaur lying where her husband once stood. Magni slowly walked behind her, panting to catch his breath.

"Now, that was one hell of a fight," Magni said and clapped a hand on her shoulder. He saw her starting to cry, she turned and hugged the older man. "I'm sorry," he said, surprised by the sudden change. "Were you two close?"

Jake and Esmy closed in around them. Dolores squeaked out, "He was my husband," in choking sobs. "How how-how am I going to support raising a kid without him?"

"Something will work out my dear," Magni said reassuringly. "Why don't you go have a seat in the Wellhouse? I find it always cheers me up." He led her to a seat in the small building, she folded her hands over her face as he left her there.

"Is she OK," Jake whispered to Magni when he rejoined them.

"She will be in time," he replied. He turned his attention to Seth, still fighting Kyle and Jesus without much effort across the destroyed grass and walkways. "We've got to go finish this though."

They crossed the corpse-strewn grounds. "Seth," Magni shouted. Jesus and Kyle saw Magni, Jake, and Esmy approach. Kyle pulled away, stepping back slowly while keeping a wall of wasps between himself and Seth. Jesus bolted to stand next to Magni at an incredible speed.

"Seth, look around you," Magni said, waving at the area. "You are defeated, your minions lay dead. Go home."

"Not until I have what I came for," snarled Seth. "Give me the remains of Horus, and I will go."

Loki took that opportune moment to step out from the falling shadow of the nearby arts building. "I don't think you need all of him, just some... bits and bobs." He held up the shriveled genitalia and imitated a bell with a tinkling sound. "Ding a ling a ling."

Loki walked around them. He stopped at an angle between the group of college defenders and Seth. "Will this finally square my little debt to you?"

Seth grinned wolfishly. "In spades," he replied, holding out his hand for Loki to pass off the detached member.

"Wait," Magni yelled. "Loki you don't have to do this. Seth, this could destabilize everything we have on Earth. I'll make you a deal, you let this go, and we'll still hold the remains here. No one gets Horus, and you can transfer Loki's debt to me. I'll take responsibility for him."

Loki looked back at Magni surprised. Seth turned and stared down his snout at Magni. "An interesting bargain, not many knew I was charged responsible for him when I got him freed. I thought Odin cursed me with him for eternity."

"Loki," Magni said. "Can this be an agreeable transfer of your debt?"

He nodded.

Seth narrowed his eyes. "Fine. Magni of Asgard, I hereby transfer all debt and responsibility for Loki to you in perpetuity." A pair of large ravens cawed ominously from atop a nearby abstract art statue.

While everyone turned their heads to the cawing birds, Seth took the distraction to dive forward and snatch the shriveled and charred genitalia from Loki's grip. He devoured it, laughing, and ran off as everyone else stood staring and stunned. Once he was across a part of the yard, a slit in reality opened in front of Seth and he vanished from sight, the slit closing behind him.

"Did he just really try to eat his brother's cock and balls?" Esmy asked pointing at the space Seth once stood.

"Nephew," corrected Jake.

"Whatever, did he just eat them?"

"Actually, that would have been the genitals from a huge goat," Loki replied, looking sheepish.

Magni shot him a suspicious glance. "Snarler or Grinder?"

"Snarler," Loki responded. "I may have also scarred your campus vegans making that little dick-ka-bob"

They all turned to look at Loki now. Magni began laughing loudly. He kept going and slowly everyone else started chuckling and laughing as well.

CHAPTER 31

ESMY

Esmy came out of the restroom carrying her broomstick like a walking staff. She changed shirts and spent over twenty minutes scrubbing her left arm up to the shoulder. Loki, Kyle, and Jake were hanging around the base of the large central staircase in the Old Bastard. She looked around. "Where'd Magni and Jesus run off to?"

Jake straightened up from leaning on the banister. "Jesus headed off, said he needed to go raid a fridge and refuel. Magni is up in his office and said he'd like to see us when you got done cleaning up."

Esmy nodded. "How about you two, you getting called to the principal's office?"

"Nope," Kyle said, sitting on the bottom step and holding his hands around his jaw. "He told me we'd catch up after the break. He made me put my swarm back in their hive and took my helmet though." Kyle looked sad about that.

"I'm apparently now a ward of the college," Loki said. "Magni said I'd be quote dealt with and used accordingly. But apparently, I'm also free to do as I want." He leaned down to Kyle. "You up for a little adventure?"

"Depends, what have you got in mind?"

"You like unicorns right?"

Kyle sat up. "They're real?"

Loki nodded. "I know a place we can go check some out."

Kyle stood up, and he started to walk away with Loki. "So, it's like a magical zoo or something?" Kyle asked.

Loki wrapped his arm around Kyle's shoulder. "More like a bar. You'll like this, have you ever heard of a 'donkey show'?"

They passed through a doorway out of Esmy and Jake's hearing. Esmy shut her eyes though., "I do not want to hear about that next week."

"I know, right." Jake chuckled. "That guy is supposed to be our great grandfather too. How did that never come up during dinner conversation when we were kids?"

Esmy grinned. "Makes you wonder, what else we don't know."

"Like how I don't know where Magni's office is upstairs?" Jake looked up the center staircase through all of the floors above him. "For that matter, when we get there, do we call him Magni or Dr. Longfellow again? Or hell, did you ever expect to spend a day off fisting Barney to deliver an explosive poison suppository?"

"It's up on fourth. I know where it's at, but I've never been there." She started leading him up the staircase. "I'm serious about this; I mean the oldest thing we ever learned about our family history now is that a mythological character is our great-grandfather. Grandma is still there, but grandpa died before we were born and no one talks about him. Mom and dad always seemed normal enough, but how can we be sure that was not all an act?"

Jake nodded as they turned to climb another flight of stairs. "We never went to any family reunions. I met Uncle Louie once when he came to town to see dad but never again since. It does seem odd too that mom and grandma were only children."

Esmy stopped at the top of the third-floor landing. "Did you ever go to dad's office? Like for a 'bring your kid to work day' or anything?"

"No, I knew he worked in some kind of finance group. He came for a few career days at school and explained what he did as commodities brokering. That it had a lot to do with the complex economics of scale and valuation."

They approached the flights for the fourth floor.

"All of our friends were going to Sunday school every week, bible camps in the summertime, but mom and dad never really took us to church. Do you think they knew? About what Loki told us, that the whole thing wasn't real?"

"I never really questioned it much until now. I mean, we got our free Sundays, I knew they weren't very religious people. Dad seemed to scare the Mormons whenever they came around, and I remember him calling them 'bible humpers 'once."

"Didn't he mean 'thumpers'?"

Jake smiled. "Funny, I tried correcting him on it too. He told me stone-faced that he meant humpers. 'I wouldn't put it past the sanctimonious salesmen to have a go at their good book if they could figure out how.'"

Esmy laughed. "Sounds like dad. Here we are."

In a short wing on the fourth floor, there were a few offices for the administrative staff of the college. The door in front of them was slightly more ornate molding around it and a nameplate that read, "Dr. James M Longfellow, Ph.D. President, Baldur College".

"Esmy, is it odd that while all the other doors in this wing are normal wood doors, this door is made from ancient thick wood planks and has this large knocker?" The knocker consisted of a large black cast iron plate and a small short-handled sledgehammer hanging beside it.

Esmy nodded, looking up and down the corridor.

"Are you going to knock, Esmy?"

"I hoped you would."

They both looked around for a moment. Jake nudged her foot with his shoe and nodded at the door.

"Oh alright," Esmy said with a huff. She picked up the

little hammer and gently hit it on the strike plate. It rang out like a blacksmith striking an anvil hard. They both stared in shock at the small hammer.

"Enter," called a voice from inside. The door creaked on old iron hinges as they walked into the office.

The office was actually a lot simpler inside than they expected. A bookshelf ran floor to ceiling along the entire wall behind him, filled with books of varying ages, sizes and thicknesses, though all of their spines were cracked and creased from use and showed the signs of being well read. The walls bore a couple of old but well cared for tapestries.

Magni sat behind a wooden desk with two thickly upholstered wingback chairs in front of the desk. There were a few stacks of folders on the desk, along with an expensive looking phone and a closed laptop.

"Come in, please, sit, there is much to discuss," Magni said, motioning to the two chairs. They walked in slowly, taking in the office. Esmy held tightly to the broomstick, she seemed to expect something to jump out from the wall. They sat, still looking around. Magni chuckled. "You two seem a bit spooked, it's safe."

"With everything else lately, I expected it to be bigger on the inside," Esmy said. "Like I'd be walking into the feasting halls of Valhalla or something."

Magni shook his head. "It would be a friendly site, but no. It would be too noticeable, and I could hardly conduct any normal business here if that were the case."

"What kind of business would that be?" asked Jake.

"We are a college, plain and simple," replied Magni.

"But you aren't. The college Jake and I attended offered majors in traditional fields of study, it wasn't run by gods and vampires, and was never attacked by other gods or magical dinosaurs."

"Point taken, we are a bit of a specialty school." He sat back in his high-backed office chair. "We offer a lot of traditional disciplines, but that does help to cover for our Preternatural

Sciences department. That accounts for about thirty percent of our student body. We pride ourselves on preparing the mystically inclined for anything they may encounter to survive a long lifetime and career with the responsible use of magic and the supernatural."

"Careers? What kind of careers are you preparing these kids for?" asked Jake.

"Any number of opportunities. Some of our students go on to just be your average member of society that can use magic to enhance their normal occupation. Some doctors use healing spells to better help their patients, for example. We have some that even go into practicing simple witchcraft and wizardry. Believe it or not, you go to some cities and look in the yellow pages you'll find an entry or two for 'wizard. 'Some of our students go into politics, becoming ambassadors between guilds or coalitions and the other worlds."

"How does that all work?" asked Jake. "The other worlds, why isn't this all more common knowledge by now?"

"It once was, but after so many centuries of killing and misunderstanding, keeping everything secret seems to work out much better for humanity in general. Science in this world is progressing nicely and not as many people are being burned at the stake anymore. You have to understand, your world is a connection point. It's the bridge between many other worlds, Asgard, Olympus, B'Shaan, the sidhe realms of Avalon to name a few. The common link seems to be here, Earth. So, it's become a hub, a port in the cosmos. Magic exists here for good or bad, and it is potent here. Some come for travel, some for trade, education or practice as well. A long time ago, we realized there were issues though, and suppression was the best strategy. There is a binding treaty to keep all of these interests in check. It allows humanity to flourish normally while allowing as ethical business practices as can be expected. At times, there are some unfortunate few that look to upset that balance. Today, you two helped to maintain that, and I thank you for your aid."

"So, is there some Federal Bureau of Preternatural affairs

to deal with all of this?"

Magni shook his head. "No, Jake, governments can't interact with the other realms. Between elected officials changing so often and inept political appointees, we can't interact with them other than through subterfuge and disguise. We have a few nation states that get masked into reality to give us representation at the UN General Assembly, but we don't want to interact with government more than we have to. Can you imagine the US Army trying to harness someone like Seth to sacrifice untold numbers of soldiers in the name of empire?"

Jake nodded, and Magni continued, "The leaders of the various realms self-police issues and deal with infractions, like what happened here, in a council. Loki will likely be called by Odin for testimony. If Odin knows my involvement, I'll likely be called too, then have to deal with my grandfather." Magni shuddered at the possibility. "He thinks I'm dead, which it's for the best that continue. There are also some minor coalitions of wizards and trade guilds that as part of their duties patrol these activities as well. Many of them hire directly from our college."

"So, what happens now?" asked Esmy. She tried to look at Magni, but something on the bookshelf kept catching her attention. "I mean," she turned back, "for Kyle, Jesus, us, or even that lady that dropped in? I thought she'd beat the snot out of you, but I don't even see the bruising anymore."

"That's the great thing about the blood of Asgard and magic, it can make healing go pretty quick. That lady you mentioned. She seemed familiar to both Jesus and I. I didn't realize until after Grann Brigitte left her, that was an old student from the college, Dolores King. She was a good student, very gifted in dealing with the Vodoun spirit realms. She is recovering in a dorm, Jesus is seeing to her after he hits the blood bank."

"Did that thing kill her husband, that man I saw run out before we blew up Dr. Neidermeier?"

"Yes, that's what really popped her out of the possession. Strong emotion can do that, and no matter how good or bad her relationship with her husband was, seeing him die so violently like that would easily end the possession. I'd like to talk to her when she comes around. I'm sure she'd make an excellent staff addition. Regardless of the possession, she went hand to hand with me for over twenty minutes. She'd be able to handle some Voodoo and Hoodoo classes, but also take over the classes for Hand to Hand combat with Demigods and Minor Deities until we decide what to do with Professor Briggard."

Jake cocked an eyebrow. "What's happened to Professor Briggard?"

"Oh great, you hadn't heard. Then we have finally got the rumors under control. Well, Jack was found giving a sasquatch a blowjob on the football field. Naturally, since the squatch in question was only fifty-seven, still considered a minor with his clans, we had to suspend Jack while we formally investigate the matter."

Esmy and Jake looked at each other suspiciously and then back to Magni as he seemed to continue as though it was still a normal conversation. "As for Kyle, well, he was just a normal Biology student, on track to graduate next year and move onto whatever. Now, though, well, there's too much memory and trauma from all of this to just remove it without causing some lasting damage. If he wants, we'll offer him some extra classes he can take. I believe he has an interest in continuing after his undergrad here to a veterinary school. If he can do well in some courses here and stop abusing arbitrary powers granted him by mischievous practitioners," he winked at Esmy, "I can also advise he continue with Dr. Gene. He likely wouldn't see a license as a vet in the classical sense you are used to but would be licensed and certified for the care of magical and cryptozoological organisms. Now there is a vastly more interesting and dangerous profession!"

"Sir," continued Jake uneasily. "What about Dr. Neidermeier?"

"Oh, she's dead." Magni sat back and folded his hands together in front of him casually.

"No bringing her back?"

"Afraid not, transformed into a dinosaur, blown up, and I believe you put poison in that can too. Nah, she's dead. Any luck, we won't be haunted by her ghost. Or at least, if we are that the ghost will be in human form, not a dinosaur. Not sure how we'd deal with a dinosaur specter."

"Are we in any trouble," Jake said, pointing to himself and Esmy. "For, well, blowing her up?"

"Nope," Magni said with a casual smile.

"Nope?"

"No, it's in her employment contracts and non-disclosure agreements, it's in the ones you signed as well. If you find yourself hurt, maimed or killed due to any actions carried out to cause damage to this institution, be those damages financial, physical or other, then you are considered the sole party responsible for those actions, and no counteraction may be brought against the inflicting party."

"But we killed someone, four people actually, won't the police investigate?"

"Esmy," Magni said, unfolding his hands and leaning forward again. "What will they investigate? We're already calling in our clean-up crew to take care of the mess on the lawn. Bodies will be disposed of, and the one you two actually killed was a dinosaur at the time. Even if they found that body, how would a police department ever determine it was once Julia? At most, they'll get calls to investigate her as a missing person once her mortgage or rent lapses. They'll leave it open as a missing person, and the investigation will get lost over the next number of decades with no leads."

"What the hell kind of cleaning crew do you have for dealing with everything out there?"

"Oh, they're quite professional. They are triple-A rated for their services. You'd be amazed the things they've cleaned up, magic can get to be a really nasty business," he joked darkly. "They offer some of the highest paying internships to our undergrads as well. I am not allowed to say I recommend the experience but trust me, it is eye-opening."

"So, what about us though?" Jake asked again. "Do we just come back to work Monday as though nothing's happened?"

"Well," he rubbed his chin, "Esmy already expressed some interest in taking some classes. I really would love for you two to continue in your roles here, you've both become quite invaluable. However, I can find some scholarship money to set aside specifically for you two to take up some continuing education in the Preternatural Sciences department. You'd do well in it. To be honest, I haven't seen this good of results and this much raw talent in a long time. It really is amazing what you two have been able to achieve in only the week since you met Loki."

Magni sat up suddenly. "By the way, I saw an interesting story on the news this morning. A naked hairless Latvian man showed up out of thin air on the corner of Wacker and Michigan in downtown Chicago last night. He couldn't explain it, neither could anyone else." Magni leaned back pointing at them both. "Any chance either of you would have an explanation?"

The twins looked to each other and back to Magni, raising their eyebrows innocently.

Esmy bobbed her head. "Depends, Upper Wacker or Lower Wacker?"

Magni scowled at her and chuckled.

"That doesn't sound like us," said Jake. "You might check with Loki sometime that sounds like his sort of prank."

Esmy saw something familiar on a shelf behind Magni. She nudged Jake's foot with her broomstick and nodded at the photograph that caught her attention. His eyes widened and looked back at her, she nodded again, this time to the phone with a light on that showed an open line.

Magni was still talking. "I guess it must be something in your genes. I remember Loki mentioned he was your great grandfather or something, that must be it."

"It must be," replied Esmy smiling. "Just one last question though. Why do you have a sexy picture of our grandmother on your shelf?"

Magni looked back and forth at them and the photo, then again. He folded his hands over his face. "Ah, shit."

A voice on the phone yelled out, "You left Mom's picture up? For fuck's sake Dad, you said you had this covered!"

Jake and Esmy looked in shock and said together, "Mom?"

AFTERWORD

I hope you have enjoyed reading "Over a God's Dead Body" as much as I enjoyed writing it. I've currently planned it to be a series with new installments written as I can find time. There are a number of stories and adventures I have planned for some of the characters you met in this novel, as well as new characters and other familiar faces that will show up.

If you did enjoy this or any of my future novels, do me the favor of leaving a rating and a review on Amazon, Good Reads or anywhere really. Ask any author and they will tell you that little blurb of enthusiasm you have for their book means as much or more than the royalties they may see from the sales.

Be sure to follow me on social media as well if you want to know when I release the next set of adventures of Jake, Esmy, Kyle, Loki, Dolores, and Magni.

ABOUT THE AUTHOR

Joel Spriggs (1982-?) was born and raised in Frankfort, IN. He graduated from Franklin College of Indiana in 2004 with a Bachelors of the Fine Arts in Computer Science and Broadcast Journalism.

Joel's first novel, "Over a God's Dead Body" was published on the Kindle platform in June 2018 and is the first in a planned series surrounding the same characters and fantasy world.

Joel has successfully defended his beard from being stolen 1873 times out of 1878 attempts by his elder brother. On the five occasions he failed, Joel immediately set about growing a new beard and refining his defenses.

Joel lives with his wife and three children in scenic Lebanon, IN. He maintains a website and blog at joelspriggs.com. He is also active on Twitter, @joelspriggs.

Printed in Great Britain
by Amazon